PRETTY MUCH SCREWED

"A brilliant blend of smart storytelling and sidesplitting humor."
—Janet Evanovich, #1 *New York Times*
bestselling author of *One for the Money*

"Jenna McCarthy takes what could have been a standard chick-lit formula—heroine gets dumped, commiserates with her BFF, ventures back into the dating jungle, finds love after a series of complications—and breathes new life into it by giving it her own smart-mouthed-yet-utterly-sweet spin. Sure, her two memoirs were hilarious, but with *Pretty Much Screwed*, her first novel, she proves she's a first-rate storyteller too. More, please!"

—Jane Heller, *New York Times*
bestselling author of *Princess Charming*

I'VE STILL GOT IT . . . I JUST CAN'T REMEMBER WHERE I PUT IT

"Everything you could want in a book *or* a best friend—blunt, truthful and dead-on hilarious."
—Jen Lancaster, *New York Times*
bestselling author of *The Best of Enemies*

"Hilarious and spot-on! . . . Made me howl. Her comic timing and quirky wisdom have never been better!"
—Celia Rivenbark, *New York Times*
bestselling author of *Rude Bitches Make Me Tired*

"Jenna McCarthy is Lena Dunham if she had kids and shopped at Costco, or Howard Stern if he had prettier hair and a thing for happy hour . . . Wildly entertaining."
—Anna Goldfarb, author of *Clearly, I Didn't Think This Through*

"Aging isn't funny; it's tragic and unavoidable and depressing as hell. Aging through Jenna McCarthy's eyes, however, is a laugh-out-loud ride."
—Jill Smokler, *New York Times* bestselling author
of *Motherhood Comes Naturally (And Other Vicious Lies)*

continued . . .

"Jenna McCarthy isn't just funny; she's an amazingly gifted chronicler of modern life."

—W. Bruce Cameron, *New York Times*
bestselling author of *A Dog's Journey*

"Jenna McCarthy is one of a handful of writers who can make me laugh until I wheeze and my eyes tear up."

—Robin O'Bryant, *New York Times* bestselling author of
Ketchup Is a Vegetable & Other Lies Moms Tell Themselves

IF IT WAS EASY, THEY'D CALL THE WHOLE DAMN THING A HONEYMOON

"If Chelsea Handler and Dr. Phil had a love child, it would be Jenna McCarthy . . . At once profane, irreverent, warm and wise . . . Brilliant!"

—Celia Rivenbark

"Hilarious, smart and utterly addicting."

—Valerie Frankel, author of *It's Hard Not to Hate You*

"At the end of the day, you'll recognize yourself in these pages and applaud her honesty."

—Lucy Danziger, editor in chief of *Self* magazine and
coauthor of *The Nine Rooms of Happiness*

"An uproariously funny, deliciously satisfying and completely accurate take on wedded bliss."

—Tracy Beckerman, syndicated humor columnist
and author of *Lost in Suburbia*

"When Jenna McCarthy turns her wicked wit to the, ahem, challenges of modern-day marriage, hilarity ensues."

—Julie Tilsner, author of *Mommy Yoga:
The 50 Stretches of Motherhood*

"This should be required reading for all brides . . . An enlightening tour of the true realities of marriage."

—Alisa Bowman, author of *Project: Happily Ever After*

Everything's
Relative

Jenna McCarthy

BERKLEY BOOKS, NEW YORK

BERKLEY

An imprint of Penguin Random House LLC
375 Hudson Street, New York, New York 10014

This book is an original publication of Penguin Random House LLC.

Library of Congress Cataloging-in-Publication Data

Names: McCarthy, Jenna, author.
Title: Everything's relative / Jenna McCarthy.
Other titles: Everything is relative
Description: Berkley trade paperback edition. | New York : Berkley Books, 2016.
Identifiers: LCCN 2015033425 | ISBN 9780425280690 (paperback)
Subjects: LCSH: Mothers and daughters—Fiction. | Domestic fiction. | BISAC:
FICTION / Humorous. | FICTION / Contemporary Women.
Classification: LCC PS3613.C34576 E94 2016 | DDC 813/.6—dc23
LC record available at http://lccn.loc.gov/2015033425

PUBLISHING HISTORY
Berkley trade paperback edition / February 2016

PRINTED IN THE UNITED STATES OF AMERICA

10 9 8 7 6 5 4 3 2 1

Penguin
Random
House

For Laurie and Brian,
the relatives I'd pick anyway

ACKNOWLEDGMENTS

You're tired. You're busy. And OMG the Internet. (Did you know the world uploads over three hundred hours of video to YouTube every single minute? The mind boggles.) And yet here you are, giving yourself permission to kick back and enjoy this book. For that, I would like to thank you. I understand there are countless demanding hordes of people and activities vying for your time and attention *all goddamned day*, and instead of stalking your exes on Facebook or pinning a bunch of crafty shit you'll never make to your dusty DIY Pinterest board, you decided to spend your precious resources on me. I'm honored and humbled (and honestly, it's time those kids of yours learned to cook for themselves anyway). Enjoy!

Prologue

⌒

Jules rested the wooden spoon on the edge of the pan she'd been stirring and turned to Brooke. "Will you please call Lexi in for dinner?" It was almost six o'clock and their mother liked dinner on the table at exactly that time, whether she was home herself or not. Of course, it stressed Jules out when she wasn't, but there wasn't much she could do about it.

"Sure," Brooke said. She cupped her hands around her mouth and shouted into them. "LEXI! DINNER'S READY!"

Jules cringed.

"YOU'RE NOT THE BOSS OF ME," eight-year-old Lexi called back from somewhere outside. She stuck out her tongue after she said it, even though she knew nobody could see her. That part didn't matter to Lexi one bit.

Brooke poked her head out the side door. Her younger sister was out on the small, weed-tangled patio doing her favorite thing in the world: frying ants with a magnifying glass.

"Lexi, Jules said it's time to eat," Brooke said as firmly as she could.

"Jules isn't the boss of me, either," Lexi said without looking up.

"Please, Lexi, come inside, okay? Jules has been in here sweating her butt off for an hour. The least you can do is come to the table."

"I can't," Lexi said. "I have two left and I need to kill them. They're squirrely little shits, too. As soon as I get them, I'll come in."

"If Mom hears you talk like that, she'll ground you for life," Brooke said, wondering if any of Lexi's second-grade classmates had potty mouths. Brooke highly doubted it. Even her own friends weren't really swearing yet, and they were two whole years older.

"Then I'll sneak out," Lexi said with a shrug. Brooke pulled the door closed.

"Any suggestions?" she asked Jules.

"I'll handle Lexi," Jules said, sighing as she scraped a pile of seasoned ground beef onto hamburger buns she'd laid open on each of four plates. She arranged slices of apples carefully on each one and brought them to the table. She knew her mom would be annoyed that she hadn't made a vegetable, but she'd gotten wrapped up in her studying and had lost track of time. She'd made a conscious choice: No vegetable was better than dinner not being on the table when Juliana expected it. The apples would have to do. Without being asked, Brooke filled four glasses with water and set one beside each place setting. She folded four napkins and tucked one neatly under the side of each plate, then added forks and knives. Jules wiped her hands on a towel that was tucked into the pocket of her shorts and opened the door to the patio.

"Lexi, I mean it, it's time to come in," she said sternly. "Mom will be home any minute."

"Got 'em! Ha!" Lexi shouted. She stood up, dropped the magnifying glass unceremoniously onto the pile of dead ants and brushed her hands on her dirty cut-offs. It was a blistering Southern California evening and sweat was leaving trails of almost-clean skin down Lexi's grimy cheeks. "What's for dinner?" She planted her hands on her hips and blew a chunk of thick dark hair out of her eyes.

"Sloppy Joes," Jules told her. "You should wash your hands."

"You should mind your own beeswax," Lexi said. She marched into the house, letting the screen door slam in Jules's face.

"Can't you just be nice?" Brooke whispered at her.

"Nope," Lexi replied. She was already sitting at the table, shoveling food into her mouth. Meat was spilling out of the sides of her bun and juice was running down her arm.

"Brooke, sit. I just heard Mom's car," Jules said, squaring her shoulders and self-consciously smoothing down her shirt.

Brooke nodded and lowered herself into her chair just as Juliana swept into the room.

"Hey, Mom," Jules said brightly. "Dinner's just ready." She added the obvious last bit as much for the announcement as to deflect attention from her filthy youngest sister.

"Hay is for horses, and I can see that," Juliana said, taking in the table and Lexi at the same time. She raised her eyebrows at her youngest daughter. Lexi, naturally, ignored her glare. "May I ask what it is?"

"They're Sloppy Joes," Brooke said in a rush. "We had them

at Kylie Bennett's birthday party and they were awesome. Jules figured out how to make them all by herself. Don't they smell great?"

"Unless they can cure cancer, I'd suggest you find a more accurate term than 'awesome' to describe them," Juliana said, taking her seat. "Did you run today?"

"Four miles," Brooke told her, beaming. "I'm the only one in my grade who can run that far without stopping." Juliana said nothing.

"How was your day?" Jules asked her mom, rushing to fill the awkward silence.

"Nothing but pure, unadulterated joy," Juliana replied, the sarcasm dripping from her words. It was no secret she hated her job as a receptionist at the uppity Salon Patine, but the girls routinely wished she would pretend to hate it a little bit less. "Where did you get the meat?"

"Ralphs," Jules told her. "It was on sale so I bought a bunch and froze the rest." Jules walked to Eastridge Junior High each day and there were several grocery stores on her route, so Juliana had turned over most of the shopping duties to her. Jules never complained about having to lug those heavy bags home every other day, not even once.

Juliana nodded vague approval before shifting her eyes to Lexi, who was licking sauce off of her wrist.

"I got a one hundred on my history test today," Jules blurted before Juliana could speak. She was in all honors classes, and spent whatever time she had left after taking care of her sisters with her nose in some gigantic textbook or other.

"You studied like crazy," Brooke said. "You should have."

"Do your lips ever hurt from kissing butt all the time?" Lexi asked Brooke.

"Try the meat, Mom," Jules urged, jumping between her sisters as she always did in the hopes of staving off a scene.

Juliana used her fork to place a tiny bite of meat into her mouth. Her grimace was small but unmistakable. Before Jules could think of anything to say, Lexi let out a gigantic burp. Her mother and two older sisters watched in disgust as she picked up her plate with both of her filthy hands and licked its entire surface clean. She had sauce on the tip of her already dirty nose, and Jules didn't know whether to laugh or cry. Lexi was such a beautiful girl; her oldest sister ached to tell her to brush her hair and wash her face, but she knew that no words would ever fall on deafer ears.

"Alexis Alexander, you may be excused," Juliana hissed through gritted teeth. "You will shower off that filth and then go immediately to bed."

Lexi shrugged and scraped her chair back so hard it tipped over. Brooke let out a yelp when it crashed to the ground. She rushed to pick it up as Lexi flounced from the room. Juliana sighed, placed her napkin on her barely touched plate of food and rose from the table.

"One serving for you tonight, Brooke," she said. "No seconds."

"Okay," Brooke said, hurt.

"And please make sure the kitchen is clean before you do anything else," Juliana said. She directed this at Jules.

"Of course," Jules said.

"Be careful scraping that pan so you don't scratch it," her mother added.

"I will," Jules promised.

"No television tonight for either of you. You can work on homework or read."

"Got it," Jules said. And with that, their mother was gone.

"Thanks for dinner, Jules," Brooke said finally. "I thought they were really good. Better than Kylie's mom's even."

"Glad you liked them." Jules smiled weakly, rising to clear the table.

Twenty Years Later

Jules

~⟋⟍~

Jules strode through the Northridge Fashion Center purposefully. She had exactly one hour and a twenty-percent-off Sears coupon burning a hole in her purse, a brown faux-leather messenger-style that happened to be on its last synthetic legs. It was time for a new one, and she'd already decided she was going to splurge on genuine leather—if she could find one on sale. Even though she was finally fine financially, Jules could never bring herself to pay full price for anything. She blamed her mother for this.

As she made her way toward Sears, a navy-and-white sundress in a shop window caught her eye. It had the halter neckline that flattered flat-chested women like Jules, and the horizontal stripes accented the mannequin's perfectly protruding middle. Jules could just see herself breezing around the neighborhood in it, a tangle of adorably mangy mutts at her feet. In a highly uncharacteristic burst of spontaneity, she ducked into Motherhood Maternity.

The sundress was on a center rack right in the front, and Jules flipped through the hangers until she found a size small. She pulled it out and inspected it from every angle, amused by the way it hung several inches longer in the front.

"Can I put that in a fitting room for you?" A grandmotherly saleslady had appeared out of nowhere. Jules blushed furiously. In her size-two flat-front khakis and tucked-in blouse, she was shocked by the question. She figured the salesladies were probably trained not to make any assumptions.

"Oh, actually I was just looking . . ." Jules said nervously, her face burning. She felt like a kid who had been caught with her hand in the cookie jar.

"Well, that dress just came in and I haven't seen it on yet, so if you try on anything else would you slip it on for me? We have fake bellies you can strap on to see what it will look like . . . You know, when you're showing. If you ever show, that is. You sure are a tiny slip of a thing!"

"I don't really have a lot of time . . . " Jules said, trailing off. The saleslady looked crushed. The mall was dead and she probably hadn't had a customer all day.

"Oh, why not?" Jules said. The woman genuinely looked as if she might cry happy tears as she led Jules to a curtained fitting room.

"The belly is in there, and my name is Ethel if you need another size."

"Right. Thank you, Ethel."

Jules closed the curtain, wondering what on earth she was doing. Not only was she not pregnant, but she and Shawn had agreed that they wouldn't even entertain the idea until he finished law school, which was another two years away. Still, it was a free country. There was no harm in just trying the thing on. It wasn't like she was secretly flushing her birth control pills down the toilet or anything. Besides, she was only doing it for Ethel.

She took off her clothes and folded them neatly on the fitting room's padded bench. She looked at her bra-and-panty-clad thirty-two-year-old body in the mirror and tried to picture herself pregnant. It was impossible. Her stomach was as pancake-flat as it had been when she was seven years old, and her thighs were still lean and taut. In fact, nothing much about Jules had changed since she was a child. She was the same nondescript plain Jane she'd always been, the sort of woman who could pass for anywhere from twenty to forty. She longed for pregnancy curves, for the assurance that she was fertile, but more so, for the promise they represented. If she could create life, after all, she could change the world. Jules wanted desperately to believe that was possible.

She strapped on the padded belly, which looked like a giant stuffed peanut glued to a stretchy Velcro-tipped belt. It certainly didn't look like any pregnant stomach Jules had ever seen, but maybe it would look more realistic when she had the dress on. She pulled it off the hanger and over her head and gasped at her reflection. The sundress spilled over and around her prosthetic baby beautifully, making her look legitimately, shockingly pregnant.

"Well?" Ethel called from outside the curtain. "How does it look? Come out and show me! Don't keep me in suspense."

Self-consciously, Jules peeled back the curtain.

"Oh my word, you're adorable!" Ethel squealed. "Come out here and look in the three-way mirror!" A quintessential rule-follower, Jules did as she was told. In the arc of the mirrors, she was transfixed. She turned this way and that, lifting her arms and admiring the way the dress's stripes created the illusion of curves where none actually existed. She instantly recalled a photo of her mom when she was pregnant with Lexi. In the picture, Juliana had Jules's slight build, and her sandy-blond hair was cut into a shoulder-length bob nearly identical to the one Jules wore now. Jules squinted at her reflection, dazed by her uncanny resemblance to a ghost.

"Julia? Julia Alexander? Sorry . . . you're the married one . . . I think it's Richards, no, Richardson, right? Julia Richardson, is that you?" Jules's eyes darted away from her reflection to the face behind hers that now appeared in triplicate in the mirrors.

"Mrs. Berkovitz!" Jules blurted. She spun around, dropping her arms instinctively in an effort to hide her fake belly.

"It *is* you! I thought so but I didn't know you were pregnant, and then I realized since Juliana's . . . passing . . . maybe I *wouldn't* know. Although you'd think some of those other gossipy biddies in the complex would have mentioned it. Or maybe nobody knows yet? Am I the first? Oh, that would just *kill* that know-it-all Judith Steinman. Tell me I'm the first." She clapped her pudgy hands together like a four-year-old seeing her birthday cake for the first time.

"Well, um, it's sort of a secret still since we're not very far along . . ." Jules started. She couldn't believe she was lying about being pregnant, especially to her mother's bigmouth neighbor. Jules never lied. It wasn't in her nature. But what else could she do? And really, what did it matter? Her mother was dead, and it wasn't like she was crossing paths with the old ladies at Garden Villas all that often. Or ever. Well, other than today, hopefully.

"I hate to tell you this, but *we* look like we've already popped," Mrs. Berkovitz said with a knowing smile and a wink. Jules cupped her fake belly protectively; Ethel stifled a laugh.

"Oh, yeah, well . . . still. Would you mind not saying anything to anybody? Until we announce it officially, that is? You know, just in case." Jules made the sign of the cross here, hoping lightning wouldn't strike her dead before she had a chance to get pregnant for real.

"Of course," Mrs. Berkovitz promised. "You know, my Aaren is expecting, too. Not due until December. She's twice as big as you are, but then again we come from Russian peasant stock and she got my birthing hips. That baby's probably gonna slide out like a wet bar of soap!" Mrs. Berkovitz laughed uproariously at this and Jules tried not to cringe at the messy image of Aaren's baby-spewing private parts. "Anyway, maybe we'll see you at the park in the spring."

"Yeah, sure, that'll be fun," Jules said. She gave Mrs. Berkovitz an awkward hug, trying to keep the woman from feeling her padded peanut belly.

"Mazel tov," Mrs. Berkovitz whispered in her ear. "I pray the Lord blesses your womb with as much fruit as it can bear." They pulled apart and Jules managed a weak smile, not sure how to respond to what sounded like a curse.

Mrs. Berkovitz followed her back to the fitting room. "It's such a shame that Juliana didn't live to see this miracle, may her soul rest in peace," she said. "She would have been over the moon."

"Thanks," Jules said. What she was thinking was, *I can add this little encounter to the long list of reasons I'm thankful my mother is dead.*

Brooke

~

"Want to go for a hike this afternoon?" Pam asked. "Hannah is coming, too, and maybe Jess, if she gets all of those all-about-me posters hung up in time." Pam was the junior teacher in the Tadpole room, a job Brooke wouldn't wish on her worst enemy. Poor Pam spent half of her day in the smelly Little Me Preschool bathroom, bribing a two-year-old Mackenzie or Jackson with a temporary tattoo or some Silly Putty to "pretty please go pee-pee in the potty." Brooke's Frog room was right next door, and thankfully the kids were almost always potty trained by the time they got there. There were occasional accidents, of course, but at least Brooke didn't have to use her classroom stipend for diapers and wipes.

"Oh shoot. I can't today," Brooke said, intentionally vague. She was pretty sure she'd used the dentist, chiropractor, gynecologist, podiatrist, rheumatologist, optometrist and hair appointment excuses to get out of one of Pam's fitness funfests already. And it wasn't like Brooke was eager to admit to her friend that she was afraid she would keel over and die if she tried to trudge up Topanga Canyon.

"Another day, then," Pam said breezily. She wrapped up her half-eaten brownie and tucked it neatly back into her insulated paisley lunch bag. *Who eats half a brownie?* Brooke wondered.

"Totally," Brooke said, trying not to stare at Pam's brownie-filled lunch bag.

"Do you want the rest of my brownie?" Pam asked.

Shoot. Busted.

"Oh, no, I'm good, thanks," Brooke insisted. She willed herself to stop staring at the forbidden bag.

Pam shrugged and surveyed the yard. It was a perfect winter day, sunny and chilly without a cloud in the sky. A lovely day for a hike—if you were into that sort of thing, which Brooke most definitely wasn't. Brooke didn't like to exercise and she didn't like to sweat. Although she'd been an athlete as a child, now she was carrying enough extra weight to make any form of physical exertion about as enjoyable as a root canal. As she watched the kids chase one another around the huge play yard, she had a faint flashback to her own days as a runner, when she was young and fit and would go out to the track and push her own limits for hours at a stretch. It seemed a lifetime ago, if not more.

"Any fun plans for this weekend?" Pam asked now, interrupting her little trip down memory lane.

Fun plans? thought Brooke. She was pretty sure trying to wrestle the remote control away from her deadbeat boyfriend and shuffling through stacks of bills she couldn't afford to pay didn't qualify as fun on any scale. "Nothing special," she said instead. "You?"

"I think I'm going to go see my old college roommate in Vegas," Pam said. "She has tickets to some Cirque du Soleil show that's supposed to be amazing. Hey, you want to go? I'll bet you can still get a ticket. We could make it a road trip! It would be a blast."

Brooke couldn't even fathom what it would be like to have the guts—or the money—to just take off and drive to Nevada on a whim. Even if she could afford the ticket and her share of the gas, which she couldn't, what would she wear to a fancy Las Vegas show? The swankiest place she'd ever been to was probably Red Lobster, and that was in high school. For *prom*. Thankfully she'd been thin then, so she'd been able to find a cute dress on the JCPenney sale rack for just twenty-five bucks. But in her current shape, which in Brooke's mind bore a tragic resemblance to Jabba the Hutt, the pickings would be slim at best. *Slim,* thought Brooke. The irony.

"Thanks for the invite, but Jake and I have a bunch of work to do around the apartment this weekend," she said. It wasn't technically a lie. Jake worked really hard at playing video games most days, and not complaining while he did it for hours on end required Herculean effort on Brooke's part.

"Another time, then," Pam said. She brushed imaginary crumbs off of her lap and stood up. "Hey, Tadpoles," she called, her hands cupped around her mouth. "Swim your cute little tails over here and let's go get washed up!" A tangle of loud, sweaty kids rushed in their direction.

"Hop this way, Frogs!" Brooke shouted over the nearby ruckus.

Brooke led her charges back to her classroom and began laying out the nap mats.

"Thank you, Miss Alexander," said Hala, her secret favorite. Hala climbed onto her mat and pulled her blanket up to her chin.

"You're very welcome, Hala," Brooke said, giving the girl an affectionate hug.

"I wish you could come to my house and tuck me in at night," Hala said. "Your breath is *way* better than my mom's."

Brooke laughed and thought about how much she loved her job. The kids were so special, and so priceless, and so funny. They didn't care that she was overweight or judge her for it like the rest of the world did. They didn't tell her that she looked *just like Kirstie Alley*, and really mean *just like Kirstie Alley before she hooked up with Jenny Craig*. Spending her days with them was the one good thing in her life. Well, that and no longer having a mother around to make her feel like a worthless loser.

Lexi

～

Lexi looked around to make sure Floyd hadn't snuck in while she wasn't looking before she slipped a twenty off the sticky bar and stuck it in the back pocket of her teeny skirt. With a what-the-fuck shrug she downed the half glass of bourbon her last customer had thoughtfully left behind. *Waste not, want not*, her mother had always said. Not that Lexi was fond of quoting Juliana, but some things just stuck whether you wanted them to or not.

The Salty Dog was slow on its best night, but tonight was abysmal. Lexi had made a whopping six bucks in tips in four hours, if you didn't count the two twenties she'd pocketed instead of putting them into the cash register where they rightfully belonged. And Lexi *didn't* count them, because she owed her roommate Brad exactly that amount, so it wasn't like she'd be enjoying any of it. Unfortunately, it didn't look like she'd be getting an opportunity to score any more cash the easy way tonight, either. She surveyed the room; it was the usual mix of regular old drunks who each had an outstanding tab a mile long. Lexi rolled her eyes at them and poured herself a fresh shot of bourbon. It landed in her stomach with a grumble and Lexi realized she hadn't eaten a thing all day, with the meager exception of the half-dozen drinks she'd pinched since she'd been on the clock. No wonder her head was so fuzzy. She stumbled backward toward the opening that looked into the kitchen.

"Hey, Jorge," she purred in her most gravelly voice. The cook snapped his head to attention at the sound. Lexi twirled a long dark lock thoughtfully around her finger and lowered her chin. "Do you think you could make me a burger on the down-low, before Floyd gets here? And maybe some fries? I'm starving out here and I haven't made a dime all night." She leaned ever-so-slightly forward when she said this, offering Jorge an enhanced glimpse of the cleavage that was purposely spilling out of her push-up bra. Jorge blinked rapidly then dragged his eyes back to Lexi's face. Her lids were half-closed over her pale green eyes, and her lips were drawn into the suggestive sort of pout usually reserved for selfies.

"Course, Lexi," Jorge stammered. Jorge had been scolded—more like verbally flogged—by their boss for giving in to Lexi's food-on-demand requests more times than any of them could count. The rule at the Salty Dog was employees only ate on their breaks, at designated tables, and they paid half the menu price. They were charged with keeping one another accountable when Floyd wasn't around, of course. But Jorge, like nearly every man with a pulse Lexi had ever met, was utterly powerless to resist her wiles. She knew the cook would willingly take a tongue-lashing from Floyd all day every day if it meant he might get a close-up look at her tits when he delivered her food.

Lexi blew him a kiss and his brown face turned crimson. *If only Floyd were that easy,* she thought with a stifled sigh.

"Well, look who decided to show up today." Speak of the devil. Floyd had barged through the heavy wooden front door, causing it to slam against the wall and startling Lexi half to death. She grabbed the bar to steady herself. "What a treat for all of us."

"Fuck you, Floyd," Lexi said, high on hunger and liquid courage. She thrust her middle finger in his direction for good measure.

"If those Friday-night dickwads didn't sit here all night spending money so they could watch you shake your ass, you'd be telling some minimum-wage schmuck at the unemployment agency to fuck off instead of me," Floyd said, pulling up a bar-stool directly in front of her. "If someone would be nice enough to give you a ride to the unemployment office, that is." He laughed when he said this, and it was all Lexi could do not to grab a glass and hurl it at his ugly, pockmarked face.

"Fuck you," she said again, wishing she could come up with a meaner, or at least more original, retort.

"No, thanks," said Floyd. "I already had crabs once, and let's just say I'm in no rush to get 'em again. Hey, Jorge, fix me a burger, would ya?"

"Coming right up, Floyd," Jorge said, looking at Lexi guiltily. Her stomach rumbled on cue.

"Wrap it up to go," Floyd added. "I'm beat. I think Spicoli here can hold down the fort for the rest of the night. That right, Spicoli?"

Lexi bit the inside of her cheek so hard she tasted blood. Then she smiled—the fakest fuck-you smile she could muster—and walked around the side of the bar toward the back bathroom. Her middle finger was raised behind her back.

"Take a piss on that burger and I'll give you forty bucks," she whispered to Jorge as she passed by him. Jorge nodded ever so slightly, a mixture of agreement and apprehension. Lexi didn't care if she had to pick up three extra shifts this week. The thought of Floyd eating Jorge's nasty piss burger would be worth it.

The Sisters

~

"Thank you for coming here today, ladies," Mr. Wiley said.

"Of course," Jules said on behalf of her sisters. She shifted uncomfortably in one of Mr. Wiley's big leather chairs.

"As I explained previously, before your mother passed she made me the executor of her will, so the purpose of today's meeting is to go over her final wishes with regard to the disbursement of her assets—"

"Do I get the Chevy?" Lexi interrupted. "Please tell me I get the Chevy. That thing is classic. Not *a* classic, mind you. But definitely classic."

"Lexi, hush," Jules said. As the oldest of the three sisters—and the only one with an ounce of responsibility in her bones, it was clear—Jules had always made it her job to keep Lexi in line. This had never been an easy task, and from the looks of things, nothing had changed. "I'm sorry, Mr. Wiley. Please go on."

"I have to say, your mother's final wishes are a bit unusual,"

Mr. Wiley told them. "It seems that she's laid out several provisions that you'll each need to meet in order to receive your portion of her estate."

"Her estate?" It was Lexi, of course. "Does that include the plastic lawn chairs on her back deck or do those get sold with the condo? Because I could really use some furniture."

"What do you mean by 'provisions,' Mr. Wiley?" Jules asked, ignoring her youngest sister. "Is this like that crazy movie where the rich old man leaves his grandson everything, but he has to jump through all of these hoops to get it? Because frankly, that only works when you have a ton of money, which unfortunately our mother did not."

"Actually, your mother was a wealthy woman," Mr. Wiley said. Jules looked around his stodgy office, wondering what his frame of reference could be. Juliana Alexander had been modestly comfortable, maybe, but she certainly hadn't been rich. Jules had never seen her buy a single thing that wasn't on sale, and all three girls had been humiliated more than once when their mother had tried to haggle over the price of this or that in a department store. "They'll always knock off at least ten or fifteen percent if you can find a pull or a tear," Juliana would insist loudly as her daughters cowered and tried to be invisible.

"Yeah, she was a regular Rockefeller," Lexi snickered. "In that case, I want the Tuscan villa *and* the Chevy."

"Lexi, please," Brooke said. As the middle sister and self-appointed peacekeeper, Brooke was uncomfortable with any level of conflict. Lexi, on the other hand, enjoyed nothing more than making others, Brooke in particular, excruciatingly uncomfortable.

"As I was saying," Mr. Wiley continued, "your mother was a wealthy woman. I should probably say a *very* wealthy woman."

"And I'm the Queen of Sheba," Lexi snorted. Brooke gave her a pleading look.

"You're talking about Juliana Alexander?" Jules asked. "*Our* mother? The woman who lived in a seven-hundred-square-foot condo and drove a 1993 Chevy Caprice and wouldn't consider shopping anywhere but the clearance rack? Are you sure you have the right person?"

"I'm quite certain that I have the right person, and believe it or not, women like your mother are not as uncommon as you might think," Mr. Wiley told the three stone-faced sisters. "Women who grew up with a financial disadvantage frequently learn the value of saving and being thrifty. Often the result is a nice, comfortable nest egg, although unfortunately, many times these ladies are so unaccustomed to spending even a single frivolous dime that the whole thing winds up being distributed among their heirs. That's partially the story in your mother's case—the bit about her not spending it, at least. Where her story diverges from most is that she managed to amass a lot more than what most would call a comfortable nest egg. Apparently she was a bit of a savant when it came to investing."

"How much?" Jules whispered.

Mr. Wiley plucked a heavy pen from its stand on his enormous desk and started to write a number on his legal pad. The sisters' eyes grew wider with each zero. He turned the paper so that it was facing them.

"Is that . . . Wait, where's the comma? Is there a decimal point in there?" Jules couldn't make sense of the number she was seeing.

"It's thirty-seven million," Mr. Wiley said.

"Dollars?" Brooke croaked. Mr. Wiley nodded.

"Shut the fuck up," Lexi said.

"Lexi," Jules hissed, "watch your mouth." Jules hadn't seen Lexi in over a year, and she'd come here today hoping her baby sister had cleaned up her act at least a little. It was clear she had not.

"Why should I?" Lexi shouted. "I'm fucking rich! I can do whatever I want! Fuckity fuck fuck fuck! How do you like me now?" Lexi had jumped up out of her chair and was dancing around Mr. Wiley's office in an appallingly suggestive manner. It didn't help that Lexi had decided that an appropriate outfit to wear to a meeting with your dead mother's lawyer consisted of painted-on jeans and a white T-shirt so sheer she might as well have been wearing her purple lace bra on the outside of it. When Jules realized her sister's racy little victory dance could go on for days, she grabbed her around the waist and thrust her back into her chair. Lexi pushed her sister's hands away and folded her own arms across her chest. Her perky nipples strained against her T-shirt and Jules fought the urge to take off her own cardigan sweater and cover them.

"Mr. Wiley, I sincerely apologize for my sister," Jules said. "She's not well, as you can see. But you started to say something about . . . I guess I'm just not even sure . . . I mean are we . . . Are my sisters and I even the beneficiaries?" Jules, Brooke and Lexi held their collective breath.

"Yes, you are," Mr. Wiley said. Brooke let out an uncharacteristic squeal; Jules was too stunned to respond.

"Fucking-a-men! Goddamn it, Mom. Way to go! Can you hear me up there? I said, WAY TO GO! I take back every awful thing I ever said about you! You're the fucking *bomb*!" Lexi had leapt up again and was shouting this at the roof, both fists raised in a double Black Panther salute.

"Alexis?" Mr. Wiley said. When he did, Lexi stood stock-still, and her sisters watched as the color drained from her perfect face. Nobody on earth called her Alexis except her mother. And since her mother was no longer *on* earth but technically below it, that left nobody. Lexi lowered herself back into her chair.

"Mr. Wiley?" Jules asked.

"As I started to say, your inheritance comes with what I suppose you could call conditions," Mr. Wiley said, tapping his pen absentmindedly on his desk.

"Conditions?" Lexi scoffed. "Like doormat over there has to get some rich doctor to marry her—like *that's* ever gonna happen—and Jules has to, I don't know, stop dressing like she's an eighty-year-old nun? Ooh, wait, she has to get knocked up! And let me guess, I have to cut off all of my hair or start flossing my teeth every day or get some stupid, shitty *actual job* or something before we get any money?" Lexi used air quotes when she said "actual job," and her sisters stifled anxious laughs. That was one of the many things they referred to as a Juliana-ism.

"Actually, you're not that far off the mark," Mr. Wiley said, nodding at Lexi.

"What does that mean?" Jules demanded. "What exactly are the conditions, Mr. Wiley?"

"Why don't I just read Juliana's note to you? I think it will answer a majority of your questions," Mr. Wiley suggested. He handed them each a copy of the letter so they could follow along.

Of course Juliana would die filthy rich, thought Jules. *How else could she control us from the grave?*

Jefferson Wiley, Esquire, cleared his throat and began:

Julia, Brooke and Alexis,

It's hard to imagine that when you hear these words, I'll be gone. I like to believe I'll be in a better place, one without pain and suffering. That's what I want for you all, too.

By now you are aware of the fact that I managed to sock away a little money before I passed, and you probably want to know how. I received a million dollars in life insurance money when your father died. Spending or enjoying it was never an option; I couldn't have lived with myself knowing that I was profiting from his death. So I invested it, and I guess I have quite a knack for picking stocks. I managed to turn that money into several dozen times what I started with. Now I want the three of you to have it. I really do. But I also don't believe that just handing it over would be doing you any favors, so instead you must earn it. In order for my inheritance to be divided in equal thirds and disbursed to each of you, you have exactly one year to meet the following conditions:

Julia: Walking dogs is not a career. I would like you to write your book and make a concerted effort to sell it. The topic can be anything of your choosing, with the explicit exception of pornography. (I don't care how well that Fifty Shades *business sold; hopefully you won't need the money anyway.) Jefferson knows some literary agents he can introduce you to; please don't embarrass him.*

Brooke: No more dating down. You must sever all ties with this Jake person Julia has told me about and be

*dating a man both of your sisters deem suitable. (Julia
and Alexis, I expect you to be discriminating.) Also, you
must take up running again. I didn't drive you to track
meets all over California for you to just throw it all away.
You have a year to train for and compete in a race no
shorter than a half-marathon. A marathon would be
better.*

*Alexis: You must get an actual job. A respectable one
with a paycheck and regular hours and, ideally, health
benefits. And no more of this "Lexi" business. Your father
and I didn't give you a stripper name; we gave you a
beautiful, elegant, classy name. It's Alexis, and you must
start using it.*

*Jefferson has an extensive file with many pages of notes
that I am confident will address any issues or
complications that arise; anything that's not covered
specifically will be decided solely at Jefferson's discretion.
Please be clear: All of these conditions must be met or the
money will go to charity. I pray you won't let your
estrangement stand in the way of what could be a very
rich and rewarding future for you all.*

Love, Mom

Mr. Wiley set down the letter and looked at the three sisters. "Any questions? Comments?"

Jules looked at her watch. January fifteenth. One year.

Brooke sat dumbly, looking as if she'd been slapped.

"She didn't even know she was going to die," Jules said, her voice barely above a whisper. "It was an accident."

"Your mother updated this letter annually," Mr. Wiley explained. Jules, Brooke and Lexi tried to process this information.

"That fucking bitch," Lexi finally said.

"Alexis, watch your mouth," Jules said.

Jules

~

Jules opened the door of her Honda and slid in, tossing her purse into the empty passenger seat. A novel, a half-marathon and an "actual job"? Had her mother been mad? Jules had made a point of visiting her weekly, and none of these things had ever come up. Sure, Jules had probably mentioned in passing that she still pined to see her name on a book cover, and she might have let it slip that Brooke had put on some weight and clearly wasn't running any longer, and certainly it would have come up when Lexi was invariably between waitressing jobs. But to lay out such specific stipulations for each of them? Who did that?

Juliana, that was who.

Jules's head was reeling as she eased onto the jam-packed 405 Freeway. Her mother had gotten a million dollars twenty years ago and had never said a word, had never stopped shopping at the dollar store, never even bought herself a single new stick of furniture? They'd stayed in their tiny two-bedroom house, the three sisters squished into a bedroom not much bigger than a single-car garage. As the girls grew up and out of that house, Juliana had watched all three of them struggle to try to make ends meet, and never once offered help. Hell, it was Jules who'd paid the ER bill the time Lexi passed out in a drunken stupor and broke her jaw; Jules who'd worked three jobs until she'd managed to save enough money to buy her own dog-walking franchise; Jules who had learned to make a week's worth of soup with just a cube of bouillon, a few carrots and a stalk of celery. And all along, her mother could have helped. Even a hundred dollars would have gotten any of them out of countless binds over the years—and Juliana could have forked over dozens of times that. But she hadn't, not even once.

None of it made sense. Why would her mother deprive herself of seeing the joy her money could bring to her daughters? Juliana Alexander had thrived on recognition, and as much as she loved to control Jules and her sisters, she could have lorded that money over them day and night. She could have bribed Jules to write her damned book and paid Brooke to dump Jake and forced Lexi to get her act together and actually been alive to witness it all. Why had her mother had her entire last wishes spelled out when she wasn't even that old or sick? Why, oh why, had she chosen this of all possible routes?

"I don't need your money," Jules said out loud, wiping away a tear that had fallen despite her best efforts to keep it together. "Shawn and I are fine. Fine, do you hear me? We have a house and jobs and I'm not a dog-walker, I'm a *business owner*. And I can grow that business as big as I want to! Shawn's going to be a lawyer, and do you know how much money they make? A *lot*, I'll have you know. I took care of myself as a kid and I'm taking care of myself now, so screw you." The tears began to fall in earnest and Jules carefully edged to the side of the freeway. At the next exit, she pulled into a Burger King and found a parking spot under the shade of a giant oak. Then she turned off her car, rested her head on the steering wheel and let the tears come.

As she cried and cried, there was no escaping the truth of the situation: She might be fine, but Brooke and Lexi certainly weren't. Brooke had let a string of loser boyfriends bleed her dry—hence her current living situation with that dreadful Jake. And Lexi, well, Jules didn't even want to think about how Lexi got by. And as much as her younger sisters had always resented her mothering ways, Jules hadn't felt as if she'd had a choice. Her mother's money would change her own life, no doubt, but it would completely transform theirs.

Jules wiped her eyes with a wad of tissues from the glove box, pulled out her phone and launched the calculator. She knew that the inheritance money would be heavily taxed, but even if the government took half of the pie, it was a big pie by any standards. Eighteen million after tax divided three ways was more than six million for each of them. *Six million dollars.* Comfortable was one thing; six million was downright rich. Jules was confident that she could write a book—a decent one, even—for that amount of cash. As for her sisters, she couldn't be sure. Certainly Brooke could break up with Jake, but could she run a half-marathon? She'd been a track star in high school, but ten years and quite a few extra pounds later, Jules couldn't really see it. And what kind of "actual job" could a high-school-dropout party girl get?

When Jules had graduated high school, every instinct in her body told her to get in her car, drive away and never look back. She'd been in Reseda all of her life and longed for a fresh start in a new place. She'd fought those urges, of course, because she still had Brooke and Lexi to think about. To her great dismay, her sisters hadn't recognized her sacrifice. They accused her of abandoning them and begged her to stay at home, but she knew she couldn't. Staying nearby was the best she could do.

Jules found a room for rent in a crappy house around the corner from the one she'd grown up in on busy Wilbur Avenue. With no skills or education, she'd taken up dog-walking, which gave her frequent opportunities to check on her sisters as she strolled by. She wasn't going to stick around forever, of course; just until her sisters had graduated, too, and were on their feet. While she was waiting, she managed to save enough money to enroll in a few classes at Los Angeles Valley College, and then she met Shawn. He, too, was just a part-time student, but he was planning to go to law school one day, and it was love at first sight. Shawn lived just on the other side of the freeway in Van Nuys, where he took care of his own sick mother. Blinded by love, Jules forgot all about her dreams of running away and starting over.

Nobody could say that Jules didn't try to keep her fractured family together. She'd kept tabs on her sisters the best she could, given them money when she had it and invited them for holiday meals and coffees out. Lexi had wanted nothing to do with her from the get-go—she didn't need anybody, she insisted—but she and Brooke had been relatively close for a while at least. But even though she'd kept her mouth shut about Brooke's weight and bit her tongue through a parade of bad boyfriends, Brooke would still accuse her of being *just like Mom* whenever they had even the tiniest disagreement. They drifted apart naturally, as people who think they have little in common often do, and Jules silently surrendered to it.

Through it all, she had been the only one to put in the back-breaking work of maintaining a relationship with their mother. Lexi couldn't be bothered and Brooke was bothered too much. So it was Jules who visited Juliana weekly, enduring her tirades alone and taking the brunt of the unhappy woman's abusive anger on behalf of her sisters. Over the years Jules had racked her brain more times than she could count, trying to figure out where she'd gone wrong or what she could have done differently to make her mother love her, and she always came up at a loss.

Seeing her sisters today, she couldn't believe the women they'd grown into. Her once athletic and outgoing middle sister was a shapeless, timid frump, and her stunning baby sister looked and acted like a strung-out streetwalker. If Brooke would let her, Jules was pretty sure she could help her get back in shape and get rid of her deadweight boyfriend. As always, Lexi was going to be the wild card. *Alexis*, she corrected herself, firing up her car engine. Jules drove home on autopilot, lost in a tangle of memories and musings.

"Well?" Shawn asked the moment he walked in the door. He'd just come from his three-hour ethics class, and he had dark rings beneath his eyes. "What did you get? Did you get the Caprice? I'll bet your mom left it to you just to piss Lexi off."

"You're not going to believe this," Jules said, throwing a container of leftover pasta into the microwave.

"Let me guess. Brooke got the Caprice? That would make Lexi even madder! I'll bet those two were going at it like a couple of cats in a bag."

"Actually, we didn't even get to the Caprice. Are you ready for this? Apparently my mom was loaded."

"Loaded?" Shawn asked. "As in rich?"

"Yup," Jules said.

"And I'm the King of Sheba." Shawn laughed.

"That is so weird, Alexis said the exact same thing! Well, she said queen, not king. But still."

"'Alexis'? Did your wacky sister decide to revamp her trampy image or something?"

"I know, Shawn, it's nuts, but apparently my mom had millions of dollars—thirty-seven of them to be exact—and she left them to me and my sisters—"

"You're not serious," Shawn said, his face a portrait of disbelief. After all, they'd spent a decade working their fingers to the bone and shopping at three different grocery stores each week to get the best deal on the cheapest cuts of meat. Now they were comfortable, by SoCal standards at least, but they had no padding, no savings, and no plan for the future.

"I'm dead serious, I swear," Jules insisted. "I mean, that's what her attorney says, and he's the executor. Oh, and that doesn't include the condo. Or the Caprice." She smiled at this last bit.

"So you're saying we are about to inherit"—he did some calculating—"somewhere in the neighborhood of ten million dollars?"

"I think it's probably closer to six million after taxes, but yes. With a catch."

"A catch? What do you mean, a catch?"

"I forget what Mr. Wiley, her attorney, called them exactly, but they're basically conditions. Things that Brooke and Lexi and I have to do before we can get the money. Oh, one of them is that Alexis has to go by her given name from now on. No more Lexi, ever."

"That is *so* your mom," Shawn said, shaking his head. "Wait, what's your condition?"

"I have to write my book," Jules said.

"That's it? Holy shit, baby, we're going to be rich! Filthy stinking rich!" He picked Jules up and swung her around in circles until she thought she'd puke. Finally, when he couldn't manage another spin, he collapsed on top of her on the couch she'd re-slipcovered at least a half dozen times.

"That's it?" Jules said, pushing him off of her. "I've been trying to write that book for ten years. And do you know how many pages I have? Go on, take a guess."

"Fifty?" Shawn said tentatively.

"Try four. Four lousy pages in ten years. But I'm sure I can whip out another three hundred or so this year—that's the deadline, one year from now. Oh, I also have to 'make a concerted effort to sell it,' which I should give at least, what, a month? Or two or three? Now I'm down to writing it in nine months. No problem."

"First of all, we're not destitute, so you don't need to freak out," Shawn said. "Although with that kind of cash in the bank, think of what we could do . . ." Shawn trailed off, lost in thoughts of fishing boats and European vacations, no doubt.

"It's not about us," Jules said. "Brooke and Lexi need this, Shawn. It's almost like this money is the only shot they've got. I can't *not* do it. I can't let them down. I couldn't live with myself."

"And you *will* do it, I don't doubt it for a second. You haven't had time to write because you've been busting your ass for me, for us, so quit being so hard on yourself," Shawn told her. "Plus, you never had a big, fat, golden *six-million-dollar* carrot dangling in your face before. Right? I mean, Christ. Talk about an incentive! You can do this, Jules. You know you can. *I* know you can. Let's do the math. How many pages is a book?"

Jules loved that about Shawn; his mind went exactly where hers went. "Three hundred. It works out to thirty or so pages a month. Finished pages, that is."

"That's a page a day! You've got this, Jules. No problem. And I'll do everything around here. All of it. The shopping and the cleaning and everything else you do. All you have to do is write."

"The book isn't all," Jules told him, cracking open a beer and taking a swig before handing it to Shawn.

"What else? Do we have to climb Kilimanjaro on our hands and knees carrying live porcupines on our heads? Because whatever it is, I'm in."

"Brooke has to break up with Jake, for good, and be dating someone who both Lexi and I unanimously approve of."

"Well, that seems . . . not impossible," Shawn said hopefully.

"Oh, she also has to train for a half-marathon," Jules added. Shawn paused, letting this information sink in.

"Wasn't she a track star in high school?" he asked.

"Yeah, that was ten years and I don't know how many pounds ago," Jules said with a sigh.

"What about Lexi?" Shawn asked. He screwed his face up as if anticipating a blow.

"Lexi—shit—*Alexis* . . ." Jules paused here and took a deep breath.

"What about her?" He wanted to know.

"She has to get an actual job."

"Oh shit." Shawn took a swig of the Keystone and handed it back.

"I know," Jules said.

Brooke

❧

"A half-marathon? Really?" Brooke asked her reflection in her dresser mirror with an angry laugh. "You're funny, Mom. Really funny. You drove me all over California and sat at every track meet because you wouldn't let me take the bus with all of the other girls! That was *your* choice, not mine! Why didn't you just come out and call me fat, or demand that I get back into my high school track shorts before I can get your money? I'm not stupid; I know that's what this is about. And do you want to know why I quit running and got fat? Because of *you*. You and your need to control every last thing I ever did. Of *course* I got fat. When I was finally out of your house and didn't have somebody scrutinizing every forkful that went into my mouth and yelling at me to *go run five more miles*, you know what? I sat on my butt and I ate whatever I wanted! And I enjoyed it! And I don't even mind being fat, so you can kiss my fat ass." Brooke didn't usually swear, and she was surprised at how good it felt.

Frustrated, she flopped across her bed and sobbed. She

sobbed because she was fat and she did mind it, and because she missed being known as "the athletic one," and because while her mother hadn't spelled out a causal conclusion, Brooke knew she used her weight as an excuse to date down. It had been that way ever since Billy McCann, her high school sweetheart and the one true love of her life. She'd been thin and beautiful, and Billy had fallen out of love with her anyway. So she ate and ate to pass the time, to fill the void that had been left when she'd been abandoned by him and Jules practically at the same time, and to punish her mother and her sister and, possibly, herself.

Since then, her boyfriend criteria had mostly consisted of one singular item: whether or not they'd have her. But Jake wasn't that bad, at least compared to some of the other guys she'd dated. At least he hadn't run off with all of her money. Of course, she didn't have any money to run off with, but that wasn't the point. She knew she could do much worse because she repeatedly had.

If she broke up with Jake, where would she go? What would she do? Brooke had moved into his studio apartment after they'd been dating only three months, when she'd been evicted (after another boyfriend had disappeared with her meager life's savings, but who was keeping track?) and had nowhere else to go. She'd insisted on paying her share of the rent when she moved in with Jake, which turned out to be just over four hundred bucks a month because his place was rent controlled and he'd lived there forever. Of course, then he'd lost his job, and it wasn't like she could kick him out of his own apartment or anything, so now she was paying the full eight twenty-five. Even so, Brooke was pretty sure there weren't a lot of rooms for rent at that price in the Valley, and with her credit card bills and on her salary as a preschool teacher, it was pretty much all she could afford.

"Why do you even need to go to college to be a *preschool*

teacher?" her mother had demanded when she'd told her she had been accepted to the community college. "That's just a glorified babysitter. I'll help you out if you at least promise to get a job in secondary education, preferably high school and ideally something to do with literature. It would make your father so proud." Brooke knew she could lie and say that was what she planned to do, but she wouldn't give Juliana the satisfaction. She didn't want her mother's help—which she was certain would only amount to a class here or a book there anyway. She was tired of being owned, and she knew what she wanted to do with her life. When Juliana had forwarded her a link to a news article titled "The Ten Lowest-Paying Jobs That Require a Degree" (preschool teacher was at the tippy top), she'd refused to even respond.

"Kiss my fat ass," Brooke said again at the memory, sniffling. She pushed herself up to a sitting position and took several deep breaths before padding on wobbly legs to her apartment's tiny bathroom. She gasped when she saw her reflection. She looked atrocious. Brooke splashed cold water on her face and then held a washcloth there, willing the redness and puffiness to go away. Neither complied. She was playing a sick game of poking her pudgy pink cheek with her finger and watching the spots turn white when her phone rang. She didn't recognize the number. She really didn't feel like talking to anybody, but it wasn't in Brooke's nature to ignore a phone call. That was just plain rude.

"Hello?" she said. Her voice was hoarse.

"Did you not pay the damned phone bill?" It was Jake and he was pissed. "My phone's dead."

"I paid it," Brooke croaked.

"Well then, what the hell is wrong with it?" he demanded.

"I don't really know, Jake," Brooke sighed. "Maybe you dropped it in the toilet one too many times." She knew she sounded robotic;

she also knew he wouldn't ask why or even think to ask how it had gone with her mother's attorney today.

Jake yelled something to someone in the background.

"Where are you?" Brooke looked at the clock. It was after eleven at night.

"Out," Jake replied.

"Are you coming home?" she asked. Sometimes he did and sometimes he didn't.

"Don't know yet," he said. "But if I do, try not to wake me in the morning when you get up."

"Okay," she said mechanically. Jake hung up without saying good-bye.

"All right, I'm going to start training tomorrow," she told her splotchy reflection. "I'll get up and run before work." She did some mental calculations, and realized that she'd have to get up at four thirty in order to get an hour-long workout in, have time to shower and dress and get to school by six fifty. That was fine. Brooke knew that she was such an awful witch when she was tired that Jake would probably kick her out anyway. She could cross that bridge when it happened. This much decided, she trudged to her computer and looked up marathon training. Five million results? Jeez, this was stupid. Brooke knew what she had to do: Run a little bit farther each day until she could run just over thirteen miles. It wasn't rocket science. It wouldn't be easy at first, but she knew she'd be motivated when the weight started falling off her. In high school, she'd had to eat around the clock to keep from getting too skinny from all that running. How could she have forgotten about that?

Relieved to have a plan, she shuffled to her tiny studio apartment's kitchenette. After surveying her options, she pulled some Oreos and a jar of peanut butter from the cupboard and grabbed the chocolate-chip-cookie-dough ice cream from the freezer. She dumped the remains of each bag, jar and carton into her giant mixing bowl and carried it to the couch. *Yes,* she thought as she shoveled spoon after spoon of cold, sweet deliciousness into her mouth, *it's going to be so great to be skinny again.*

Lexi

❧

"Fuck her," Lexi said, pouring another shot of rotgut tequila. "Seriously."

"Okay," said Brad. He took a deep drag off his huge glass bong and gave her a thumbs-up.

"I'm talking about my *dead mother*, you disgusting perv," Lexi said. Plumes of smoke shot out of Brad's nostrils and mouth as he burst out laughing, which led to a loud fit of coughing and sputtering.

"Damn it, Lexi, that was a good hit, too," her roommate said, cupping the smoke toward his face and trying to inhale it.

"It's Alexis now, asshole," she slurred, reaching for the bong.

"Slexis? Sweet. I'll try to remember that. Slexis. Slexis. Slexis. Yeah, it'll never happen. Besides, that's a pretty fucked-up name. What's wrong with Lexi?"

"It'll cost me ten million bucks, that's what's wrong with it."

"No shit? Damn. I'd change it then, too. Wait, what's the new one again?"

"Alexis," she told him, trying her best to enunciate the awful word. Without the "it's" in front of it, it was nearly audible.

"That's pretty fancy," Brad said. "Could you just be, like, Mary or Jane or something? Hey, *Mary Jane*. Get it? I totally didn't even do that on purpose." He exploded with cough-laughter again and Lexi couldn't help but laugh, too.

"Nope, it's gotta be Alexis. I know, it fucking sucks. Hey, what's a good job? I have to get one and I don't want it to be some lame-ass, douche-y job like secretary or teacher or anything. I can't think of a single job that's not lame-ass or douche-y."

"Blow job?" Brad suggested.

"You're a moron."

"Okay, for real. What about, like, a massage person? I forget what they're called. You could practice on me any time you wanted."

"I am so not touching disgusting hairy bodies all day long," Lexi said with a shudder.

"I'm not *that* hairy." Brad thought for a while. "What about Victoria's Secret? My girlfriend works there and can probably get you in."

"You have a girlfriend? Dude, we just fucked last night."

"Sorry, she's more like an ex-girlfriend. Whatever. I hardly ever see her but she's chill. Want me to call her?"

"Yeah, I don't think selling skanky underwear fits the bill for an 'actual job.'"

"Maybe you could go work for your sister?" Brad asked, offering her the bag of Doritos. Lexi had told her roommates all about Jules and her dog-walking "business." They'd laughed and laughed—who called walking dogs a job anyway? Besides, dogs were smelly and gross, and Jules would probably pay her three dollars an hour.

"I'd rather sell skanky underwear," Lexi said, stuffing a Dorito into her mouth. She'd figure something out. For ten million bucks, she was going to have to.

Jules

~

Jules had been very busy enjoying a simple, mostly happy childhood when her dad had dropped dead of a heart attack. They were at the park, the whole family, on an otherwise perfect summer Saturday, eating ice-cream cones and watching him play softball with some of the other dads from school. Jules was just twelve when it happened, and his death rocked her world in every way imaginable. Her parents had had one of the few happy, intact marriages she knew of, even though they struggled financially. John Alexander had been a writer, and from the looks of things, publishing was a tricky, fickle business to be in. He'd sell something one year and nothing the next two, and they were all just waiting for something he'd written to hit it big. Her dad would always say "not if but when," and of course they believed him. He was talented, everyone knew it; they just had to be patient. Jules and her two younger sisters didn't complain about sharing a room or having only one small bathroom in the house, because they knew it was temporary. Any day now John Alexander would hit a bestseller list and then they'd be rich and famous. They'd probably move to Malibu or Pacific Palisades or maybe even Beverly Hills. When that happened, the very first thing he was going to do, he promised, was build them a swimming pool. Jules had the floating lounge chairs all picked out. And then he died.

Their mother was inconsolable. Brooke and Lexi were only eight and six, so it was Jules who picked up the slack. She taught herself to cook and took over as the head of the household, making sure her sisters did their homework and brushed their teeth and had clean underwear. She practiced Juliana's signature until it was perfect so she could sign school forms and permission slips without having to bother her mother while she sat and stared at the wall. Her sisters, Lexi in particular, weren't old enough to notice or appreciate her efforts, but Jules wasn't doing it for the recognition; she was doing it because it was the right thing to do, the *only* thing to do, and because somebody had to do it.

At the time, Jules would have said that first year was the worst. Her mother was present in body only, leaving Jules with nowhere to turn with her own grief. Their tiny house, once made a home with laughter and jokes and music and games, became unbearably lifeless and tense. Jules prayed every night before bed. She knew it was silly to ask God to bring her dad back, she told Him, but if it wasn't too much trouble, could she pretty please have her mom?

Jules could remember the exact day Juliana had awoken from her stupor. Nearly a full year had passed since her father's death, and Jules had felt the need to mark or acknowledge it in some way. "Tomorrow is the anniversary," she'd said to her mother tentatively. Juliana had exploded with fury.

"Anniversaries are things you *celebrate*," her mother had screamed. It was the first time Juliana had shown any emotion other than dejection in months, and Jules hoped it was a turning point. And indeed it was—but not in the direction she was longing for. To her daughters' great dismay, Juliana was no longer the warm, free-spirited, fun-loving mom they'd once known. Almost overnight she became critical and demanding and obsessed with micromanaging every detail of her daughters' lives. It had taken years of painful processing, but finally Jules believed she understood: Something inescapably beyond her mother's control had robbed her of her husband, her life, her entire future. She was bitter and angry and would be damned if she was going to let that happen again.

Jules thought about her mother now, about how hard it must have been for her, and felt guilty for the ten thousandth time that she hadn't been more compassionate toward this broken shell of a woman. But damn it, Juliana had made it impossible, she truly had. She'd hovered and criticized, and nothing Jules or her sisters did was ever good enough. She wasn't quite Joan Crawford, because she didn't drink and she'd only hit Jules twice that she could remember. But Jules couldn't count the times her mother would demand she change her clothes, or forbid her from reading a certain book all of her friends were reading, or rip apart the bed she'd just made and insist she do it again. "You'll thank me someday," she'd say. Jules was still waiting for someday to come.

In the meantime, she had a novel to write. She'd called her top dog-walker and had her take over her usual routes. She cringed at the thought of spending the extra money, but it was for the greatest good. She pulled up the story she'd started a decade ago and reread her own words, surprised at how unfamiliar they felt. The writing was fine, good even, but the problem she was having was the same one she'd had since she started: There was no plot, no story. There were lovely and lyrical descriptions of her main characters, and the setting was palpable from her narrative. But what was going to *happen* to them? She had no idea.

How hard can this be? Jules wondered. Bookstores were lined with billions of stories, each crafted exactly the same way: by putting one word after another. Why did this feel so impossible? Did she even want to write a book? Or was she just doing it to please her dead parents? How had this become the sole focus of her life? And was money really that important anyway?

Money? Please. Six million dollars wasn't money; it was freedom. It was never again having to stress about bills or student loans or saving for the future. It was no longer tossing and turning every night worrying about her sisters or wondering if she'd get a call from the cops or the hospital or both. It was the family she and Shawn desperately wanted to start—but only when they were sure they could give their children everything they never had, from cars on their sixteenth birthdays to prepaid tuition to the colleges of their choice. Jules had read online that babies go through an average of eighty dollars in diapers alone every month. Eighty bucks! Not to mention food and clothes and toys and everything else they needed—or that the clever marketers made you think they needed, at any rate. With a few million in the bank, she could finally relax and splurge a little on herself. She could buy a fancy stroller like the ones she saw the cute young moms pushing around the mall. The eight hundred dollars the popular day-care center charged every month for full-time care would be couch change. Which was ironic, seeing as she wouldn't need full-time care because she'd no longer be working around the clock.

Was there a book idea there? Something about a mom . . . or a baby . . . or somebody buying a diaper company? Jules sat at her keyboard, her fingers hovering at the ready in their proper positions, but nothing came.

Maybe she just needed to do some research, get inspired. Jules thought about the sitcoms she and Shawn watched; wasn't each twenty-three-minute episode a mini story of its own? She could just watch a bunch of them and then steal one of the plotlines, which wasn't really stealing because at the end of the day, how many stories were there to be told in the world? People rewrote and modernized classics all the time. *Bridget Jones's Diary* was *Pride and Prejudice*; *The Lion King* was *Hamlet*; *My Fair Lady* was *Pygmalion*. Writing was more than putting words on paper; there were ideas and inspiration to consider. Just because she hadn't yet found her muse didn't mean she wasn't working.

Jules poured herself a cup of coffee, which was now ice cold. She nuked it for a full minute and then dumped in several spoonfuls of sugar and a generous helping of milk. It was lukewarm and bitter, but she drank it anyway. The effect of this was that she was wide awake and jittery all day as she watched TV and completely forgot that she was supposed to be looking for a plot.

Brooke

〜

Brooke shot straight up in bed and looked at her phone. Four thirty? Who was calling her at four thirty in the morning? Then she remembered: It was her alarm. She was supposed to go for a run, which would surely be more like a walk. Her heart pounding, she tentatively felt around in the bed; at least Jake hadn't come home. She shuddered to think of the outrage that would rain down if she'd dared to disturb his precious sleep.

Two hours later, Brooke heard the sounds of birds chirping in the distance. She peeled her eyelids open and reached for her phone. Six thirty-five. Cripes. She'd fallen back asleep, missed her workout, and was supposed to be at work in fifteen minutes.

"Shoot, shoot, shoot," she mumbled, flying out of bed and scrambling around the room for her clothes. Good thing she *hadn't* exercised, because there was no time for a shower. Fortunately everything she owned was a solid color and pretty much went with everything else, so she grabbed a skirt and top and some shoes and quickly ran a brush through her thick, wavy hair.

Then she raced to the kitchen and pulled a bag of gummy bears from the cabinet, indelicately stuffing a fistful into her mouth. She could brush her teeth when she got home. She shoved the bag of candy into her purse, grabbed her keys and raced out the door.

It wasn't until the noon bell rang that she remembered she'd forgotten to bring a lunch.

"Want half of my sandwich?" Pam offered, holding up a turkey on wheat.

"Oh, that's okay," Brooke said, thinking she could sneak into the art room and eat her gummy bears.

"Really, I never finish it all anyway," Pam insisted. Brooke finished her lunch every single day. Always. And she was still starving when she got home. Pam must be some sort of genetic mutant, that was all there was to it.

"If you don't mind, that would be great," Brooke said gratefully, wondering if she had ever not finished a meal in her life. "I can bring lunch for both of us tomorrow." *And when I'm rich,* she added in her head, *I'll bring us lunch every day, I promise.* She couldn't tell Pam about her mom's will, and she certainly couldn't tell her about the ridiculous conditions. Pam would probably suggest they start running stadium steps after work or something crazy like that, and then when would Brooke get to catch up on her favorite reality TV? No, it was definitely best to keep the whole inheritance nightmare under tight wraps.

When she got home from work, Brooke was even hungrier than usual. She knew she should go for a run, but food was fuel, after all. She'd run much harder and farther if she had something in her stomach. She made a beeline for the fridge and pulled out the leftover chicken-fried steak she'd made two nights before.

"I was just about to eat that," Jake announced. He'd been playing video games when she'd gotten home and had barely looked up to say hello. He must have been there awhile, as he had clearly worked up quite an appetite.

"Well, now you're not because I'm starving and I got here first," Brooke told him. She didn't usually talk back to him, but she was hungry and cranky.

"Yeah, you really look like you're *starving*," Jake said, still absorbed in his game. "What the hell am I supposed to eat?"

"I don't know, but I'm sure you can figure something out," Brooke said, stinging from the insult. He could eat rat poison for all she cared. She had shopped for the food, she'd paid for the food, she'd cooked the food, and now she wanted to eat the food. She was pretty sure she was well within her rights to do so.

"Where's your purse?" Jake asked, throwing the game controller aside angrily and leaping to his feet. He was wearing the Santa Claus pajama bottoms she'd bought for him last Christmas and a ripped Led Zeppelin T-shirt, and Brooke wasn't sure which looked crazier: his outfit or his eyes.

"On the hook," she told him.

"Why don't you get it for me?"

"Why don't you get a job?" she asked.

"Why don't you find somewhere else to live?" he countered. She watched as he snatched her purse off the hook and pulled the lone ten-dollar bill from her wallet.

"I'm taking your car," he announced, grabbing her keys and shoving his feet into the pair of flip-flops he always left by the door. "I'm out of gas." She was about to point out his clothes but he slammed out the front door before she could get the words out. It served him right.

Brooke popped the chicken into the microwave, then she pulled the cottage cheese container from the back of the fridge. She dumped the contents into a bowl, congratulating herself on the clever decoy. She knew Jake wouldn't touch that tub unless he was actually starving to death, so her chocolate-covered almonds were perfectly safe. They were even better cold, she thought now, as she shoveled them into her mouth with a spoon.

By the time she finished her steak, Brooke was too stuffed to move. Clearly there was going to be a learning curve with this whole becoming-an-athlete-again plan.

That's when she had an epiphany: Obviously she couldn't train for a half-marathon, break up with her boyfriend and change her entire living situation at the same time. It was too stressful. The breakup would be quick—as soon as she got up the nerve to do it—and she was positive she could find an affordable place to live in a month or two, three max. Then she'd have nine months to work up to running thirteen lousy miles. That was more than doable. She could do it in half that time, no problem.

Brooke celebrated having come up with a perfectly reasonable plan with a beer and the rest of the chocolate-covered almonds.

Lexi

~

"Are you going to answer that damned thing or not?" Ryan asked. "I can't take it anymore."

"Word," added Brad.

"Why does it matter if I answer it or not? It still makes the same sound." Even as buzzed as she was, Lexi was pretty sure this was an airtight argument.

"Yeah, but it stresses me out," Ryan said. He was chopping a rock of coke into a fine powder on the side of her hand mirror that wasn't cracked.

"Me, too," Brad agreed.

"It stresses you out? You guys are so fucked up," Lexi said. She stretched her long legs out on the coffee table. It had been there when she moved in and was an ugly, beat-up mess. When nobody currently in residence claimed ownership of the thing, she'd found some paint in a storage closet and given it a makeover. There hadn't been much of a paint selection, so she'd used purple as the base and then painted a giant red cannabis leaf in the middle. It had looked great when she was finished, too, but now it was scuffed and covered in burn marks. Oh well. That was what happened when you lived with a bunch of slobs.

The Pad, as their house was known, could accommodate as many as ten people at a time, so it may as well have had a revolving door for roommates. At the moment, Ryan and Brad were the only two who weren't gay or uptight assholes and also liked to sit around and get high as often as possible. They were like brothers to Lexi. Well, if you didn't count the fact that she occasionally slept with both of them.

Lexi looked at her phone. Jules, of course. Her pain-in-the-ass sister had been calling her every day and leaving these annoying chirpy messages. "Just checking in! How's the job search going? Let me know if I can do anything to help!" Lexi fumed every time she heard one of them. Of course Jules wanted to help her now, when there was something in it for her. Where had she been the last fifteen years, that's what Lexi wanted to know. Her oldest sister had moved out of the house the day after she graduated high school, leaving her sisters with Juliana the Terrible. Lexi had been just twelve, although she had looked and acted much older. By that point she had already discovered boys and booze and pot, and she used all of them to escape the hell that was her life at home. Juliana's increasingly overbearing posture seemed to multiply when Jules left and she could only divide her intrusive attention by two. Lexi had had to be incredibly sneaky about it all, which to her had been the best part. She knew that her mom suspected she was doing *something* she shouldn't be, and Lexi savored the feeling of having something all her own, something her mother couldn't control.

"Hey, Slexis," Brad said now. He couldn't remember "Alexis" to save his life, but "Slexis" he had no problem with. "Don't forget we need a buck-fifty for rent. Bump?" He wiped his nose on his sleeve and offered her the mirror.

"Fuck," she said, taking the mirror. Blow wasn't her favorite, but Lexi wasn't one to turn down a free buzz. "I think I've got like ninety. Maybe you guys could cover me? I'll pay you back." She licked her full lips suggestively. That was almost always all it took.

The guys shrugged. "Sure, okay," Brad said. "That cool, Ry?" Ryan nodded.

Lexi sat back, feeling proud that she'd figured out how to take care of herself. Certainly no adult had ever taught her. The guys would be happy to fork over the sixty bucks she was short if she let them screw her a few times. She could wait disgusting tables at the Salty Dog all night and not make half that much. Besides, they were her friends and she didn't really mind, especially since it hardly ever took either of them longer than two minutes to get the job done. If she was actually getting paid, that would translate into a few hundred bucks an hour. Lexi was pretty sure whatever "actual job" she got to please her dead mother wouldn't pay anywhere close to that.

Jules

~⁓~

Jules stepped out of the shower and pulled the damp towel that Shawn had just used off the hook. She'd been fourteen the time Juliana had yelled at her and called her selfish for taking the last dry towel, and she'd never done it again. She couldn't. Jules wondered now if there were people in the world who took a fresh, dry towel every single time they showered. She'd bet there were, and she wondered still if she would ever feel like she deserved to be one of them.

"I won't be home until after midnight tonight," Shawn said, spitting toothpaste into the sink. He'd taken a security job at night so that she could cut back on her dog-walking clients and pay her employees to take her place. She was still taking a few trips a week, mostly because she needed to get out of the house. Plus, she could be plotting out her book while she was walking the dogs, so it wasn't like she was shirking her responsibilities. Theoretically, at least.

"I feel awful for you," she told him. "You're working yourself to death." Even though they were almost definitely going to be loaded in the very near future, Shawn had insisted that he could never be a lazy, jobless loafer. He'd been putting in fifty hours a week as a workers' comp claims adjuster while he was putting himself through law school, and he was still doing both. But instead of feeling pressured to pursue an in-house position with an oil and gas conglomerate or some other ridiculously high-paying (and soul-stealing) path, in light of their imminent wealth he had decided he was going to become a public defender. Like Jules, he'd been raised in near poverty by a single mom, but unlike Jules, he had a father who had been a wife-beating asshole before he died. Shawn dreamed of putting men like Adam Richardson behind bars. In the meantime, they had bills to pay. Jules certainly couldn't finish her novel if they couldn't pay their mortgage and became homeless before she hit her deadline.

"Yeah, you should really feel *awful* for me," Shawn joked. "Sucks to be married to a millionaire bestselling author. However will I cope?" He feigned wiping his brow.

"You're funny," she said now. "But seriously, you're working yourself to death and you never complain about everything you're doing around here and you're my biggest fan and just, you know, thanks." How had she gotten so lucky? Most days she felt like pinching herself to make sure she wasn't dreaming him up. Shawn stepped in for a hug, but she pushed him away. "I'm dripping wet! You'll get soaked."

He wrapped his long arms around her anyway.

"Do you think I care?" he said. "About my shirt getting wet or about working a little harder than usual? It's just for a year, and I'm so proud of you I can't even stand it. Honestly. When can I read something? I know you hate it when I ask that, but

I'm dying for a peek. I promise I won't try to edit it or offer any suggestions. How about just a page? The first page, that's it. And then I'll leave you alone."

"Nope, sorry," she said. She gave him a quick kiss and pulled back to survey the damage. The front of his T-shirt, as she had predicted, had a giant wet imprint of her body on it. "Look at you. I told you."

"And I told you, I don't care. It'll dry. And fine, be stingy about your book. I guess I'll have to wait with all of the other nobodies to enjoy your brilliance. But tell me one thing: Am I in there? Even, like, thinly veiled? Come on, throw me a bone."

Jules laughed. "Of course you're in there. You're one of the main characters."

"Excellent," he said with a grin. "Now get to work. You've got all day to whip out one solid, finished page."

Or twenty or thirty, she said in her head.

It was already February, and Jules had yet to come up with a single viable idea. She tortured herself daily with the new, updated calculations for how many pages she needed to write a month, a week, a day. *Write about what you know,* people always said. What did Jules know, exactly? Death and hardship and miserable mothers and messed-up sisters who wouldn't return your texts or phone calls. Who wanted to read about *that*? No, she needed a big idea, something she could sink her teeth into and really run with. Her dad had written thrillers teeming with espionage and international terrorism and nuclear war, and Jules could confidently say that none of those things would fall into the what-she-knew category. Then again, her dad didn't have firsthand experience with any of those things, either, that she knew of, and he had managed to crank out a half-dozen books in the genre. The more she thought about it, the more confusing and daunting the whole prospect became.

She sat down once again at her desk. A book about a man . . . a good, honest, hardworking husband who loved his wife and dreamed of being a millionaire. She couldn't think of a thing to write—or anything more god-awful boring.

Brooke

Brooke turned her back to the floor-length mirror and let her bathrobe slide to the floor. It had been years since she'd actually looked at herself without clothes on, and she had no desire to break her stellar record of avoidance anytime soon.

She stepped into the shower, thinking about how good it was going to feel to be a runner again, to actually use—and maybe even like—her body after all these years. She'd been tall and naturally thin as a child, and the junior high cross-country coach had sought her out on these qualities alone. Brooke had never been sought out for anything, ever, and she'd been both thrilled and terrified by it.

"You run?" Coach Bradley had asked, sizing up her gangly limbs. He'd been watching her class play field hockey, and apparently had liked something he'd seen.

"Not really," Brooke had admitted. "I mean, just in PE I guess."

"Well, you do now," Coach had insisted. "See you on the track at three o'clock." When Juliana insisted on driving her to her first meet, Brooke hadn't just shown up; she'd *shone.* For the first time since her father died, she thought maybe she saw something in her mother—a spark of interest, an inkling of something almost resembling encouragement. Brooke had never wanted to excel at anything so badly. What nature hadn't given her in the way of innate talent, she made up for in sheer drive. She pushed herself until she puked, and then she pushed herself some more. There were girls out there with far more experience and athletic ability than she had, but none had her determination. She won meet after meet, often beating her own records. Where had that girl gone? she wondered now as she dried herself. Where was the girl who would endure self-inflicted pain to get what she wanted?

"Goddamn it, hurry up in there," Jake barked through the door, banging on it for emphasis. "Are you taking a monster dump or something? Jesus, Brooke. Would it kill you to think about somebody else for once in your life?"

Brooke sighed as she picked her bathrobe up off the floor and wrapped it tightly around her. Then she counted to one hundred in her head as slowly as she possibly could before opening the door.

"Sorry," she said as she brushed past a furious Jake. "All yours."

She slipped one of her standard tent-style dresses over her head and grabbed her phone to check the time. The home screen told her she had one new text and one voice mail, both from Jules. She deleted them both without reading or listening to either. She had no desire to hear how great Jules's novel was coming along, or to be grilled for details about Lexi's job hunt, of which Brooke knew exactly nothing. And she certainly wasn't keen on having to admit that she'd taken a grand total of zero steps toward either of her two goals.

"Brooke, bring me a decent bar of soap, would you?" Jake shouted. "This sliver you left in here is worthless."

She knew she could pretend not to hear him, but it wasn't worth the tirade he'd unleash if she didn't bring him the stupid soap. She grabbed a new bar of cheap, store-brand soap from a crowded shelf in the single broom/clothes/junk closet and brought it to Jake.

"You're welcome," she said when he failed to acknowledge the gesture in any way.

"Your trophy is in the mail," he sneered.

Pretty soon I am going to be filthy, rotten rich, she said in her head as she quietly closed the bathroom door behind her. *I won't ever—and I mean ever—have to take this sort of abuse from anyone again. I'll be able to do whatever I want and buy whatever I want and live wherever I want.* Even as she issued this silent promise or threat or whatever it was, Brooke didn't quite believe it.

She thought now about what she would do with millions of dollars. The truth was, her mind really couldn't wrap itself around what being wealthy would look like. Would she keep all of that money in the bank, or would she have to learn how to invest it? Would she walk into a Realtor's office and pick a house out of one of those catalogs that came with the newspaper and write a check for the whole thing? Would she quit her job? She obviously wouldn't need the money, but she loved her kids as if they were her own. Besides, if she did quit, what would she do all day? She'd probably have people to cook and clean and do awful chores like grocery shop and mow the lawn for her. What did rich people do with their free time? Volunteer, she supposed. Shop a lot, certainly. Count their money, maybe. Brooke thought all of those things might get boring after a while. Maybe she'd open her own private preschool that underprivileged kids could attend for free. Surely six million dollars was enough to fund something like that. She wondered how much she was going to have to pay an accountant to figure all of this out for her. She'd heard stories of people who won the lottery going back to being broke in a matter of years or even months, and she made a mental note to make sure to learn how to budget. She certainly wasn't about to jump through a year's worth of painful, flaming hoops for nothing.

Lexi

~

"You guys are both moving out?" Lexi sat up too quickly and swooned, knocking over her beer and Brad's bong when she grabbed the table to steady herself.

"Yeah, Slex, you know, sorry," Brad said. He looked around for a towel or something to catch the beer and bong water that was racing toward the edge of the table. When his search proved fruitless, he pulled his LEGALIZE IT T-shirt over his head and dropped it onto the foul, wet mess. "My brother has an extra room and he said me and Ry can live there for free. You know, so we can work on our music and shit. There's not enough room for all three of us. Plus my brother is kind of a dick. You'd hate him."

"When?" Lexi asked.

"First thing in the morning," Brad told her.

Lexi was screwed. What were the odds she'd get two new totally cool, straight guy roommates who would be willing to pay her part of the rent in exchange for the possibility of maybe someday getting laid? Why did nothing ever go her way? Why?

It was her mother's fault, obviously. She'd dropped the parenting ball in the biggest way possible, pushing Lexi away with her need to dominate everything in her path. For some reason, Lexi thought now about when she was thirteen years old and had gotten her first period. She'd asked her mom to buy her some tampons, but Juliana wouldn't even entertain the idea, insisting that she was "too young" for tampons because that area was "sacred." Lexi tried the pads her mother gave her; the gigantic, stiff, generic-brand kind that felt like she had a stale hoagie roll or a wadded-up hand towel in her underpants. She couldn't run or swim or even sit comfortably in one of those things. Lexi had fought the urge to inform her mother that she'd already gotten intimately familiar with the orifice in question and was pretty sure it was far from sacred; instead she took to stealing spare change from Juliana's purse—just a quarter here or a handful of dimes there, never paper money—until she had the six dollars she needed to buy a lousy box of tampons. Sometimes she would replace what she took with pennies from her piggy bank so her mom wouldn't notice the difference in her wallet's weight. It was a bittersweet practice that made her feel guilty, angry, ashamed and proud all at the same time, and she'd had no choice but to endure it for years.

"Who's going to be in charge of collecting bill money now?" Lexi asked. Not that it mattered, she thought, doodling absent-mindedly on the wet kitchen table with a Sharpie.

"Sita," Ryan said. "Sorry."

Sita was the nickname Lexi had come up with for their roommate Rachel, and it stood for Stick in the Ass. To say Rachel was a bit of an uptight priss was like saying molten lava was a tiny bit warm. Sita definitely wasn't going to be into the freeloading-roommates-with-benefits thing, and besides, Lexi wouldn't touch her nasty freckled ass with a ten-foot pole. She'd live on the street if she had to; she'd done it before. She put her head down on Brad's wet, smelly shirt.

"Fuck," was all she could say.

Her portion of the utilities was already past due, but Ryan was usually cool about it. Lexi looked in her wallet; she had exactly eighteen dollars. She called Floyd, the owner of the Salty Dog, and asked if she could pick up a few shifts.

"Are you fucking out of your stoned-out mind?" he shouted at her. "You didn't show up for your last four shifts, Lexi. Do you know how fucked I am when you pull that shit? I had the goddamned Mexican cooks serving the fucking food. Jorge probably spilled fifty bucks' worth of beer. No way. Never. Not if you were the last hot little ass on the planet." Floyd had slammed the phone in her ear.

Well, maybe this was just the kick in the pants she needed, Lexi thought bitterly. It was something Juliana would have said.

When the boys finally stumbled off to bed, Lexi hatched her plan. She needed to get out before Sita started riding her ass for her share of the bills, which would surely be five minutes after Ry and Brad drove away with their crappy things. At least she didn't have much stuff; that simplified things a bit. She grabbed her phone and started punching at the keys. Desperate times called for desperate measures, and if Alexis Alexander was anything at all at this particular moment besides high and broke, it was definitely desperate.

Jules

❦

"No way," Jules said, staring at her phone screen.

"What is it?" Shawn asked. She had waited up for him to get home—she barely saw him at all these days—and they had just crawled into bed. Jules was hoping he'd have enough energy to have sex, something they hadn't done in weeks. Half the time she was already asleep when he got home, and the other nights he passed out before she could even ask him about his day.

"A text from Alexis," she said, showing him her phone. He read it out loud.

"'Need to talk to you have a favor not a big deal call me.'"

"What do you think she wants?" Jules asked. "I'm scared."

"Probably money," Shawn said. "And how funny that she texts you and asks you to call her. Why didn't she just call *you*?"

"That's Lex—Alexis. Passive-aggressive all the way. This way if we get in a fight she can scream, 'Well YOU called ME so WHATEVER.' She wouldn't ask me for money, would she? Not after she hasn't returned a single call or text in almost two months.

Maybe she got a job, or an interview at least. Maybe the favor is that she wants to borrow something to wear that didn't come from the hoochie-mama store. That could be it, couldn't it?"

Shawn raised his brows but said nothing.

"Crap. Of course not. Should I call her now? Is it too late, do you think? It's after midnight."

"She just texted you, Jules. And I'm pretty sure your sister *Alexis* has only been awake for a few hours. She's probably just getting started. I'm thinking the sooner you call her, the better."

Jules dialed her sister's number.

"Hey," Lexi said.

"That's how you answer your phone?" Jules said.

"I knew it was you, asshole. God, could you be any more like Mom? I can answer the phone any fucking way I want to, okay? It's my goddamned phone, so don't tell me how to answer it."

"So what's the favor?" Jules said, her jaw clenched. She could hear horns and sirens in the background and wondered where Lexi was calling her from. Hopefully the sidewalk in front of some seedy bar and not the police station. Again.

"Oh shit, right. I sort of need a place to stay for a few days. Maybe a little more than a few days. But I was thinking maybe it would be a help to you, you know?"

"Are you planning to pay rent?" Jules asked.

"Well, no, not . . . not really . . ."

"Going to cook and clean for us, then?"

"Yeah, right," Lexi said.

"So how would you staying with us help me out exactly?" Shawn raised his brows again when she said this; Jules shook her head as if to say, "Don't worry, it'll never happen."

"How's your book coming?" Lexi asked, ignoring Jules's question.

"It's going great, thanks," she said, seething quietly. "You didn't answer my question."

"You didn't answer mine, either," Lexi said. "How many pages have you written?" Jules could just picture the smug smile on her sister's beautiful face.

"A bunch, okay?"

"I'll bet you a thousand bucks you haven't written a single page," Lexi taunted.

"Oh, and where are you going to get a thousand bucks, Alexis? Huh?"

"I guess I can't borrow it from my inheritance, because you're never going to write that fucking book. Never."

"And you're never going to get a fucking job, so I guess we're even."

A painful silence hung between them. Lexi took a deep breath.

"Look, I'm fucked, okay? I have no job, no money and nowhere to live. If you let me stay with you guys, you can help me get my shit together and get a job, and in a way that's helping us both. Plus, I'll help you write your book. I don't know how, but I will. I could tell you stories that would make your eyes pop out of your head."

Jules laughed. "Mom specifically said no porn."

Lexi laughed, too. "I have one or two clean ones."

"I need to talk to Shawn," Jules said. He rolled his eyes and grimaced.

"I'm out of options, Jules. I wouldn't ask if I could think of a single alternative, I swear it. I can't look for a job if I'm homeless. Who knows? It might even be fun. Maybe I can get you to lighten the hell up a little bit. I'm kidding! Honest."

Shawn leaned in and whispered in her ear, "God help me, but yes. The crazier of your two crazy sisters can stay with us."

"Ha-ha," Jules said to Lexi. "You sure know how to butter a person up. Fine, Alexis, you can stay with us for a little while. But listen to me: No drugs, no sex and none of your junkie friends dropping by and eating our food or crashing on our floor or stealing our stuff. Your job will be to get a job."

"Sounds like a blast," Lexi said.

"Alexis, I mean it. Do you swear to God you won't pull any of your famous stunts?"

"Yes, Mom. I swear," Lexi said. "To *God*."

"Little bitch," Jules said under her breath. "So when is this happening? You know all we have is an air mattress, and you'll be in my office, so you can't sleep all damned day, either."

"How does now sound?" Lexi said. "I'm sort of halfway there already."

"You're halfway here? What do you mean? How?"

"I'm walking," Lexi said.

"At twelve thirty at night? Jesus, where are you? I'll come get you." Jules tried to ignore the fact that it was happening already. She was getting sucked into her sister's crazy and Lexi hadn't even set one foot in the door yet.

"I just crossed under the freeway and I'm turning onto Fairview right now," Lexi told her.

Wonderful, thought Jules. They called that part of town Crack Alley.

"Can you see the 7-Eleven from where you are?" Jules asked.
"Yup."

"Okay, tuck in there and read some magazines or something. Try not to get arrested. I'll be there in fifteen."

"You want anything? Oh shit, I don't have any money. Never mind. See you then. Thanks, Jules. I mean it."

Jules hung up her phone and looked at Shawn. He was struggling to keep his eyes open.

"I love you," she said, kissing him. "I didn't have a choice, right?"

"Right," he said, closing his eyes.

She threw on some sweats, grabbed her keys and headed out to the Honda. It purred to life instantly, clearly oblivious to where they were headed.

"I hope you're happy," she said to her dead mother as she backed her car carefully out of the driveway.

Brooke

❧

"Hello?" Brooke said tentatively. She didn't recognize the number, which meant it was probably Jake using somebody's borrowed phone. *What awful thing have I done this time?* Brooke wondered. She braced herself for the verbal beating that was surely coming.

"Is this Brooke Alexander?" a woman demanded.

"May I ask who's calling?" Brooke said.

"My name is Nikki Reeves," the woman said. The name was vaguely familiar. Did Jake have a sister? Reeves was his last name, too. Maybe it was a cousin or something. His mom was dead, just like hers. And just like in all the Disney movies. Strangely, that thought was comforting to Brooke.

"This is Brooke," she said finally. "Can I help you?"

"Oh, I don't know. Do you happen to know where my husband is?"

"I don't even know *who* your husband is," Brooke said with a nervous laugh.

"It's Jake, Einstein. Your boyfriend." Brooke was amazed at how much venom this woman managed to squeeze into that word *boyfriend*.

"My Jake?" Brooke said.

"Well, legally he's mine, but believe me, you're welcome to him. I only want him long enough to try to squeeze some money out of him and get him to sign a few pieces of paper. Then he's all yours."

"Jake . . . is . . . um . . . well he's not here at the moment." The truth was, Brooke had no idea where Jake was. He'd taken her car, again, and the few bucks she'd had in her wallet, and said he was going "out." That had been yesterday afternoon. Brooke had been waffling between worry and outrage ever since she'd woken up at three in the morning and realized he hadn't come home.

"Well, I've been calling his phone and it goes right to voice mail, so the asshole probably dropped it in the toilet again. Tell him to call me if he ever drags his sorry ass back there."

"How did you get my number?" Brooke asked. *How did she know he habitually dropped his phone in the toilet?*

"He said he was living with a fat preschool teacher from Reseda. I could have gotten your driver's license number and social security number if I'd wanted to. I'm a PI. That's a private investigator."

"I know what a PI is, thanks," Brooke said. That Jake had told his private investigator wife he was living with a *fat preschool teacher* was worse than the fact that he had a wife at all.

"Just tell that asshole to call me," Nikki said.

"Please," Brooke said.

"Please what?" Nikki demanded.

"You should say please," Brooke said. It was an automatic

response—she said it to her preschool students a thousand times a day when they barked their tiny commands at her. She realized how silly it sounded saying it to Nikki only after the fact.

"*Please* tell that asshole to call me," Nikki said.

"Can I give him a message?" Brooke said. It was a knee-jerk question; she couldn't help it.

"Sure. Tell him I'm pregnant. Thanks."

Brooke was struggling to formulate a response when Nikki disconnected the call.

She was living with a married man who had a pregnant wife. Was Jake the father? Of course he was. He had to be. Why else would his wife be calling?

Brooke dashed to the closet and grabbed her suitcase, the one that still had the faded, battered tags on it from the one time she'd been on an airplane in her life. She'd been sixteen and her grandmother had sent plane tickets for her and Lexi to visit her in Florida. Juliana had forbid it at first; with Jules out of the house, she kept a tighter rein on Brooke and Lexi than ever. That was the year she'd forced both girls to chop their waist-length locks into boyish little matching bobs ("I will not have my daughters looking like hippies," she'd said), and had grounded Brooke for a month after she found a candy bar wrapper ("Who said you could eat *that*?") beneath her bed. Brooke had been terrified to fly, terrified to spend a week with an old lady she barely knew and whom her mother had nothing kind to say about whatsoever, but the thought of seven days away from Juliana was enough incentive to overcome just about any fear she could imagine. So she'd worked her mother very carefully, pointing out how nice it would be for her to have the house to herself and not to have to shuttle her and Lexi around for a few days. Eventually, miraculously, Juliana had given in, and it had turned out to be one of the best weeks of Brooke's life. Her father's mother, who asked them to call her Nonnie, had been sweet and doting and had spoiled the sisters rotten, teaching them to play canasta and baking cookies with them and even taking them to get matching pedicures. She'd told them stories about their dad that they'd never heard before and taught them songs she'd once sang with him. When the sisters got back and told Juliana what a great time they'd had, their mother hadn't said a word. Nonnie had never invited them to visit again, at least that they knew of. The next time they saw her face was in her obituary picture two years later; they hadn't been allowed to attend the funeral.

Now Brooke stuffed clothes and shoes and toiletries into the suitcase. She huffed and puffed and tugged and pulled and finally got the zipper closed. It was straining at the seams. When she stood it up it popped open, the broken zipper dangling limply over the spilled contents. She looked around and finally pulled a pillowcase off the bed, then scooped up her things and shoved them angrily into it. She kicked the broken suitcase as hard as she could afterward and watched it spin across the floor. When it stopped, she ran over to it and ripped the American Airlines tag off of it and stuffed that into her pillowcase, too.

She grabbed her purse and began fishing in it for her keys when she remembered: Jake had her car. That married, probably-about-to-be-a-father, pathetic excuse of a man had her car. And she didn't have a single dollar. Or anywhere to go. She slumped into a chair. Defeated, Brooke put her head down on her pillow-case full of fat-girl dresses and granny panties and sensible shoes and wept.

Lexi

~

Lexi was watching TV when Shawn came home. It was after one in the morning. She mumbled a surly hi and was relieved when he padded off to bed without trying to make polite small talk with her. All she wanted was to be left alone.

When she heard the grumbling that was her brother-in-law's snoring, she tiptoed to the refrigerator and pulled out a beer, muffling the top with her hand as she cracked it open. She felt like she was fourteen years old again, sneaking around behind Juliana's back. She'd gotten caught only once, after downing her mother's vodka and foolishly refilling the bottle with water before putting it back in the freezer. She hadn't known that water would freeze and expand and crack the bottle, although she could have predicted Juliana's reaction. Lexi had been grounded for six months—no television, no friends, and certainly nothing resembling fun. It was just enough time to really hone her delinquency skills. She'd learned how to slip out her bedroom window undetected, forge her mother's signature perfectly and catch a nice little buzz by stuffing moth balls into a bag and inhaling the fumes. Although she'd gotten remarkably proficient at staying below her mother's radar, she'd been sure those days were far behind her. How the fuck had she wound up here, in her sister's shitty little boring, ugly-ass house, when there were people living on yachts and in mansions and traveling the world and walking down red carpets? Life was so not fair. Then she remembered: She was about to be a millionaire. This was all temporary. In five minutes—relatively, at least—she could have and do whatever the hell she wanted. All she had to do was get a job.

Lexi rifled through Jules's desk until she unearthed a fat pad of paper and then fished around in vain for a decent pencil. Her sister was supposed to be a writer, and she didn't even have one pointy pencil with an eraser on it in the house? That couldn't be a good sign. Lexi found one broken one with a nice, sharp tip and another with a nub of an eraser and no lead at all and curled up on the couch with her supplies.

She'd intended to make some notes of things she might be good at, jobs that might be suitable for her, but instead she began sketching. Drawing was the one way Lexi knew—besides snorting or inhaling or injecting something deliciously mind altering—to quiet her mind and collect her thoughts. When she was lost in a sketch, hours could pass before she realized she hadn't eaten, hadn't gotten up to pee, hadn't worried about money or life or tried to count how many guys she'd screwed in her lifetime. Plus it was free, a fact that trumped all of the other advantages combined.

Her pencil flew over the page as she sketched now, pulling haunting faces with piercing eyes and perfectly proportioned limbs out of thin air. She'd never had a single art lesson, yet she understood on a cellular level how to contour and shade and shadow things to remarkably realistic effect. Very few people had ever seen her drawings, but she'd been busted drawing in the library in high school once, and the librarian had insisted that her work had "an incredible M. C. Escher quality" to it. Lexi had nodded and pasted on her best fake smile, refusing to admit that she didn't know—and frankly, didn't give a rat's ass—who that was.

Without even realizing it, Lexi had drawn a woman and three young girls. The woman was tall and beautiful with the graceful body of a ballerina; she stood alone, far apart from the little girls. The sketch was rich with detail, with the pattern on the woman's skirt disappearing into the folds of fabric and popping back out again. The three girls were identical, save one identifying marking apiece. One had a skinned knee, one had a bandage on her hand and one had a tiny tattoo of a broken heart on her arm. The picture was so lifelike it could almost have been a photograph but for the fact that Lexi had drawn the woman with no eyes at all; the little girls had no mouths.

Lexi sketched and sketched until she could barely keep her eyes open, then flipped the pad closed. She looked around the living room for a place to hide it, finally sticking it between two tall books on the small bookshelf. She scanned the other titles with amusement: *Why We Write. Advice to Writers. The First Five Pages.* Her amusement quickly turned to dull despair when she realized that if her sister had to read books about how to write one, her odds of actually doing it were up there with her own odds of ever landing an actual job.

Jules

~

"I'll be back in an hour," Jules told Lexi, shaking her sister's shoulder as she did. "Did you hear me?"

"'Kay," Lexi slurred. She pulled the blanket over her head and curled up into a tight ball.

"Alexis, please get up and get this bed picked up before I get back, okay? That was one of our deals. You promised."

"'Kay," Lexi mumbled again. Jules sighed, grabbed her things and headed out to fetch her dogs. Of course, Lexi would be right where she was now when Jules got home, but it's not like anything Jules said would change that. Lexi had been with her and Shawn for two weeks and it felt like they were living in a pressure cooker. Jules had hoped that Lexi would be gracious and thankful, but instead she was as touchy and sarcastic as Jules had ever seen her. She commandeered the TV and growled when Jules or Shawn suggested watching a different show, and she ate the meals Jules prepared in stony silence, without so much as a "this is good" or "thanks." Jules realized that what she was offering wasn't much—she was hardly a gourmet chef, and they tried to keep to a strict budget—but it was certainly better than any other option available to Lexi, as far as she could see. But her sister refused to show an ounce of appreciation. She didn't come right out and say anything directly, but Jules got the distinct feeling that beneath every interaction between them Lexi was silently screaming, *You're not my mother so quit acting like you are.* Jules certainly didn't want to be Lexi's mother, but there was no question her baby sister needed somebody to assume that position.

Jules hadn't gotten a half mile with her charges when her cell phone buzzed in her pocket. She put all four dog leashes in one hand and fished the phone out to see who was calling. Brooke's name was flashing on the screen.

For a split second her heart stopped. Brooke and she rarely if ever spoke on the phone. In fact, the last call she'd gotten from Brooke had been to deliver the news that their mother had been in an accident. Jules had been paying bills at the time and had ignored a call from an unknown number. She routinely didn't answer the phone when she was crunching numbers, but when Brooke's call came in moments later, she'd known she needed to take it. And if she hadn't, she wouldn't have gotten to see her mom take her very last breath. Jules wasn't sure if she was grateful or regretful now.

"Hey, Brooke, what's up?" Jules tried to keep her voice light even though she was annoyed that her sister hadn't returned a single one of her dozens of calls or text messages since their meeting in Mr. Wiley's office. *There are millions of dollars at stake here and you need them more than I do*, she wanted to scream each time, either with words or all capital letters, but instead she usually just said something benign like, "Just checking in, call me!" Her sisters obviously resented her for trying to keep them accountable, but somebody had to do it, and it wasn't like there were people lining up at the plate.

"Jules . . . I . . . need . . . help . . ." Her sister was sobbing and Jules nearly dropped the phone.

"Brooke, what is it? Are you okay? Are you hurt?" No matter how pissed off she was at either of her sisters, a lifetime of feeling responsible for them and worrying about them was knitted tightly into the deepest fibers of her being. She couldn't ignore her concern if she wanted to.

"I . . . have nowhere . . . to go . . ." Brooke howled.

"Okay, calm down and tell me what's happening. What do you mean you have nowhere to go? Where are you?"

"I'm in Woodland Hills . . . near the bank and Sharky's . . . I had to leave, Jules . . . All I have is a pillowcase . . . He took all of my money . . . and she's a private investigator . . . and she found me because I'm a fat preschool teacher and I'm pretty sure that asshole got her pregnant and he has my *car*."

"I have no idea what you're talking about," Jules shouted. If Brooke had been standing in front of her she would have hauled off and smacked her across the face. That was what you were supposed to do with hysterical people, wasn't it?

"Jules, please . . . can you come get me? Please. I don't know what else to do. I had to get out of there. I . . . I need you."

Jules didn't know what to do. She couldn't leave her hysterical sister wandering around town with a pillowcase and no money, that was for sure. She didn't even want to ask about the pillowcase. Or the pregnancy. Or the private investigator, for that matter.

"I'll come get you," Jules finally said despite herself. "But then what? Where are you going to go? I don't know if you know this but Alexis is staying with us right now. We're sort of maxed out at the moment."

"I don't know. Please, Jules. Please? We'll figure something out. I'll figure something out. Just come get me. I'm scared."

Jules yanked on the tangle of leashes and twisted the mess to turn the dogs around. "Give me an hour or so, okay?" she said. *That should be enough time to get these dogs back home, leave Shawn the message that might end our marriage and get over to Woodland Hills to rescue another sister.*

Brooke

 ∽

"You have to call him eventually," Jules told her. "He has your car. And a bunch of your other stuff, right? Just call him, Brooke."

"And say what, exactly?" Brooke pouted.

"How about, 'Hey, douchebag, give me my fucking car back or I'll sit on you and smother you to death with my gigantic ass,'" Lexi suggested.

"Helpful," Jules said, shaking her head.

"Drive me over there and I'll get it," Lexi said. "I'm serious. I'll walk right in and grab the keys, and if that fucktard so much as looks at me funny, I will karate-chop him in the nuts."

Brooke hated to admit it, but the fact that her scrappy little sister would do that for her filled her with something close to joy. Plus, she wouldn't mind watching that happen.

"Would you?" Brooke asked with a sniffle.

"Totally," Lexi insisted. Brooke looked at her sister now and felt the familiar pangs of envy. She knew she shouldn't be jealous of Lexi; after all, her little sister was what people commonly referred to as a hot mess. But Lexi was ballsy and confident and she didn't take orders from anyone—or even care what they thought. Plus she really was ridiculously, unreasonably gorgeous. With her long, lean legs and minuscule waist and perky, perfectly proportioned boobs, it was hard not to begrudge her a little bit. If Brooke looked like that, her life would be completely different, she just knew it. It wasn't fair that she'd gotten her dad's sluggish metabolism. Not that he'd been fat; nobody in the family had ever been fat. But Juliana had been a dancer and had died with a dancer's body at fifty-nine, so obviously Brooke had gotten her genes from *somewhere*.

"I don't know if this is such a good idea," Jules said.

"Lighten up, Francis," Lexi said. Jules stared at her in surprise.

"It's a movie line," Lexi said.

"I know," Jules said. "From *Stripes*. Shawn and I say it all the time."

Lexi looked disinterested in this and turned back to Brooke. "Anyway, I probably won't karate-chop him in the nuts, okay? How about only if he hurts me first? Then can I?"

Brooke tried to stifle her excitement; Jules laughed outright. "Fine," Jules agreed to Brooke's delight. "If he hurts you first, you may karate-chop him in the nuts."

"Shotgun!" Lexi shouted as they walked out the door to Jules's Honda. Brooke had already assumed she'd be in the backseat; the front seat had always been Lexi's, even when they'd been kids. Although she was the baby—or maybe because of it— she'd been born with an excess of confidence and a grandiose sense of entitlement. If she wanted something, she got it . . . one way or another. Brooke wondered now if she'd ever once sat in the front seat of their mother's giant Buick Century station wagon. She couldn't recall it if she had.

"I'm thinking when we get our money, you might want to spring for a new car," Lexi said.

"What's wrong with this car?" Jules wanted to know. It was clean and dependable, and she thought sort of cute even.

"Who buys a *gray* car?" Lexi asked. "It's like the ugliest color ever invented."

"Beggars can't be choosers," Jules said, astounded by her sister's insolence. "At least I *have* a car."

"I have a car," Brooke said from the backseat. "Well, sort of."

"Tell us when you see it," Jules said as they drove up and down the streets around Jake's apartment.

"There it is!" Brooke shouted.

"Please tell me it's the Volkswagen," Lexi said.

"It's the Kia," Brooke told her, pointing at a powder-blue minivan.

"You drive a fucking minivan?" Lexi asked with a sneer. "That's awesome. And by awesome I mean whatever the total opposite of awesome is."

"I'm a preschool teacher, I drive kids around a lot," Brooke said.

"They make these things called SUVs now that hold a ton of people and are actually pretty cool," Lexi said. "You should check them out."

"Who are you to talk? You don't even *have* a car, Lexi," Brooke said, doing a terrible job of hiding her hurt.

"ALEXIS," Lexi and Jules shouted in unison.

"Sorry, *Alexis*," Brooke said.

Jules found a spot and parallel-parked her Honda. The three sisters got out and Brooke led them to apartment 4G.

"Should I knock or just walk in?" Brooke whispered at the door. Lexi rolled her eyes and shoved open the door. It bounced off the wall behind it with a crash and she stopped it with her hand. Jules and Brooke jumped a little bit.

"Honey, we're home," Lexi called out, storming into the tiny one-room apartment without a backward glance at her sisters.

"What the fuck?" Jake shouted. He was in his underwear on the couch playing a video game. He grabbed a pillow and covered his crotch.

"That was probably a good call," Jules said under her breath. Brooke laughed nervously.

"We're just here to get Brooke's car and a few of her things," Lexi informed him. "We won't be long, so no need to get up. Nice tighty-whities, by the way. It's a good look for you."

"You've got three minutes to get the fuck out of here or I'm calling the cops," Jake spat.

Brooke moved automatically to the hook and grabbed her keys off of it, marveling at the fact that they were there. Jake had never put them back in their proper place when she'd lived there; not once, despite her frequent, pleading requests for him to do so. She looked around the apartment now; most of the beat-up, mismatched furniture was Jake's. She'd sold all of her things since his studio was "furnished" and she didn't want to pay to store her equally crappy belongings.

"What's yours?" Lexi asked now. Jules stood awkwardly, visibly uncomfortable with the whole situation and unsure what to do next.

"Just the TV," Brooke said.

"You're not taking that TV, you bitch," Jake said, glaring at Brooke.

"Of course she's not," Lexi said. "I am." Then she marched over to the set and started wildly ripping out wires. Jake threw the pillow aside and leapt up, grabbing Lexi by the arms to stop her. She kicked and hissed and struggled to free herself.

"Jake, stop!" Brooke screamed, rushing into the tangle of limbs. Jake let go of Lexi long enough to give Brooke a rough shove with one hand. She fell to the ground, landing on her plump butt. Jules lifted her sister to her feet, and as soon as she did, her face melted into a portrait of shock, awe and possibly even admiration as Brooke hauled back and karate-chopped Jake right in the nuts.

"No fair," yelled Lexi as Jake fell to the ground writhing in pain, cupping his privates and muttering obscenities. "I was supposed to get to do that."

"Sorry," Brooke said. "I mean, sorry, *Alexis*. Not you, Jake."

Lexi swiftly lifted her hand and Brooke threw up her own hands and cowered beneath them. "I'm not going to hit you, dumbass. I was going to high-five you," Lexi said with a laugh. The sisters slapped hands.

Jake was still on the ground firing off a nonstop string of profanities and insults as the three women trudged clumsily out the front door with Brooke's beat-up TV.

Lexi

❧

"I have to run out for a few hours," Jules said as she fished her keys out of her purse. "You're welcome to use my computer . . . You know, if you want to work on your résumé or anything."

"My résumé?" Lexi scoffed. "That's a good one, Jules. Let's see: education? I went to at least half of my classes in high school, so that's good. Work experience? Bar wench, waitress. Wait, you're not supposed to list jobs you've been fired from, are you? If not, then scratch both of those. Work experience, none. Skills? I'm guessing 'expert joint roller' would be inappropriate, so we're back to zero. At least I won't waste a lot of your printer ink."

"Okay, fine, you might not need a résumé anyway. Do you want me to drop you off downtown and you can maybe walk into some places and ask if they're hiring? Or you could go to the library. They have all of the local papers and you could go through the Help Wanted sections if you didn't want to do that online. It's just a thought . . ."

Jules trailed off and Lexi could tell she was trying not to be pushy, which was next to impossible for Jules. When their dad died and Juliana disappeared—first emotionally, and then physically because she had to work to support the family—people worried needlessly about who would take care of the "orphaned Alexander girls." Jules had jumped right in and taken over, going so far as scheduling her sisters' annual physicals and teeth cleanings and forcing them to practice their cursive and study their math tables. Lexi and Brooke had called her "the boss of everyone" behind her back, and had resented her for acting like she was their mother. At twenty-six, Lexi found she despised it more than ever. But a free ride downtown? That she'd take.

"Sure, I'll go," she said now.

"Go get dressed, then," Jules said. "I'll pick up your bed."

"I am dressed," Lexi said, looking down. She was wearing ripped cut-off shorts and a hot-pink T-shirt that said FUBAR across the front. She'd cut slits in the back of the shirt in such a way that the holes formed a giant skull—through which you could plainly see that she wasn't wearing a bra, something that was equally evident from the front view, even minus the holes.

Jules looked her up and down. "What's FUBAR?" she finally asked.

"Just a brand," Lexi told her. *It certainly doesn't stand for something inappropriate like Fucked Up Beyond All Recognition, if that's what you're getting at.*

"Would you like to borrow something a little more . . . professional looking?" Jules offered. "I'm not suggesting you go out there in a business suit, but maybe a nice pair of khakis and a blouse wouldn't kill you?"

"A blouse? Is that even a word anymore? Do you have a pocketbook I can borrow, too?"

"Sure," Jules said. "And some panty hose, if you'd like. Come on." Lexi made a face but she followed her sister into her tiny, tidy bedroom. Jules opened the closet she shared with Shawn. It was jam-packed but remarkably neat and organized.

"Are all of your clothes actually arranged by color?" Lexi asked, surveying the contents.

"Well, yeah, and also by type and season," Jules admitted. "Winter stuff here, from dark to light, and summer stuff here, same order, long sleeves then short sleeves and then tanks. Shoes go by heel height."

"That's totally fucking psycho, you know that, right?"

"I like knowing where to find my things," Jules told her. "It just makes things easier."

"Whatever you say," Lexi said. "Just show me the blouse section. This ought to be fun."

Jules pulled out a handful of shirts and Lexi tried not to cringe. Who dressed like that, in bright, flowy tops that looked like a flower shop threw up all over them? She made a puking, gagging sound at each one Jules held up for her.

"Look, I'm trying to help you," Jules said. "If you want to walk around and be laughed at, go right ahead. You're not a kid anymore, and you have to find a job. If you think you're going to be offered some amazing position—or land any job at all for that matter—looking like a homeless meth addict, good luck with that." Jules jammed the tops back into her closet and stormed out of her room, leaving Lexi standing there. "I'm leaving in ten minutes, with or without you," she called from the kitchen.

Lexi sighed. If she didn't put on one of these awful outfits she'd be stuck in this godforsaken house all day. She flipped through the tops and found a black one that wasn't too hideous. It was pretty sheer, and she knew Jules would have a conniption if she didn't wear something underneath it, so she rifled through the tank top section until she found a black one with skinny straps. Then she slid a pair of white jeans off their hanger and pulled them on. They were baggy and too high-waisted—Lexi guessed Jules had probably had them for a decade or more—but she supposed they'd do. She grabbed a pair of black gladiator sandals from the floor, since all she had were ratty flip-flops and one pair of what she was pretty sure people called hooker boots.

"You clean up pretty well," Jules said when Lexi came out of the bedroom. She'd pulled her hair back into a messy bun, which on Lexi—at least in a presentable outfit—looked more chic than sloppy.

"I feel like a jackass," Lexi said.

"Well, you don't look like one," Jules told her.

They sat in silence in the car, and Lexi was grateful for it. What would they talk about? Jules's boring marriage or her stupid book? Lexi's job hunt? What they'd both been up to for the past ten years? Lexi was pretty sure Jules wouldn't want to hear about her creative rent-financing practices or all of the drugs she'd done or about the time she'd downed a bottle of hand sanitizer she'd stolen from a port-a-potty and her friends had been kind enough to drop her unconscious ass off on the curb outside of the ER.

"Here's ten bucks in case you need to make some copies or anything. Pick you up here at three?" Jules said. They were idling outside the West Valley Library.

"Sure," Lexi said, taking the money and hopping out of the car. "See ya." She pretended to be searching for something in her bag while she waited for Jules to pull away. When the Honda was out of sight, she crossed the street and turned left, where she made her way to the dollar movie theater, the one that showed last season's movies and served five-dollar pitchers of beer. She saved just enough money to buy a pack of gum afterward so Jules wouldn't smell the beer on her breath. Lexi sat in the cold, dark theater, thinking it was too bad that sneaking around wasn't an actual job.

Jules

~

"It won't be forever," Jules told Shawn, stroking his chest.

"No, it won't," Shawn said. "It will just feel like it."

"What else was I supposed to do? Let them both live on the street? I didn't have a choice; you know I didn't."

"I lived with my sister for a while before we got married, remember? I get it. They're family. They're screwed-up crazy people, but they're family. It's what you do."

Jules wondered how she ever got so lucky. She hated thinking about it, because it made her feel guilty. She'd had twelve years to watch and absorb what a loving, healthy marriage looked like, and she knew that had given her a distinct advantage over Brooke and Lexi. At eight and six, they'd still been in that la-la land of innocent, immature narcissism that most kids—the lucky ones, at least—are supposed to exist in. What did their parents' marriage have to do with them? They were happy, big deal. They were supposed to be. It was right there in all of the fairy tales: You met a boy, you fell in love, you got married and you lived happily ever after. But as a much more mature almost-teenager who had been navigating the landscape of boys and betrayal herself already, Jules knew better. She'd watched how her parents interacted, how her dad doted on her mom, how he told her she was beautiful and that the dinner was delicious and even kissed her and grabbed her butt in front of them. Jules knew that was special, and she wanted it someday, too. And somehow, miraculously, she'd gotten it. Poor Brooke and Lexi never had the same road map, at least not when they needed it most. It was no wonder they were so messed up; Jules couldn't even blame them.

"I just wish we had more space," she told Shawn now. She realized that if they lived anywhere but Southern California, they could have four times more house than what they had now for the same amount of money. Even though their two-bedroom 1930s Spanish-style house was small even by L.A. standards, she and Shawn owned it and she was proud of that fact. Still, her sisters were taking turns sleeping on the twin air mattress in the tiny bedroom they called the "cloffice"—for closet-office—and on the couch in the living room, both of which were pretty miserable options. If one had been unmistakably superior, they all knew Lexi would have claimed it as "hers." As it was, the couch was too soft and the air mattress was too hard, so flip-flopping back and forth offered both girls a rotating measure of relief.

"It'll be good practice for when we have a baby," Shawn said.

"When we have a baby," Jules reminded him, "we'll also have millions of dollars, so unfortunately all of this practice sharing sardine-can quarters will have been for nothing."

Shawn laughed. "Good point. I keep forgetting about that. I mean, I never really forget about it *completely*, but it still just doesn't seem real. Which reminds me—"

"It's coming along really well," Jules interrupted, anticipating his how's-the-writing-going question.

"Sorry. I mean it. I'm just so damned excited for you. I know you won't believe this, but I think I'm more excited for you to finish that book than I am about the whole inheritance. The money will be great, don't get me wrong, but being able to say, 'This is my wife, Jules. She's a novelist' is going to be epic. Not to make it all about me or anything." Shawn smiled sheepishly.

Jules had fantasized about that very scenario countless times, and it was always some version of the same setup. "And what do *you* do?" the snooty stranger would ask. "Me? Oh, I write," Jules would say vaguely, knowing this would prompt further probing. "What do you write?" the stranger would invariably want to know, clearly waiting for her to say something like "bank brochures" or "appliance manuals." "I'm a novelist," Jules would reply, a cat playing with her freshly caught mouse, batting it this way and that, not ready for the fun to end. "Would I have heard of anything you've written?" the now-impressed stranger would say next. And then Jules would rattle off a string of bestselling blockbusters and bask in the stranger's satisfyingly nervous fawning.

"Yeah, that will be great," Jules said now. She wanted to tell Shawn she was stuck, that she was suffering from the biggest and most crippling case of writer's block the world had ever known. She wanted to beg him for an idea, a plotline, a character sketch or two; hell, even a single decent sentence to get her going would be more than she had now. But for some reason, she couldn't. Shawn was her biggest fan, her greatest supporter. Nobody had ever believed in her the way he did, except maybe her dad. She wanted Shawn to be proud of her, and how could he be if she couldn't even come up with a stupid idea?

This was her deal, her challenge, and she'd just have to buckle down. No pain, no gain. And the payoff of being able to say she did it all alone? She could practically taste the satisfaction.

"What are we going to do about Alexis?" Shawn asked after a long pause.

"What do you mean?" Jules asked.

"She has to get—and yes, I'm using air quotes here—*an actual job*, remember?"

"I know, and I've been looking on Craigslist and I even walked the dogs over to the community college the other day and checked out the jobs board. She has a high school equivalency degree, no college credit at all and, from what I can see, absolutely zero skills or experience. There aren't a lot of Fortune 500 companies looking for a Lexi."

"At least she's got a GED," Shawn said. "It's better than no high school degree at all."

"I guess," Jules said.

"Hey, remember how my brother Randy got his job in Germany?"

"Wasn't he waiting tables or something?" Jules asked.

"Yeah, he was working at that little German pub that used to be over by all the car dealerships. The Festhaus, I think it was called? Anyway, he waited on this guy one night who happened to own a bunch of pubs in Germany. And the guy was so impressed he hired Randy to oversee the whole operation. Randy never waited on another table again."

"What do you suppose are the rough odds," Jules asked, "of Alexis landing a waitressing job at somewhere decent enough to have rich, important customers, and then keeping it long enough for the opportunity to wait on one of those rich, important customers to present itself, and then bowling this rich, important customer over with her winning personality and bottomless charm and professionalism and being hired immediately into an overseas middle-management position?"

"Somewhere between slim and none?" Shawn asked.

"I'd say more like somewhere between none and none," Jules said.

"What about vo-tech? She could take some quickie course in, like, cutting hair or fixing computers or something."

"I have a list of courses in my desk but I'm afraid to give them to her. She's so damned touchy. I was trying to give her some time to figure it out on her own. She doesn't want my help, Shawn, you see that every day."

"Well, want and need are two entirely different things," Shawn reminded her needlessly.

"Let's give her a few more weeks," Jules said.

"I wouldn't wait too long. The clock is ticking. I'm just saying."

Nobody knew that better than Jules.

Brooke

❧

"Yeah, I'd say you're just about marathon ready," Lexi jeered.

"Alexis, leave her alone," Jules said, pausing for a moment. "But honestly, Brooke, I thought you said you've been training after work?"

"I'll have you both know I'm the only one who's made any progress at all toward getting our inheritance, so maybe you could both get off my back," Brooke said. She stopped to catch her breath, and when she did, a pocket Pomeranian named Precious darted between her legs and got tangled there. Her sisters kept walking. Brooke untangled Precious and struggled to catch up. All of the houses looked the same in Reseda—cement block squares with tidy lawns and identical squat driveways. If she got separated from her sisters, she might never find her way home.

"How do you know how much progress I've made on my book?" Jules demanded, her one free arm pumping.

"If you had written anything at all, you'd be begging us to

read it," Brooke said. She was gasping for air, which she supposed was the point. When Jules had begged for help walking her dogs, Brooke knew it was her sister's not-so-subtle way of getting her to exercise—and getting Lexi to do anything at all. And since Brooke needed any nudge she could get, she had feigned ignorance and agreed to pitch in.

"When you wrote those short stories when we were little, I remember you making us read them eight thousand times each," Brooke reminded Jules now. "We had to reread them every time you changed a word or put in a comma."

"Well, this time I want it to be a surprise," Jules said.

"Yeah, sure." Brooke smirked.

"Well, what did *you* do? You left your loser dickhead boyfriend, big whoop," Lexi chimed in. "It's not like he tried to stop you or anything. So like I was saying, how far are you running these days? Three miles? Five?"

Brooke cringed. The truth was, she *had* tried to run a few times, but it had been unseasonably hot lately and every step had been brutal—she'd barely been able to jog a few hundred yards—so she was waiting for the fog to roll in to start training in earnest. They called it "June Gloom" and you could set your clock by it. It was nearly April, and that would still leave her plenty of time to get in shape. She was sure muscle memory would kick in once she got going. It was going to have to.

"I'm not sure," she admitted. "I don't have a pedometer or anything yet, and I'm not very good with judging distances."

"Maybe we should get you a ruler," Lexi said. "I'm guessing we could measure your distance in inches."

Jules glared at her baby sister and then looked back at Brooke. "Seriously, Brooke, you *should* get a pedometer," Jules said. "I think that could be motivating."

"Maybe when I get paid next week," Brooke said, hoping they'd forget about it by then.

"Mom, can we borrow twenty bucks so we can buy sissy a fancy device to tell her how many inches she ran today?" Lexi asked Jules, batting her eyelashes. *Sticks and stones,* Brooke reminded herself, just as she told her kids all day long. Brooke thought a sharp stick in the eye would hurt less than some of Lexi's barbs.

"Knock it off, Alexis," Jules scolded.

"Isn't it going to be so great not to have to wait for the next paycheck to have and do whatever we want?" Brooke said wistfully, desperate to change the subject. "Have you guys thought about that? I mean, I seriously can't even imagine. You walk into a store and see something—some boots, a watch, a flipping pair of diamond earrings—and bam! They're yours. Right then and there, no waiting, no wondering, no questions asked. No worries at all. Are you kidding me? Hey, can we rest for a second? I'm dying over here." Brooke stopped in a shady spot and leaned against a tree. Jules and Lexi joined her.

"Why do you guys think she did it?" Brooke asked. "Why did she keep that money a secret? Why didn't she help us when she was alive, when she could have? Why did she have to make all of these stupid conditions?"

"Because she's Mom," Lexi said simply. "It's what she does. Or what she did. She controlled. And I bet she thought we'd fall flat on our asses. So I say we suck it up and get this shit done so that we can get the last laugh. I'm serious. Who's in?"

"I'm in," said Jules.

"In," said Brooke.

"In," said Lexi.

They walked in silence for a while before Jules started blabbing about how nice it was having company when she walked the dogs and something about fresh air and exercise. Brooke wasn't really listening. She was too busy imagining how amazing it was going to feel to take off her sweaty sneakers and sit on her butt for the rest of the afternoon.

Lexi

~⚬~

"I told you, I'm going to a movie with a friend," Lexi said with a dramatic sigh. She turned her back to Jules and eyed her reflection in the hall mirror: microscopic pleather skirt clinging low to her hip bones; skintight, belly-baring tank top; knee-high boots with six-inch heels. *Not bad,* she thought to herself as she wrapped a gold cuff bracelet that looked like a snake around her upper arm.

"A movie, huh? Dressed like that? Won't you freeze to death? You know how cold it gets in movie theaters," Jules said.

"I'll bring a sweater," Lexi said. She fought the urge to stick her tongue out at Jules's reflection behind her in the mirror.

"Do you even own a sweater?" Brooke asked.

"Stay out of it," Lexi spat at Brooke, spinning around to glare at her, then stalked past both of them into the kitchen area.

"Nice ink," Jules said, referring to the tattoo on Lexi's lower back. It was three rounded triangles joined by a circle and surrounded by an intricate tangle of thorns. Lexi was pretty sure that Jules wouldn't be a big fan of permanent body art, so she'd been keeping it hidden to avoid yet another lecture. Tonight she'd decided she didn't care anymore. If not the tattoo, Jules would just find something else to rag on her about.

"Thanks, I drew it," Lexi told her.

"How did you draw a tattoo on your own back?" Brooke asked.

"You actually get paid to teach kids?" Lexi snorted. "I drew it on a piece of paper and the tattoo guy copied it." She shook her head. Could Brooke really be that dense? Juliana had insisted she'd regret not getting a college education, but a fat lot of good it had done her sister.

"How are you planning to pay for your movie?" Jules asked. Lexi's first reaction was to tell Jules to go fuck herself, but she realized her big sister was just doing what she always did—trying to play peacekeeper between her and Brooke. Jules was nothing if not predictable.

"My friend is paying." Lexi decided to just keep the peace herself. She was standing in front of the fridge now with both doors swung wide open, not exactly sure what she was looking for and definitely not finding it.

"Is your *friend* picking you up or are you planning to walk to the theater in those ridiculous shoes?" Jules asked.

Lexi slammed the refrigerator doors and shot her nagging sister the bird. "I'm meeting him on the corner. There's no fucking way I'm letting him come in here and get grilled by Sergeant Bossypants and Deputy Shit-for-Brains." Brooke looked away, but not before Lexi saw the kicked-puppy look on her face. Lexi felt bad for a split second, then thought better of it. The world was a hard, mean place. People were cruel. Brooke needed to toughen up, grow some skin. Lexi was actually helping her, although she knew there would be no thank-you card for her efforts.

"Well, that's a perfect outfit for standing around on a corner, that's for sure," Jules said to Lexi.

"Why don't you go have a baby or something so you have someone else to boss around and you can get off my ass?"

Jules bit her tongue and Lexi knew exactly what she wanted to say: *As long as you live under my roof, you will abide by my rules.* Lexi raised her eyebrows at her sister, silently daring her to say it.

"What time can we expect you back?" Jules said instead.

"You can *expect* me any fucking time you'd like, but I'll be back when I'm back. See ya." Lexi could feel her sisters' eyes on her back as she sashayed out the door, letting it slam behind her.

I'm twenty-fucking-six years old, Lexi seethed as she stumbled on a root poking up out of the sidewalk. She felt guilty for barking at Jules, and she did not like that feeling one bit. Instead, she channeled her discomfort into the much more comfortable, more familiar emotion: angry defensiveness. *Jules isn't my fucking mother. Hell, my mother wasn't even my goddamned mother. I don't have to answer to anybody. I'm an orphan. Orphans can do whatever the hell they want. And right now, what I want is to go out and get totally fucked up.*

Lexi had texted Brad and Ryan and begged them to pick her up and take her to Rusty's. It was the seediest bar in town, smack in the middle of Crack Alley, but it had an outdoor patio where they could smoke and nobody would bother them. She prayed the boys would have some dope.

"Hey, hot stuff! Need a ride?" Brad shouted out the window. He was in the passenger seat of Ryan's rusty Dodge Ram, and he pushed the door open for her. She hiked her tiny skirt up even higher and pulled herself into the truck.

"Hey, Slexis," Brad said, sliding his arm around her shoulder and giving her a friendly squeeze. "How're things?"

"Other than the fact that I'm living on my sister's floor and I'm still broke as shit and I have like eight months to get an actual job and my psycho sisters are driving me batshit crazy, things are practically perfect," Lexi said, reaching for the open beer between Brad's legs and taking a huge sip. Then she belched.

"Sorry, but I haven't had a beer in two weeks," she told her friends. "They buy one six-pack for the whole week and they fucking share a can a night. And they don't drink real booze or take any pills so there's nothing else. I took one of those beers once—I didn't know they had a fucking *beer-drinking schedule*—and Jules about had a conniption. She's a total nightmare. No, she's worse than that. She's my mother. You should have seen her flip her shit when I left some hair in the shower drain. Big fucking deal. It's hair. Pick it up and get over it."

"What do they do the other day?" Ryan wanted to know. He took a drag on his fake-cigarette pipe and offered it to Lexi. She inhaled deeply.

"What?" she finally asked. She'd forgotten what they were talking about already.

"They buy a six-pack a week, and there are seven days," Ryan explained.

"I don't know," Lexi laughed, loving the buzz she was building. "Maybe they take Sunday off for God, or maybe they make one last two days. They probably have a special beer Tupperware for it. It wouldn't surprise me. Oh, and, you guys, just so you know, I don't have a dime."

"We got you tonight," Brad said.

"God, I've missed you guys," Lexi said, downing the last of Brad's beer and thinking how lucky she was to have friends like Brad and Ry, friends who loved her and didn't lecture her and looked out for her because they wanted to—not because they had to.

Jules

~

Jules was still smarting from Lexi's words. *Why don't you go have a baby or something so you have someone else to boss around and you can get off my ass?* Damn Lexi and her brutally offhand blows. Did her self-absorbed sister even know that Jules's greatest fear in life—ten times greater than her fear of writing a novel or not writing a novel or writing a novel that was awful or even being eaten alive by alligators—was that she would be a bad mother someday? Of course she didn't. She didn't know a thing about Jules. She had never wanted to and she probably never would. She was a narcissistic little user who only thought about herself and how she could get what she wanted. And since that was partially Jules's fault—for moving out the second the opportunity had presented itself and leaving Lexi in Juliana's care (or lack of it)—she felt obligated to endure the abuse.

Jules was going to be a great mother, she was almost positive. She knew that unhealthy cycles like alcoholism and abuse tended to repeat themselves in families, but she also knew that plenty of people managed to stop those cycles by going in the polar opposite direction. Kids of alcoholics became teetotalers; adults who were abused when they were younger refused to even raise their voices at their own children. Jules looked at her relationship with Juliana after her dad's death and considered it a guidebook on how *not* to parent. If she just approached every parenting quandary and conundrum by asking herself, "What Would Juliana Do" and then doing the exact opposite, she was pretty sure she couldn't go wrong.

"Brooke, would you please take out the trash?" she asked now. Jules had pulled the overflowing bag out of the can, tied it up, placed it by the door and replaced it with a clean bag. All Brooke had to do was walk the thing out to the curb. And Jules would insist that she do it, too, because you didn't get to live room-and-board-free without at least contributing to some of the upkeep. But at the moment, Brooke was very busy sitting on her butt, watching TV and painting her fingernails a hideous bright pink color. Jules was dying to suggest maybe she go for a walk or do a few lunges, maybe pop in an exercise video, anything to start building up some strength and stamina.

"I'll take it out as soon as my nails dry," Brooke said, not looking up.

Jules sighed. How had she wound up here again, she wondered, playing mom to her two irresponsible, troubled sisters? Would this be happening if Juliana hadn't died? Jules had barely had any contact with either Brooke or Lexi in years, and now she could remember why: They had nothing at all in common. But they were family, the only family any of them had until they created new ones of their own. Did their shared genes even matter anymore? Jules genuinely wasn't sure.

"I'm going to jump in the shower," she told Brooke. Brooke

was now far too absorbed in the taxing double task of blowing on her awful manicure and watching *America's Funniest Home Videos* to respond.

Jules lathered up her body as quickly as she could and then turned off the water while she shaved her legs. She was shivering, and the goose bumps made the job miserable, but she was conscientious by both nature and nurture. Besides, water was expensive and now there were four of them. Brooke was pretty good about getting in and out, but Jules had to bang on the door every time Lexi showered and ask her to wrap it up. And Jules couldn't prove it, but she was convinced Lexi's shower schedule revolved around the laundry—the laundry she made copious amounts of but never helped with—because she invariably managed to get herself a clean, dry towel. Jules knew she should let Lexi do her own laundry, but the problem was that when Lexi ran out of clothes she'd either wear them filthy, not wear underwear or take something from Jules's closet. It just wasn't worth it.

She got out of the shower and put on a sundress and some makeup. This was Shawn's one night a week that he'd be home for dinner and she wanted to look nice for him. He'd been so patient and understanding and hadn't grumbled once when he had to wait for the bathroom or tiptoe through his own house, stepping around sleeping bodies when he got up at the crack of dawn.

She'd splurged on some steaks—the more expensive lean kind, for Brooke—and was going to make a big, nutritious, high-protein salad. She'd seen the nutrient-void junk Brooke inhaled when left to her own devices, and Jules was worried her sister would never be able to get in half-marathon shape if she didn't change her eating habits. She just hoped her not-so-subtle efforts wouldn't backfire and send Brooke screaming down to Jack in the Box as soon as her back was turned.

She wondered if Lexi would even eat dinner at all.

Jules hated the fact that she couldn't stop wondering and worrying about Lexi. What would she do if Lexi didn't come home? Call the police? File a missing-person's report? She didn't know any of Lexi's so-called friends, nor did she want to. She was positive her sister wasn't heading off to any movie, but it wasn't like she was going to follow her or anything. If she didn't come home, she didn't come home. Jules would deal with it then. *Is this what being a parent is like?* she mused. If so, maybe she and Shawn should just get a dog. A nice, well-behaved, cuddly, predictable, hairless dog.

Brooke

~

Brooke could smell the steak broiling in the kitchen and her mouth was watering. She wondered if Jules would dole out a tiny portion for her and then watch her eat it. It was fine if she did; Brooke had her secret stash of chocolate-covered almonds and peanut-butter-filled pretzels hidden in the single drawer Jules had cleared out for her. She hoped Jules and Shawn would go to bed early, and prayed Lexi wouldn't be home when they did. It was next to impossible to sneak any food in this tiny house, and Brooke really needed a treat without anyone giving her a guilt trip.

More than four months had passed since their meeting with Mr. Wiley, and Brooke could barely jog a single mile. In part, she blamed the extra weight, and she cursed the catch-22 of it all. The other problem was finding the right time. She'd tried running in the morning, but she had no energy before she ate and felt sick if she tried to exercise on a full stomach. She'd tried running after work, but she was exhausted by then and even lacing up her sneakers had seemed too great of an effort. She'd done some research, and full marathon training plans ranged anywhere from fourteen to thirty weeks—and she only needed to complete a half-marathon. She still had plenty of time. It said on the Internet that you could get ready for a half-marathon in as little as eight weeks. *Not overweight, totally sedentary people who hadn't run in over a decade,* her subconscious reminded her. Brooke politely asked her subconscious to stay out of it.

"Hey, Brooke, do you think you could set the table?" Jules called from the kitchen. Brooke put down the two-year-old *Redbook* magazine she'd been flipping through and shuffled into the kitchen. She watched as her sister moved skillfully about the small space, adding spices to this pot and adjusting the flame on the burner under that one. She was beyond impressed. Their mother had stopped cooking completely when their father died, although Brooke had a few fuzzy memories of her doing it earlier. Jules didn't even seem to use or need recipes, a fact Brooke found staggering. Even when she followed a recipe to the letter, half of the time what she made was inedible.

"How did you learn to cook?" she asked Jules now. She placed three matching plates on the small kitchen table and tucked a neatly folded napkin under the edge of each.

"I don't really know," Jules said. "I guess I just sort of figured it out. Trial and error, you know? I'm no Julia Child now, but I used to be god awful. You probably don't even remember this, but once, right after Dad died, I tried to make a baked pasta dish I'd had at a friend's house, and I just threw everything in a big casserole pan. Uncooked pasta, a few whole tomatoes I'd crushed with my hands, some cheese and carrots . . . then I cracked a few eggs on top of it—I'd seen Julia Child do that on TV—and threw it in the oven."

"You did?" Brooke asked. She had so few memories of that time in her life, probably because she'd been in shock and had blocked everything out. She thought now how awful that must have been for Jules, having to be so mature and industrious and responsible.

Jules nodded, lost in the memory.

"Did Mom freak out?" Brooke asked. Juliana had lived by the motto "waste not, want not," and she'd been particularly fanatical about food.

"Nah, this was early on, when she was in zombie mode. She didn't even seem to notice. She actually ate it. You and Alexis just looked at me with these huge eyes and then we all watched while Mom crunched her way through that disgusting mess without saying a word. After she went to bed I threw the rest of it away—I buried it in the backyard so she wouldn't know—and then I made us peanut butter and banana sandwiches."

"That was nice of you," Brooke said. She pulled out a chair and sat down heavily. Her heart hurt for Jules; for all three of them, actually. She thought of her sweet, innocent preschool students and realized she hadn't been all that much older than them when she'd lost her dad. She was glad she couldn't remember most of it.

"I started checking cookbooks out of the library after the pasta disaster," Jules told her. "I looked for ones with titles like *Five-Ingredient Dishes* and *One-Pot Dinners* and *Eat on the Cheap*. I guess we got by. None of us has scurvy or got really— Oh, sorry." She obviously had been about to say *fat*.

"It's okay, you can say it. I'm fat. It's not like it's a secret."

"You're not fat, Brooke," Jules said, sitting down next to her at the table and touching her arm gently. "You're a little plump. 'Round' is a nice way to put it. What about 'Rubenesque'? That's a good word."

"That would be like calling Alexis mischievous or playful when we both know she's just plain trouble."

"Do you want any help with the running?" Jules asked hesitantly.

"Do you want any help writing your book?" Brooke countered.

"Fair enough," Jules said. She stood up and went back to chopping salad vegetables.

Brooke made a promise to herself: Tomorrow she would run two miles if it killed her. She stifled a bitter laugh at the thought, and wondered if her mother had a clause in her will for what would happen if one of them died. Knowing Juliana, she probably did.

Lexi

Lexi tiptoed around the room, looking for her clothes. Her head was pounding and the place was a disaster. She found her skirt wadded in a ball near the door and one boot in a corner. The bare mattress sat on the floor, so there was no sense trying to look under it. She had only fuzzy memories of the night before and wasn't even sure whose house she was in. It might be Brad's brother's, but if it was, where was Brad? And who was the guy sprawled out naked on the mattress? She leaned over him and peered in close. His neck was covered in tattoos and he had about a dozen piercings up the ear that she could see. She didn't recognize his face at all. She hoped it wasn't Brad's brother. She remembered Brad saying he was a dick.

She'd woken up because she had to pee, but now that she was up and mostly lucid, she got the feeling she should probably get out of this skanky place.

She grabbed a dirty towel from the floor and was about to wrap it around herself, but the stench of it—coupled with the hard, crusty patches that met her fingers when she picked it up—made her drop it. *Fuck it,* she thought, swinging open the bedroom door and walking buck naked down the hall in search of clothes and clues.

There were naked, passed-out bodies in every room she passed, sometimes three or four to a bed. The living room was a post-orgy scene of scrawny limbs and limp dicks and tramp stamps and enough drug paraphernalia to open a head shop. Lexi scanned the comatose faces, looking for Brad or Ryan or anyone at all who looked even a little bit familiar, but they were all complete strangers.

"Goddamn it," she muttered under her breath. She had no idea where she was or where her other clothes were, and she was so ravenous she was shaking. She walked to the refrigerator and opened the door, but there was nothing in it but a few shriveled-up slices of pizza covered in a spongy layer of mold. She slammed the door.

"Keep it down, you stupid bitch," someone shouted from somewhere in the house.

"Go fuck yourself," Lexi shouted back. She stomped into the closest bedroom and fished around until she found a guy's button-down shirt. She put it on and tied the tails together high under her boobs. The three bodies in the bed didn't move. She coughed quietly, a test; still nothing. She kept her eyes on the bodies as she walked carefully to a heap of clothes and found a pair of pants with a wallet in the pocket. Twenty-two bucks. Score. She tucked it in the shirt pocket and tiptoed out, then did the same thing in two more bedrooms. Ninety-one bucks richer, she went back to the bedroom where she started to retrieve her skirt. She cleared another sixty-five dollars there. She was pissed about the boots—they were one of two pairs of shoes she owned—but she wasn't about to hang around this hellhole any longer. Plus, she had more than a hundred fifty dollars now. She grabbed a pair of scratched-up sunglasses off the kitchen counter and stumbled outside, barefoot, into the midday sunlight.

She walked along the strange street, trying to get a sense of where in the world she was. If Lexi knew anything, it was that she couldn't call Jules to come get her again. *Call Jules.* Shit, her phone. Where was her phone? Had she left it at that house? Or in Ryan's truck? Or at Rusty's? She had no idea. She turned around now to retrace her steps only to realize that she had no idea what the house she'd just left looked like or even which direction she'd come from. There was no use trying to find it, especially when her phone might not even be there.

From the looks of the houses around her, she guessed that she was on the north side of town, not far from Rusty's. If she could get there, somebody would probably know how to get in touch with Ry and Brad, who hopefully had her phone. She realized she didn't even know their last names *or* their numbers—she'd always just dialed them directly from her contacts. If she'd had her phone she might even have called Jules. Not for a ride, God forbid, but just so her Nazi big sister wouldn't totally freak out on her ass when she did come home. But she realized when that thought crossed her mind that not only did she not even know her oldest sister's married name, she didn't know a single phone number in the world other than her own; not Jules's, not Brooke's, nobody's. Was that normal? Sad? A sign of something? Lexi had no way of knowing.

It took her a good four hours of walking before she made it to Rusty's. Her feet were black and blistered but at least she'd finally eaten something. She'd found a cheap greasy spoon and inhaled a cheesesteak sandwich and fries and a gigantic fountain

Coke. It was heavenly. She'd even left the right amount of money on the table—plus a pretty decent tip—when she left. She was surprised at how nice it felt to actually walk out of a restaurant and stroll casually down the street instead of sneaking out and trying to disappear immediately into the crowd. She wondered if she'd miss the occasional thrill of dine-and-dash when she was filthy-fucking-rich. She decided that if she did, she could always do it just for fun. She might even go back and sneak a crisp hundy onto the table later, just to fuck with the server.

After Lexi washed her feet and her face in Rusty's grimy restroom, she counted her stolen money. A hundred and forty-three dollars left. She could sit at the bar and eat and drink for the next three days and not have to bolt out when the bill came or suck up to a disgusting drunk for another round. Sure, she had no idea where she was going to sleep, and she was exhausted and hungover and might never see her phone again, but at least there was that.

Jules

~⸒~

Jules held her breath and said a silent prayer as she stood outside
her office, even though she knew from painful experience that
asking God for anything was futile. Besides, she would have
heard Lexi come in because she hadn't slept more than ten minutes all night. She'd tossed and turned and paced and fretted,
and poor Shawn had been a wreck when he left for his fifteen-
hour day at five o'clock this morning. Now she pushed open the
office door. The air mattress sat undisturbed on the floor against
the wall, neatly made (by Jules) and exactly as it had been the
fourteen other times she'd checked it.

"Goddamn her," she muttered to herself as she pulled the
door closed.

"She's probably fine." Brooke was on the couch, sipping a glass
of murky water with a lemon slice floating on top. Jules was painfully aware of the fact that Brooke didn't want her help or advice
directly, so she'd begun casually leaving magazines lying around,
opened to various diet and fitness articles. A recent one had called

water spiked with lemon and cayenne pepper "one of the easiest, most effective tools in your weight-loss arsenal." Jules had practically had to sit on that page to make it stay open, but it had worked. Brooke had been drinking the disgusting concoction daily. Jules had been glad her sister had taken the bait, otherwise the $4.50 she'd spent on lemons and pepper would have been a total waste.

"She's just so selfish and irresponsible," Jules grumbled, pouring herself a cup of coffee.

"I know," Brooke said.

"Do you think I should call her?" Jules asked.

"It'll probably make you feel better to know she's okay," Brooke said.

Jules dialed Lexi's number. It rang and rang. Just as she was about to hang up, a gruff male voice answered.

"Um, hi, I'm looking for Alexis?" Jules said, her voice rising in question.

"I don't know who that is," the guy said, "but if it's the bitch who stole my sunglasses and all my money, you can tell her I plan to call my cousin in China today and talk to him for about six hours before I throw her fucking phone off the bridge."

Before Jules could process his words and formulate a reply, he was gone. She set her phone on the counter and scratched her head.

"That didn't sound promising," Brooke said. "What did he say?"

Jules repeated what the guy who had answered Lexi's phone had said.

"We need to find her," Brooke said, jumping up. Jules was positive she'd never seen Brooke move so quickly in her life, at least since she'd been staying with her. And because of Lexi, no less. Maybe she and Brooke weren't that different after all.

"She'd do it for us," Brooke insisted. "Remember how she went totally nuts about Jake having my car? She didn't miss a beat. She was all, 'I'm going to go over there and kick his ass RIGHT NOW.' And then she did. Well, I sort of did, but she started it. That was so awesome, wasn't it?"

Jules smiled at her sister. "I'll deny I ever said this, but yeah, that was pretty awesome."

"So do you want to do it? Go find this guy who has her phone?" Brooke looked a little bit more excited than she should have, if you asked Jules.

"For one thing, Alexis lives for any excuse to kick *anyone's* ass, so don't get too crazy with the warm-and-fuzzies over there," Jules reminded her. "Secondly, I don't think you and I together could take out a fifth-grade boy, no less some probable cokehead; no offense. And third, where would we even start? How do we know she's even in town? She could be anywhere on the entire planet. She could have jumped in some stranger's car and be on the other side of Lake Havasu by now. She could be in a hotel room or a bar or someone's house or their secret underground dungeon or at the bottom of some random pool."

"Well, we can't just sit here and do nothing," Brooke said.

"Wait, shouldn't you be at work?" Jules asked, suddenly remembering it was a weekday.

"I called in sick when I saw that she never came home. I didn't want you to have to deal with that alone."

Jules stopped scrubbing at an invisible spot on the kitchen counter.

"You did?" she asked.

Brooke nodded.

"That was really sweet of you," Jules said.

"No problem," Brooke said. "And also lice is going around the school like crazy right now and a bunch of my kids have it. I'm sure it's just psychological but my head's been super itchy, so I was going to go get some of that chemical shampoo and just try to knock it out sometime this week anyway. I figured it might as well be today."

"Lice? You think you have *lice*?" Jules shrieked.

"I might not." Brooke shrugged. "Whenever it's going around I always totally think I have it, but I've only gotten it like five or six times."

"Brooke, my head has been driving me crazy for three days. I scratched it until it bled last night. I thought it was stress. Will you look?" She sat down at the table and Brooke stood up and pulled her hair away from her part.

"Oh yeah," Brooke said. "You're infested, all right."

"I'm *infested*? Brooke, that's disgusting! What do I do?" Jules was on the verge of hyperventilating.

"It's not that big of a deal," Brooke insisted. "The kids love it when they get it, because the home lice kits come with a box of jelly beans to shut them up while their parents comb them out. I'll pick up some jelly beans when I get the shampoo." She tried to rub her sister's shoulders, but Jules jerked away.

"Go get it *now*," she barked. "And hurry."

"You're just freaking out because you don't have kids and this is all new," Brooke told her. "After you do the hazmat shampoo three or four times you just wrap up your hair in oil for a few weeks and it smothers the bugs *and* the eggs. Then you have to pick all the dead ones out with this little metal lice comb because they stick to the hair even after you shampoo. The combs are kind of expensive, too—like twenty bucks, I think—but you can borrow mine if you want. Oh wait, you're not supposed to share those. Oh, and you have to wash all of your sheets and pillows and blankets and towels in really hot water a couple times a week, and put all of your brushes and combs and stuff like that in the freezer. There's also this spray they make for your car. Hang on, I have a sheet that explains everything in my school bag . . ."

Jules wanted to vomit. Or shave her head. She'd vomit on her own shaved head if she thought it would help. She felt dirty and violated and worried and frustrated and very, very itchy.

When Brooke got back from the drugstore with the insecticide shampoo, Jules locked herself in the bathroom and took the longest shower of her life. She lathered and rinsed and repeated and scrubbed and scrubbed and she didn't even care about the money she was pouring down the drain. She was stuck mothering her two irresponsible, apathetic sisters and she was infested with lice, and from the looks of it, only one of those things was ever going to change.

Brooke

❧

Brooke had the whole setup arranged by the time Jules got out of the shower: clear bowl of water, comb, magnifying glass, big cup of warm salad oil and spray bottle with watered-down conditioner to make the combing easier. Oh, and the movie theater–size box of jelly beans. She hoped Jules didn't like the red or green ones, because she'd already picked all of those out and eaten them. It wasn't her fault; Jules had been in that shower forever.

Jules slumped into the kitchen chair Brooke had pulled out for her and Brooke went to work, first massaging the warm oil into Jules's scalp. She tried not to picture the little bugs on her sister's head drowning and gasping for air, and hoped that the massage part might help Jules relax a little bit. Brooke worked methodically through her sister's head, one minuscule section of hair at a time, and Jules swayed gently in her chair with each tug of the comb. For a few minutes, she even forgot about Lexi.

"Will you check me when I'm done?" Brooke asked. She popped an orange jelly bean into her mouth and grimaced. Why did they even bother making the other colors when reds were the only good ones? Greens were okay in a pinch, but if she were in charge, it would be an all-red-jelly-bean world.

"I don't really know what I'm looking for," Jules mumbled, half-asleep.

"They look like this," Brooke said, holding the bowl of water in front of her sister's face.

"I don't see anything," Jules said.

"Oh, sorry, you have to look through the magnifying glass," Brooke explained. She handed Jules a tiny plastic child's magnifying glass and watched as her sister peered into the bowl.

"All I see are these tiny flesh-colored dots floating on top of the water," Jules said.

"That's them," Brooke explained.

"You have got to be kidding me," Jules said.

"My hair will be easier than yours because it's dark," Brooke insisted.

"Do I have a choice?" Jules asked.

"Only if you don't want to be passing these things back and forth forever," Brooke told her.

After Brooke had gone over Jules's entire head with a fine-tooth comb—in the most literal sense possible—twice, she wrapped tinfoil around the whole oily mess.

"Is this really necessary?" Jules asked, patting her tin-covered head.

"It keeps the oil from getting everywhere, plus it helps in case I missed one—which I doubt I did—so it can't jump or crawl off," Brooke said. "But wait, I'm not done." She rolled a long length of foil into a pointy cone, and then tucked it into a fold on top of Jules's head. Brooke reached for a hand mirror and handed it to Jules.

"You're a unicorn!" she said, crying with laughter.

"This just keeps getting better and better," Jules said, shaking her head but smiling at her sister.

"You ready to do me?" Brooke asked.

"As ready as I'll ever be," Jules told her.

Jules worked her way around Brooke's head, massaging and combing and picking and drowning each tiny critter and tinier egg she found in the bowl of water.

"I think we're good here," she finally told Brooke, putting the finishing touches on her sister's tinfoil unicorn hat. "How long do we leave the foil on?"

"The longer the better," Brooke said.

They couldn't look at each other without laughing.

"I'm going to run that race," Brooke said out of nowhere. "Just so you know. I even have one picked out, the SoCal Surfside Half-Marathon. It's in December, so the timing is perfect. You're probably halfway finished with your book, I know. And I can't speak for Lexi, obviously, but I'm not going to be the one to ruin this for all of us, I promise."

Jules looked down at her lap. "I haven't even started," she said. She kept her head bowed low and picked at the skin around her fingernail.

"You haven't?" Brooke gasped. "It's already May!" She saw the guilt on Jules's face and tried to backpedal. "Hey, that's okay," she added hastily. "You'll do it. I mean, won't you? Why haven't you started?"

"Because I don't have a story," Jules said. She looked inconsolable.

"Are you serious? Anything is a story. You need to come to work with me for a day. My kids can spend forty-five minutes telling me about the potato bug they squished on the sidewalk."

"You don't understand," Jules told her. "A novel has to have a plot and characters you care about and some sort of conflict and then a nice, neat ending where everything gets all wrapped up. You can't just talk about a dead potato bug on a sidewalk for three hundred pages and call it a book."

"Hey, Mom never said your book had to be any good, did she?" Brooke asked hopefully.

"I'm not even sure I can write a crappy book at this point," Jules said.

"You'll think of something," Brooke told her. She nodded her head emphatically, and Jules couldn't help but laugh at the way her foil horn bobbed up and down when she did.

"Don't tell Alexis, okay?" Jules said. "The last thing I need is her getting on my case."

"Speaking of Alexis . . . What are we going to do?" Brooke wanted to know.

"The only thing we *can* do," Jules said. She got up, flipped on the TV and settled in on the couch. "Absolutely nothing."

Lexi

~

The cute guy across the bar had been eyeing her for close to an hour, and Lexi was working it with everything she had. She knew she was drunk, but he was definitely hot, there was no question about it. Dark hair, dark eyes, tall and lean with the chiseled features she loved. She'd unbuttoned her shirt all the way down, so now there was just a knot between her boobs. If she played this right, she might even have a bed to sleep in tonight. She locked eyes with him and sucked on her straw suggestively. He smiled and gave her a little wave.

Bingo.

She picked up her glass and sauntered over with one hand in her skirt pocket, pushing it way down to give him a good look at her impossibly flat stomach. She stumbled just before she reached him, and he caught her deftly before she went down.

"Hey," she slurred, steadying herself. "You're pretty cute."

"And you're pretty drunk." He laughed and held out his hand.

His teeth were so white and straight they looked like the picture on the box the toothpaste tube came in. "I'm Rob."

"Lex—Alexis," she said, shaking his big warm hand. "Nice teeth."

"Nice to meet you, Lex-Alexis. And thanks."

"Sorry, it's just Alexis," she said. She sank into the seat next to him and moved in close to him, resting her hand high on his thigh. "And you're welcome."

"What brings a pretty girl like you to a dump like this?" Rob asked, moving her hand closer to his knee.

"Oh, you know, I was going to hook up with some friends but they bailed on me." She pushed his hand away and moved her own hand all the way to the crook between his leg and his crotch.

"I think you should probably go home," Rob said, grabbing her hand harder this time.

"I think I should probably go to *your* home," she purred. She leaned in as close as she could and rubbed her breast on his arm. Her nipples perked up immediately and she watched him pretending not to notice.

"I don't think that's such a great idea," he said, pulling away from her.

"Come on, it'll be fun, and you don't even have to buy me anything. I have a bunch of cash tonight. I give great blow jobs, ask anybody."

"Alexis, how about I give you a ride home? To your home. Alone."

"What the fuck is wrong with you?" she spat. She wobbled as she got off her barstool and he grabbed her arm to steady her again. She pulled away. "You've been practically raping me from over here with your eyes all night. I just offered you free head—and that was just going to be the beginning, by the way—and you want to give me a ride home? Are you married? Because I don't give a shit if you are, I'll still blow you. Or are you fucking gay? Is that it?"

"Actually, I'm a cop," he said. He pulled his wallet out of his back pocket and flipped it open on the bar. There was a shiny metal badge in there, just like in the movies.

"I didn't do anything wrong," she said instinctively, pulling away from him. Did he know she'd stolen money from that house? She hadn't propositioned him, had she? No, she'd offered it for free. She was positive.

"You came pretty damned close," he said, standing. He threw forty bucks on the bar. "I've got you tonight. Look, you're a beautiful girl, Alexis. Stunning, actually. And you're right, I couldn't take my eyes off of you. But you're drunk, and you're trouble, and I'm taking you home." He put his arm protectively around her and tried to take a step but her feet were planted firmly in place.

"Come on, Alexis, let's go. You'll thank me tomorrow. Where do you live? It doesn't matter if it's far. I don't have anywhere I need to be." He smiled at her warmly.

"I live in the pit of hell," she said. She released her death grip on the floor and let him guide her out of Rusty's and into a squad car.

"Can we put on the siren and go really fast?" she asked with a hiccup as he slid into the driver's seat.

"I could lose my job if I did that," he said. "But keep your eye out for perps. If you see anything going on, you tell me and we're on it." She wanted to melt into that sexy smile of his.

"Do you ever do it in here? I'm not saying I want to or anything, so don't arrest me, okay? I'm just curious."

Rob just laughed. "Where am I going, Alexis?"

"Head up Tampa to Plum or Plummer or whatever it's called and take a right," she told him. "I live back there. I don't know the name of the street but I'm pretty sure I can find it."

"New to town?" Rob asked.

"I'm sort of staying with my sister for a while," she told him. "Hey, can we pretend that you're there to arrest her when we get there? That would be so awesome." Lexi doubled over laughing at the thought of it.

"Again, my supervisor probably wouldn't think that was so awesome," he chuckled.

"You sure you don't want to go back to your place first? I'm not a hooker or anything, I swear."

"Then why did you say I didn't even have to buy you anything?" Rob wanted to know.

"I was just being straight up," Lexi said with a shrug. Men had offered her money for sex before, but they were usually fat, disgusting old creeps she wouldn't touch with a ten-foot pole. But with this guy? She'd gladly give it up for free all night long.

"You know that sex in exchange for anything is prostitution, right? And that it's against the law?" Rob asked.

"Of course I do," Lexi assured him. "My friend Tiffany makes serious bank banging these rich Arab guys who come to L.A. all the time. She's been trying to introduce me to her pimp forever. I think his name is like Brock or Beck or something fucked up like that—"

"Hello? Cop over here, remember?" Rob said, shaking his head. He turned onto Plummer. "Where now, Julia Roberts?"

Lexi instructed him to take a right here, and then another right, and then three lefts and a right.

"Alexis, we just went in a giant circle," Rob said.

"Fine," she said. "Third shithole on the left."

He pulled up to the curb in front of Jules's ugly little house and Lexi could see the living room lights were on. She hoped it was just Brooke watching some sappy Hallmark movie and not Jules and Shawn, too.

"You sure you can't come in and fake-arrest my sister?" she pleaded.

"As much as I'd love to, no, I can't," he said. "Let me walk you up."

"That would be great. My sisters probably wouldn't murder me in front of a cop." He jumped out and raced around the front of the squad car to open her door for her. When he slammed it behind her, the neighbor's dog started barking like crazy.

"Do you have a stun gun on you?" Lexi asked as they walked up the front path.

"For that dog?" he laughed.

"No, for my sisters," Lexi told him.

Jules

～

"Oh shit," Jules said, peering out the window. Brooke jumped up from the couch, spilling the air-popped popcorn that was in her lap all over the floor. The two watched as Lexi stumbled up the path with a strange guy who either was a police officer or had stolen a squad car. Neither would have been a surprise.

"Mom, I'm home," Lexi called, swinging the door open dramatically. She gasped when she saw her sisters' foil-wrapped heads. "What the *fuck*?" Brooke patted her head self-consciously.

"'What the fuck' is right," Jules said, marching over to Lexi and the undeniably hot man she had in tow. "Is this guy a cop? Did you get arrested?"

"No, I didn't get arrested. This is my friend Rob. Officer Rob. He just gave me a ride home. It's all good," Lexi slurred.

Rob stuck out his hand. "Officer Robert Cooper. Nice to meet you."

"I'm Alexis's sister, Jules Richardson," she said, shaking his hand.

"Richardson! Shit, I knew that," Lexi said. She thumped herself on the head and stumbled.

"This is our other sister, Brooke Alexander," Jules said, nodding at Brooke.

"Nice hats," Rob said. He shook Brooke's hand and she blushed deeply.

"Oh, this, we . . . well . . . we were doing deep-conditioning treatments," Jules said, touching the foil. "It's all the rage in the fancy spas."

Rob laughed. "The horn's a nice touch. You might want to get your sister some aspirin and some water and put her to bed."

"So she's really not under arrest?" Jules asked. Relief flooded over her. Bail money was definitely not in her budget this month.

"Not at the moment," Rob said. "But if I were you, I'd keep a close eye on her."

"Easier said than done," Jules told him.

"Thanks for the ride, Rob," Lexi said, giving him a hug. "Sorry—Officer Cooper."

He pulled out his wallet and handed her a business card. "You call me if you ever need anything, okay, Alexis?"

"You might regret that offer," she said, tucking the card into her front pocket. She was grinning like a fool and swaying like a flag in the breeze. Jules watched her, unsure how she should feel. Lexi was alive and she wasn't in trouble. And it was indeed a rare treat to see her sister looking genuinely happy, she had to admit. She just wished Lexi didn't need mind-altering chemicals to flip that switch, and she was furious she hadn't even had the decency to let them know she was okay.

"I'm sure I will," Rob said to all three sisters, flashing a cartoon-hero smile. "Good night, ladies."

When Rob was gone, Jules unleashed the full force of her fury.

"You couldn't even *call*, for God's sake? You know that we were worried sick, right? And that we had no idea how to find you or where to even start looking? And we called your phone and got some guy who said you'd stolen all of his money and he was throwing your phone off a bridge. Alexis, what the hell happened? And why aren't you wearing any shoes?" She knew it was a ridiculous thing to add, but honestly, who went around barefoot at night?

"I lost my phone." Lexi shrugged. She wobbled dangerously as she walked to the kitchen. "Hey, you got anything to eat? I'm starving."

"Alexis, don't walk away when I'm talking to you," Jules shouted.

"I *love* that song!" Alexis said. She closed her eyes and belted out an incomprehensible tangle of lyrics. She was stumbling and swaying, and Jules had had enough.

"Alexis, I mean it," Jules said, grabbing Lexi's arm and spinning her around so that they were nose to nose. Her fingers were digging into Lexi's flesh. "I know I'm not your mother. But as long as you're staying here for free, you have to be respectful. And responsible. And if you can't, you can find somewhere else to live." Sure, it was exactly the same thing as "As long as you live under my roof you'll abide by my rules," but at least she'd paraphrased it.

"You're killing me with the alien brain shield," Lexi said, pulling her arm from Jules's grip. She must have jerked harder than she meant to, and when she did, she began to tumble in slow motion toward the floor. Before Jules could even lift an arm to try to stop her, Lexi's forehead smacked the corner of the kitchen table with a sickening crack. Jules watched help-lessly as she landed facedown on the linoleum, her face resting in a widening pool of blood.

"Lexi!" Jules shrieked, reaching for her.

"Don't move her!" Brooke shouted, racing toward them. "I've seen it on TV. You're never supposed to move the body!"

Lexi lifted her face a tiny bit and groaned. Blood was gush-ing from a deep gash above her eye and running down the side of her head and puddling in her hair. Jules grabbed a dish towel and held it on Lexi's head. The color drained from Brooke's face, and she held on to the kitchen counter to steady herself. She'd never had a stomach for the sight of blood, Jules recalled.

"I'm okay," Lexi said, wincing from the pain. "Heads just bleed a lot. Happens all the time. Trust me. I'll be fine."

"Brooke, get her some ice," Jules commanded. Brooke did as she was told, obviously grateful for an excuse to look away. She handed Jules a few cubes of ice wrapped in a paper towel and then lowered herself into one of the rickety kitchen chairs. It let out a groan and Jules hoped it wouldn't break. That was all they needed.

The girls sat in silence while Jules held the ice on Lexi's head for several minutes. The blood flow finally started to slow.

"Do you want to try to get up?" Jules asked. Her own hands were covered in blood.

Lexi nodded, and her two sisters helped her carefully to her feet.

"I think we should get you into the shower," Jules said. Lexi's hair was a rat's nest of knots and blood and Jules didn't even want to imagine what else.

Lexi nodded, looking dazed.

"Actually, I'll get her cleaned up and you take care of this mess, okay Brooke?" Jules said. "I don't want Shawn having to come home to that." Brooke nodded. Her face was starting to look normal again.

"I actually would have called if I hadn't lost my phone," Lexi said as Jules led her to the bathroom. "I don't know your number by heart, and I couldn't remember your last name. I'm an asshole. I'm sorry."

"Okay, it's okay," Jules soothed. She'd forgotten all about being pissed off at Lexi, and besides, it was hard to be mad at someone who was crusted in blood and calling herself an asshole. "We'll talk about it tomorrow. Let's just get you cleaned up and into bed, okay?"

Jules turned on the water for her sister and helped her undress, trying not to stare at the scars that were scattered around her perfect body or let herself wonder how they got there.

"I'll wait here in case you need me," she said as Lexi stepped into the steamy shower. Jules sat on the toilet and waited, a fresh, dry towel folded in her lap.

Brooke

❧

"Sorry about the lice thing," Brooke said to Jules. It had taken two full weeks of combing and sticky, messy oil treatments, but Brooke was pretty sure they were bug-free. Mercifully—and miraculously, what with all of the bed swapping—Shawn and Lexi had been spared. Brooke cringed at the thought of combing through Lexi's lush mane a hundred or more times, or having to get up close to that angry-looking gash on her head. At least it was finally starting to heal up.

"It's okay," Jules whispered. Lexi was still asleep in the office and Brooke knew why she didn't want to wake her. Things were always easiest—and calmest—when Lexi was asleep. "You were right. It wasn't as bad as I thought. Just gross. And my hair looks really great after all of those oil treatments. I'm thinking the whole thing could make a good scene for my book. I just have to figure out the big picture and where it might fit in."

"Maybe that's it!" Brooke shouted. "Maybe you can write a book about us. An autobiography, or a memoir. Mom never said you had to write a novel, did she? She just said a book. Just make me skinny, is all I ask. What do you think?"

"I'm not sure we're interesting enough for a memoir," Jules told her.

"Are you serious? Awesome dead dad, wacko dead mom, the will, the conditions, Alexis and all of her crazy antics . . . What else could anyone possibly ask for?"

Jules considered this for a moment. "The problem is," she said finally, "I'd have to finish it without knowing how the story ends."

"What do you mean, you won't know how the story ends? We get tons of money and you're a famous author and I'm a runner and have a fabulous new boyfriend and Alexis . . . Alexis is . . . well, she's employed *somewhere*. That's all I know. But I think that would be perfect. Seriously, you'd probably sell the movie rights, too." Obviously Megan Fox would play Lexi, and Scarlett Johansson without makeup would make a pretty good Jules. Who would play Brooke? It was too bad Kate Winslet was so old; she had a killer body, curvy and strong and not *too* skinny . . .

"I like it, I do," Jules said, interrupting her fantasy. "Let me see if any of my writing books talk about memoirs." She pulled a fat stack of books from her bookshelf. When she did, a pad of paper slipped to the floor. "Holy crap, look at this," she said as she picked up the pad and began flipping through its pages. She held the pad up so Brooke could see. "These are the most incredible sketches I've ever seen. Did you do these?"

"Are you kidding me?" Brooke asked, peering over her shoulder. "I can't even draw a stick figure! My students make fun of me all the time when I even try."

"I can't draw, either," Jules said. "Do you think Lexi did them?"

Brooke shrugged. Wouldn't they know it if their own sister was some sort of art prodigy? "Does Shawn draw?" she asked. She took the pad from Jules to get a closer look.

"I guarantee you that your stick figure would kick Shawn's stick figure's ass in a fight," Jules insisted.

"Wait, remember she said she drew her own tattoo?" Brooke asked. She winced a little at the memory of Lexi's dig: *You actually get paid to teach kids?*

"She did say that." Jules nodded.

"Dang," Brooke said. She stopped flipping pages when she got to the image of the eyeless woman and the three little girls. "Jules, I think this is us. That's you with the broken wrist from the time you fell out of the avocado tree in the backyard, and that's my scraped knee—remember when I wiped out on my bike riding home from school and Lexi had to carry all of my stuff home?—and that must be her." She turned the pad around so it was facing Jules, and Brooke watched the pain register on her sister's face.

"With the broken heart," Jules said.

"Did you know she was so talented?" Brooke asked.

"How would I?" Jules asked. "It's not like she's going around bragging about it or anything."

"How crazy is that?" Brooke demanded. "God, she pisses me off. She's the prettiest one of all of us—no offense—and she's got that ridiculous body; she could be a model for sure. And she's smart as a whip—you can't be funny if you're not smart, and she's downright hilarious—and she's got an incredible singing voice and now we find out she's practically Michelangelo! And she does nothing with any of her talent, not one stinking thing. I sort of want to punch her right now."

"Just not in the face," Lexi said. "It could ruin my future

modeling career." She was standing in the doorway of the office, stunning as ever despite her oversized tie-dyed T-shirt and bed-head.

"Alexis, these are amazing," Brooke said, holding up the sketch pad. "Why didn't you ever show them to us?"

"What, so you could put a pretty gold star on them? Who cares? I like to draw. It's a fun way to kill time. And it's free, so that's a bonus." She shrugged and reached for the pad, but Brooke pulled it away.

"You need to do something with these, Alexis, you really do," Brooke said. "This could be your job."

"She's right, Alexis, they're incredible," Jules added.

"Have you guys ever heard the phrase 'starving artist'?" Lexi asked. "There's no shortage of talent in this world, but you need to have a business head to make a living at any kind of art, and I really don't think that description fits me. Besides, I draw for fun. If it was my job, I'd probably start hating it."

"You'd hate any job you had," Jules countered. "Might as well hate a job you're already really good at, right?"

"Everything is done on computers these days, and I don't even *have* a computer," Lexi said. "I don't know any of the graphics programs or anything. Artsy jobs are for rich kids whose parents send them to fancy private colleges and basically pay their way into that world. Maybe when we get Mom's money I'll go to rich-kid art school. In the meantime, you find me an art gig that asks for a GED, no experience and a rap sheet three miles long, and I promise you I'll take it."

Brooke started hopping up and down. "Oh! There's a career fair at the convention center in a few weeks! I don't know why I didn't mention it sooner. My friend Pam from work told me about it. She's the one who has to wipe all the butts in the

Tadpole room? Anyway, she said it's supposed to be really fun and that they give away a ton of free stuff. I wasn't planning to go, but I could go with you if you want?"

Brooke smiled hesitatingly and then braced herself, waiting for Lexi to shoot down the idea as being stupid or say something horrible to her. But for some reason, she didn't.

"Did somebody say free shit?" Lexi asked, giving her sister a thumbs-up. "I'm in."

Lexi's response was unnerving. Did her rebellious baby sister have some crazy scheme up her sleeve, or was she actually changing? Brooke said a silent prayer that it was the latter.

Lexi

∽

Lexi stretched out on the air mattress, wondering what a good way to kill a dog would be. The neighbor's little shit-eater had to announce it to the entire block any time a car drove down the street. Usually it would pipe down once the suspicious vehicle in question was out of sight, but that little bastard had been barking for a solid fifteen minutes now. Shawn and Brooke were off at work and Jules had mercifully gone to walk her stupid dogs, and Lexi was kicking herself for not suggesting she take the asshole next door with her.

"Would you SHUT THE FUCK UP ALREADY?" Lexi yelled, shoving off the covers and stomping to the front door. She wasn't sure what she was going to do—throw a rock at it, maybe?—but she had to make it stop. She was cranky and exhausted; without booze and drugs to help her pass out, she'd had a stretch of sleepless nights under her belt and was not in the mood to relive the call of the wild. She flung open the door and gasped.

"Hi, Alexis," Rob said. He was holding a bouquet of orange Gerbera daisies. "I take it the doorbell doesn't work?"

Lexi crossed her legs self-consciously. She was wearing a ratty old wifebeater and the smiley-face boxer shorts she'd stolen from some guy's dresser after a drunken one-night stand.

"Oh, Rob, hey," Lexi said, wrapping her arms around herself. Why did her damned nipples always feel the need to make their perky presence known whenever a guy was in the vicinity? And why did this suddenly bother her? "Yeah, it's broken. Nobody around here is very handy." She didn't make a move or invite him in.

"I hope it's okay that I just stopped by," Rob said nervously. "I didn't get your number the other night and I just wanted to say hi and make sure you were okay . . . and that your sisters didn't kill you."

"I don't have a phone at the moment, so if I'd given you a number it would have been bullshit." Lexi laughed and swept her hair off of her face.

"Ouch, that's a nice gash," he said, noticing it for the first time. He reached out and traced the fresh pink scar on her forehead tenderly with one finger. Her nipples perked up even more. "Did Jules do that to you?"

"Oh, no. I just . . . tripped," she said. She took a step backward into the house. "Did you want to come in or anything? It's sort of a mess. I was just about to pick up." Lexi heard the words coming out of her mouth and wondered where on earth they'd come from. She'd never given a flying flip about how messy any place was, or thought twice about trying to impress a guy with her housekeeping skills, of all things. All she normally cared about was what she'd have to do to get a guy to buy her food, drinks or drugs—preferably all three.

"Sure, if it's okay and doesn't mess up your vacuuming schedule," Rob said. "These are for you." He handed her the flowers.

She didn't know what to say. No man had ever given her flowers before, or looked at her with such concern and what she would dare to call affection. What did Rob see in her? she mused. She certainly couldn't have made a great impression on him the night they'd met; she'd been totally hammered. She barely even remembered him driving her home; even the fall in Jules's kitchen was nothing but a blur.

The closest thing Lexi could find to a vase was a ceramic water pitcher. It was yellow with a giant red rooster on it, and Lexi thought it might be the ugliest thing she had ever seen. She filled it with water and stuck the flowers in it.

"My mom has that same pitcher," Rob said. "Actually, she has the whole matching set." Lexi couldn't tell by his voice whether he hated it or not, so she decided to say nothing.

"Would you like some . . . water or something? Sorry, we don't have much in the house right now. I was going to go shopping after I cleaned up." Honestly, was this *Invasion of the Body Snatchers* or something? She was going to go shopping? To the store two miles away, on foot, and pay for a bunch of groceries with her charm and good looks?

"I'm fine, thanks," Rob said. "Like I said, I really just wanted to stop by and say hi . . . and also to tell you that I'd like to see you again. You know, if you're not dating anyone or anything."

Lexi sat on the corner of the couch and curled her legs under her. She pulled the itchy brown afghan off the back of it and wrapped it around herself. Rob sat next to her.

"I'm definitely not dating anyone," Lexi told him. "I'm sort of starting over, I guess. Let's just say I've had a rough couple of years. Anyway, I'm staying with Jules and trying to get back on my feet."

"Well, I don't want to pry or anything, so I'll just focus on the part about you being free to go out with me." He smiled at her sheepishly and a swarm of butterflies took flight in the pit of her stomach. "Are you working or going to school or anything?"

"Actually, I'm looking for a job," she admitted. She didn't mention how halfhearted or unsuccessful her search had been to date.

"What are you good at?" Rob asked. "Besides blow jobs, I mean. Not that I'd know firsthand or anything, but you did make a point of telling me how great you are at giving them."

Lexi winced, then shifted swiftly into self-protection mode. "So is that why you're here, to find out for yourself? And then are you going to arrest me? Because I'm pretty sure that would be called entrapment." Her face had turned angry and hard.

"God, no," Rob said. He reached for her hand in her lap and wrapped both of his around it. "Not at all. I'm so sorry. I meant that as a joke. I thought you'd think it was funny. Alexis, I like you, okay? You're funny and tough and sexy as hell, and I can't stop thinking about you. And I realize you're probably a world of trouble, but I figure if a cop can't handle you, who can?"

A smile played at the edges of Lexi's mouth. Every instinct in her body told her to fight it; showing emotion made you weak, and when you were weak you got hurt.

"I can help you find a job if you want," Rob said, squeezing her hand. "I know lots of people, and everybody wants to do a favor for a cop. It's one of the perks of my job. You should take advantage of it."

"You'd do that for me, call in a favor?" She was being weak—and vulnerable—and she knew it. But for some reason, Rob made her feel safe. Maybe it was the gun.

"I already have something in mind," he said.

"Let me guess. You're going to have me pose as a hooker to try to get guys to pick me up so you can arrest them?"

Rob laughed. "You have to be a cop to do that, otherwise it's just prostitution."

"Oh, well, that's good, I guess," Lexi said. "So what is it?"

"Let me make a few calls and I'll let you know, okay? Is there any way I can get ahold of you without dropping by unannounced?"

Lexi gave him Jules's number and he promised he'd call her in the next day or two. Now Lexi really wanted a job. She'd need one to pay for the phone she suddenly didn't want to live without.

Jules

～

Jules couldn't stop thinking about what Brooke had said. The truth was, she hadn't ever really thought about writing nonfiction. In Jules's mind the assignment, the goal, was always to write a novel. Like her dad. That was what she wanted more than anything, the prestige of saying that she was a novelist and the confirmation that she was like him—and not Juliana. But she could write a memoir first, to satisfy her mother's ridiculous demand, and write her novel later, couldn't she?

She sat down at her computer and opened a new document, which she titled "MEMOIR WORKING." She'd checked out a half dozen books from the library on memoir writing and read them all cover to cover. Now tidbits of advice flashed across her mind. "When writing becomes painful, remember that the word *memory* is derived from the same root as the word *mourn*." Well, that was a bit daunting. "What you leave out is often far more important than what you include." Interesting approach. "Your stories are probably not as interesting as you think." Isn't that exactly what she'd told Brooke? "Thinking that memoir is the same thing as autobiography is a mistake. Memoir isn't about you; it's about universal, relatable truths and experiences." Gulp.

You have a story, she told herself. *Just tell it.*

"I stood at the counter, trying to choose between bubblegum and rocky road," Jules wrote. "Everyone else had their ice cream and I was holding up the line. Dad took his sunglasses off, wiped them on his T-shirt and laughed. 'You're not picking out your future husband, you know, Juju,' he'd said, ruffling my hair. 'Whichever one you don't get today you can get next time.' I'd gone with the bubblegum, blissfully unaware that there would never be a next time."

Was that what he'd said? Were those his exact words, *Whichever one you don't get today you can get next time*? She was pretty sure they were.

Just write, she scolded herself. *You can critique later. This is about getting the words down.*

Jules went through half a box of Kleenex as she wrote and wrote. She thought starting with that awful day would be a powerful hook; then she went back and tried to paint a picture of her life, before, as best she could. She was careful to abide by the maxim *Show, don't tell.* Her mom wasn't just happy and easygoing; she whistled while she folded laundry and swatted her husband when he pulled a shirt from the bottom of his pile and toppled the thing. Lexi wasn't simply a free spirit; she flounced around the house, naked save a tutu and too-big pink cowboy boots, a wizard's hat perched on her head. She never said Brooke was thoughtful and selfless; instead she recounted the time when she'd threatened to run away from home when their mom said they couldn't keep the puppy that had wandered into their yard, and Brooke had cracked open her piggy bank and spent her life's savings on a stuffed dog for Jules that looked exactly like the stray.

Writing about Juliana was the hardest, harder even than writing about her father. John Alexander had a distinct advantage, she knew. Because she was a child when he was taken from them, she still saw him through adoring, almost reverent eyes. The fact that he'd died full of so much promise and potential further immortalized him in her mind. Had he ever raised his voice, or been grumpy or distant or demanding or disappointing? He had to have done and been all of those things; he'd been human, after all. But Jules had no real memories of anything like that. In her recollections he might as well have been James Dean: devastatingly handsome, wildly talented and forever young.

But Juliana was a different story. Jules could vividly recall her at both extremes, and she could draw a straight line from one to the other and plot out her mother's entire heartbreaking life on it. She was careful not to rewrite the early history; her mom hadn't been perfect, because no parent could be. Sometimes she was uptight, but when their dad pointed it out, she would laugh at herself and suggest they play a silly game. She lost her temper on occasion, but she always apologized. More than anything, she'd been present in both body and spirit, a gift her children hadn't much noticed or thought to appreciate until it was taken away.

Jules mentally walked the timeline of her mother's life. Her earliest memories were a fuzzy blur of piggyback rides and picnics in the park; after that, countless hours of cuddling in bed reading books or hovering over the kitchen table tracing the alphabet on wide-ruled paper, with Juliana gently guiding her hand. There was her twelfth birthday, the last one BDD—before

Dad died—when Juliana had baked dozens of cupcakes and let the girls decorate them to look like frogs, with green frosting faces and mini-marshmallow eyes and long red licorice tongues. That year her parents had created an elaborate scavenger hunt, hiding clues all over the house that eventually led to Jules's present, hidden in the trunk of the car: the lava lamp she'd seen at the mall and wanted more than anything in the world. "You only live once!" Juliana had chirped when she saw the look of surprised joy on her daughter's face. There had been no more birthday parties after that; no cupcakes or gifts, either. Occasionally Juliana would wait until that day to present her with a new package of socks or a pair of gym shorts or some other practical thing she'd have gotten for her anyway. Brooke always had something small for her—a rainbow lollipop, a tiny pot of lip balm, a gently used book—wrapped neatly in newspaper because Juliana had long ago stopped buying wrapping paper. Had she gushed over her sister's thoughtfulness at the time? Her heart ached to admit she probably hadn't; surely not enough. *It's like pouring peroxide on a cut; it hurts because it's healing,* she told herself as she cried and typed and cried some more.

Jules's chest was heaving as she detailed a horrific knockdown between Brooke and Juliana. Brooke's boyfriend Billy was heading off to the Coast Guard Training Center in Virginia and Brooke wanted to drive him to the airport. Juliana had refused to let her take her ancient, rusty Buick, so Brooke had called Jules begging to borrow the equally decrepit Ford truck she'd managed to buy for herself. Juliana had ripped the phone from Brooke's hand mid-request, catching a lock of her hair in the process. Jules could still hear her sister's piercing wails in her mind.

"Damn it, Mom, why couldn't you have just let her go?"

Jules wondered aloud, and when she did, the answer hit her like a sucker punch. Juliana had been consumed by fear; the fear of losing everything she loved. Jules knew from personal experience that when people felt powerless, the natural reaction was to try to gain control of something, anything. She and her sisters had been the nearest, and most natural, targets. The fact that it all made perfect sense did little to ease the pain of this new insight.

Jules grabbed a tissue and blew her nose hard into it just as Lexi swept into her office.

"Holy crap, you look like shit," Lexi said.

"And you actually look presentable," Jules said, dabbing at her nose. She wouldn't have admitted it, but she was grateful for the intrusion; she'd had enough gut-wrenching epiphanies for one day. Now she eyed her sister approvingly. Lexi was wearing one of her pencil skirts—probably the shortest one she owned but it was still quite modest—and a crisp button-up top, also pinched from Jules's closet. "By the way, yes, you can borrow my clothes. And obviously you're free to do as you please, but the clothes have to be home by eleven. That's their curfew."

"Your boring clothes will be home and all tucked in by eleven," Lexi promised.

"Hot date?" Jules asked, trying to sound casual.

"Rob's taking me for ice cream," Lexi said, rolling her eyes.

"You're dressed awfully nicely to be going for ice cream," Jules said. In actuality, her sister was dressed more appropriately for a job interview or an actual job, but Jules didn't dare say that out loud—or even hope it was the case.

"Yeah, well, I didn't have any other clean clothes." Lexi shrugged.

"Tell Rob I said hello," Jules said.

"It's not a date," Lexi said.

"I never said it was."

"Well, quit acting like it is."

Jules smiled but said nothing. Worse things could happen than her sister going out with a cop, that was for damned sure.

Brooke

❧

"Hey, what time is Alexis coming home, do you think?" Brooke asked Jules, trying her best to sound casual.

"She's wearing my clothes and I told her they had to be home by eleven," Jules said with a smile. She turned and began pulling food from the refrigerator, methodically checking expiration dates. It was something Juliana had done when she was creating her own shopping list, Brooke recalled now. She'd never thought to do it herself, although she wasn't surprised that Jules had picked up the habit.

"Clever," said Brooke. "So Shawn's home tonight, right?"

"He should be here any second," Jules said, squinting at a milk carton. She looked so much like their mother when she did it that for a split second, Brooke thought she was seeing a ghost.

"I'd like to take you guys out to dinner," Brooke said, shaking off the eerie feeling of déjà vu. "Well, actually, I'd like to *send* you guys out to dinner. My treat. It can't be anywhere crazy, because I only have forty bucks right now. But I want you to have it." She'd been living with Jules for three months, but she'd been using the money she'd saved by not paying Jake's rent to pay down some of her credit card bills. She'd been surprised at how good it felt, actually being able to put a dent in that ominous number. Still, forty dollars seemed a small price to pay for all Jules had done for her—not to mention, to get her out of the house.

"Why? Are you trying to get rid of us or something?" Jules asked.

"Not at all," Brooke said in a rush. She grabbed her bag off the counter and began rifling through it for her wallet. "I just, you know, want to thank you for everything you've done for me. And you and Shawn could probably use some time together somewhere fun. You haven't been out or even alone in months, and I feel bad. I want to do this, Jules. Please let me." She held out two twenty-dollar bills.

Jules hesitated and Brooke gave her a pleading look. "It's rude to refuse someone's gift," Brooke added. It was something Juliana used to say.

"That's really generous, not to mention unnecessary," Jules said. "But if you're going to insist, I guess I have no choice. I hope Alexis left me something clean to wear!" She looked giddy as she kissed Brooke on the cheek and dashed to her bedroom.

As soon as the Honda was out of sight, Brooke pulled Lexi's notebook from the bookshelf. For the first time, she was grateful that Jules's house was so tiny that there was nowhere for Lexi to hide it. She flipped through it for the hundredth time, as blown away now as she had been when she'd first laid eyes on her sister's remarkable sketches. She closed the notebook and tucked it gently into her messenger bag, careful not to bend any of the pages. Then she grabbed her car keys and locked the front door behind her.

She drove the familiar route to Little Me Preschool, watching needlessly in her rearview mirror. Who would have any reason to follow her? Still, it wasn't in Brooke's nature to be breaking into her place of employment, although it wasn't technically breaking in if she had a key, was it?

She parked around the corner from the school's main entrance and made her way to the side door of the teachers' lounge. Her hand was shaking as she slid her key into the lock. She wished now that she'd brought a flashlight with her, and smirked at the realization that if she'd brought Lexi with her, her impish sister surely would have thought of that detail. But she hadn't said anything to Lexi for the obvious reason that it was easier to ask for forgiveness later than permission first. She locked the door to the teachers' lounge behind her.

Inside the pitch-dark room, Brooke felt her way toward the copy machine and turned on the tiny desk lamp that sat on the metal table next to it. Then she switched on the copier. It took forever for the thing to warm up, and Brooke stared at the locked door the entire time, reciting preemptive Hail Marys in her head even though she hadn't set foot in a church in more than two decades.

Her first few copies were terrible; too dark, too light, too crooked, too blurry. She adjusted the settings and tried again and again until the machine spit out a perfect, crisp copy. Brooke repeated the process over and over for dozens of sketches until she had a warm, thick stack of papers. Satisfied, she switched the machine off, lifting the lid one final time to make sure she hadn't left anything behind. After triple-checking that the door was indeed locked, she darted into the shadows and raced—marveling at the speed her own stout legs were indeed capable of—back to her car. *It's going to be so great to get back in shape,* she thought as she huffed and puffed and willed her heart rate to go back to normal.

Brooke nearly wept with relief when she got back to Jules's house and nobody was there. She snuck into the office and sat down at Jules's computer, unsure where to start. What went into an artist's portfolio? She had no idea. Lexi didn't have anything to put on a résumé, so Brooke typed up a page of basic contact information, including their address along with her own phone number, as Lexi still didn't have a phone. She went to her drawer and took out the fake-leather art portfolio she'd bought at the craft store that gave teachers a discount. The real leather ones had been far more striking and had price tags that reflected their cachet. The fake-leather one was good enough, she told herself now, as she carefully slipped each copy of Lexi's artwork into a sleeve of its own. The contact sheet went inside the front cover.

It was impressive, she had to admit. The filled portfolio was heavy and fat, and anyone flipping through its pages would have to be blown away. There was no way they couldn't be. When she had decided she wanted to help Lexi, she wasn't sure what she was going to do, or even what her wildest dream for her sister's artwork was; she just knew that it was too amazing to stay tucked away on a shelf. So she'd done what anyone in her situation would do: She turned to Google.

She started with a simple query: HOW DO ARTISTS GET DISCOVERED, in all caps, because she was serious about this. As usual, Google delivered.

*To be in the right place at the right time, you have
to be in a lot of places.*

*If you're waiting to be discovered, you'll end up
waiting tables.*

*The foolproof secret to getting discovered is BE
MORE DISCOVERABLE.*

Be more discoverable? How did one do that? In a flash, Brooke recalled a coffee shop near Little Me Preschool where they occasionally held staff meetings. The Perk had rotating art installments on the walls, and even though none of the ones she'd seen came close to Lexi's in terms of talent, she'd heard that several now-famous artists had been "discovered" there. The best part was, Lexi would never have to know she'd set it up. It was hardly a sure thing, but probably not as unlikely as, say, getting struck by lightning or dying in a plane crash or inheriting millions of dollars—and all of those things happened in the world, at least on occasion. More important, it was the only plan she had.

Lexi

~

"Remember," Rob said. "You're new to town and you just love interacting with people, kids in particular. That's why you've been volunteering all over the place and don't have a job at the moment. Got it?"

"I hate kids," Lexi said petulantly. "And ice cream."

"Nobody hates kids and ice cream," Rob told her.

"I do," she said definitively.

"Well, you'd better learn to love them both."

Lexi couldn't get over how weird it was to be riding in the front seat of a squad car, or to be riding in one at all and not be handcuffed or shitfaced or both. *Is this a date?* she wondered. No, it wasn't a date. It was a job interview, even though the interviewer didn't know it yet. Rob had called her (on Jules's phone of course) to say he'd talked to a buddy of his, actually his sister's husband, who owned an ice cream shop in Northridge. The place had seen some serious turnover recently, and Benji, the brother-in-law, was in desperate need of someone mature

and responsible who could come in and hit the ground running, particularly since his wife had just had their first baby and
wanted him to be home more. The hours were long but the pay
was above average, and Benji was willing to shell out even more
for someone who could take on scheduling and payroll and
other non-scooping duties.

"Benji's a dog's name," is what Lexi had said when he first
proposed the idea of bringing her by for an impromptu introduction.

"It's short for Benjamin, and he's a great guy," Rob had insisted. "Please do not tell him that he has a dog's name."

"I thought you said Benji was looking for someone mature
and responsible to hire," Lexi said now. "What on earth made
you think of me?"

"If I'm being honest, I was thinking of you anyway," Rob
said. His face turned pink when he said it. "But seriously, Alexis,
you need a job. You're a good person, I can tell. And I'm pretty
sure you won't screw over—or, God forbid, screw—a guy whose
best friend and brother-in-law is a cop. Benji's married, okay?
Happily married. *To my sister, Susie.* Plus, you may not know
this, but cops don't like donuts anymore. Nope, we're all about
ice cream. You can ask any of the guys in my unit. So this way I
can keep an eye on you, since I'm in there all the time anyway.
It seemed like an all-around perfect solution to me."

"You know it's sick and perverted for you to be attracted to
me, right?" Lexi said now. "Or is that another cop thing I didn't
know about?"

"I always trust my gut," Rob said. "You may have gotten yourself into some fucked-up situations and done some things you
regret in your life, but when you've seen the shit I've seen, you
learn to recognize the difference between someone who's going to

hurt you and someone who's just been hurt. I'm banking on the fact that you fall into the latter category."

Lexi didn't know what to say. Nobody had ever talked to her like this in her life, or gone out of their way to help her. And certainly no man had ever believed in her or shown her that she was worth putting his own ass on the line for. The feeling was dizzying.

"I'll try not to give him a hand job during the interview," Lexi said.

"That would be helpful," Rob laughed. "And remember, it's not an interview."

"If I put on a fucking skirt and a stupid old lady blouse, it sure as hell better be an interview," Lexi told him. She crossed her arms over her chest for emphasis.

Rob shook his head. "What have I gotten myself into?" he said. But he was smiling, and so was Lexi.

Jules

～

Jules had been averaging an easy three thousand words a day. She couldn't believe how quickly the words were coming now, or how much better she felt not lying to Shawn—and her sisters and herself—about what she did all day long. She was emotionally and mentally exhausted when she fell into bed each night, but it was a blissful sort of exhaustion, peaceful and resonant, like the feeling you'd get after a grueling workout or a good long laugh with a girlfriend. She pictured her dad, sitting at his antique rolltop desk in the corner of their living room and typing away with a distant smile on his face, and wondered if this had been how he had felt, too. She'd give anything for the chance to ask him.

Normally when those feelings of longing arose she quickly and almost mercilessly shoved them deep down into the untouched recesses of her heart and did whatever she could to shift her mental gears to something else, anything else. But now, now that she was a writer, she let the painful sensation sit.

What did it feel like, she asked herself? It wasn't the sharp sting of a blunt blow but more of an ache; a dull, relentless throbbing. She zeroed in on the feeling now, probed it, poked it, examined it from all sides. What would he look like today? What would he *be* like? Would they have been close when she was a hormonal, weepy teenager? Would they be close now? Would her mother be alive? Would they still be happily married? Would her life have taken an entirely different course? With each question the ache deepened. She squeezed her eyes shut against the tears that were threatening to come and took a deep breath. Did every grown woman who still had a living father appreciate what a luxury it was to be able to pick up the phone any time she wanted and hear his voice? She wanted to strangle the ones who didn't.

Use that rage, her inner writer told her now. *Harness it and use it.*

The words poured out of her like blood from a fresh wound, and as they did she felt as if a lifetime of sadness were being lifted off her. When Juliana died, Jules had been plagued with guilt. She'd just buried her mother; she should be devastated. Only she wasn't. As she lost herself in her writing, she realized that she didn't yearn for her dead mother in that moment because she didn't have to. She'd already done that, twenty years earlier, when her father died and she effectively lost them both. She was free now to mourn not what could have been but what never was, and the relief from understanding that distinction was indescribable. Jules wrote until her eyes were burning and she could barely see the screen anymore, then she saved her document and shut down her computer.

It was after midnight, but she cracked open a beer and settled onto the couch, exhausted but also surprisingly content. It was finally looking like she and her sisters might actually all be on track. That cute cop had somehow managed to nudge Lexi into a job, one that might even meet the criteria of an "actual job" if her sister showed some initiative and took on at least some of the extra responsibilities that were available to her. Rob had even lent her his bicycle so she could get back and forth without having to take the long way around town on the bus. Lexi had saved enough money for a new cell phone and a few presentable pairs of pants, and mercifully The Inside Scoop employees wore company T-shirts on the job. Lexi hadn't even tried to tie hers up Hooters-girl style, which Jules thought surely must be a sign of some newfound maturity. The other day, she had even caught her baby sister washing some dishes in the sink, ones she hadn't even dirtied, and she was actually whistling as she did it. Jules had smiled to herself and not said a word.

Brooke, surprisingly, was proving to be the stubborn one. Jules had dusted off her own running shoes and offered to run with Brooke several times, but her sister insisted she was already well on her way. Jules didn't see how that was possible. Brooke claimed she was running with some friends most days after work, but she never came home sweaty and spent. And as far as Jules could see, her sister hadn't dropped any weight, either, which she probably would have if she were running regularly. Jules didn't just need to light a little fire; this called for an inferno.

She racked her brain and finally she came up with what she thought was a halfway-brilliant plan. She was going to tell Brooke that the dog-walking was too much for her now that she was so engrossed in her writing; that she had to write when inspiration struck and if she had to drop what she was doing and rush out to wrangle a bunch of ankle-biters, she'd never meet her deadline. *Their* deadline. She needed Brooke, and

Brooke needed to be needed. She had a few obnoxiously high-energy dogs in her rotation, the sort that would drag Brooke at top speeds, oblivious to any kicking and screaming on their walker's part. She just prayed that Brooke would get bitten—hopefully mauled—by the exercise bug.

"I know what you're doing," Brooke said, looking hurt, after Jules made her exaggerated plea for help. "Jules, I've got this. Really."

"Brooke, you *don't* have this. You watch at least two hours of TV a day, and you're huffing and puffing when I ask you to sweep the front porch. Please. Don't blow this for us. For Alexis. Besides, I really need your help."

Brooke's face flushed.

"You get to keep all the dog-walking money," Jules taunted.

"I'm not going to need the money soon anyway," Brooke said.

"If you can't run thirteen miles, you will. And then what? You can't live here forever, you know."

Brooke looked down, ashamed. A tear slipped down her cheek.

"Brooke," Jules said gently. "Have you been running at all?"

"Not really," Brooke admitted.

"So you'll walk the dogs?" Jules asked.

Brooke nodded.

"And you won't eat chocolate-covered almonds or peanut-butter pretzels while you do it?"

"How did you know about those?" Brooke asked. She looked both shocked and pitiful.

"It's a small house. You can't keep secrets here." Jules smiled at her sister. Brooke really was beautiful, as pretty as Lexi but in a softer, subtler way. Brooke was a classic beauty and Lexi was a bombshell. She was Elizabeth Taylor to Lexi's Marilyn Monroe; Mary Ann to her Ginger.

"Fine, I'll do it," Brooke said. "But will you come with me the first few times, in case I have a heart attack and drop dead from the exertion? It does run in our family, you know."

"Is that what you're afraid of?" Jules asked.

"Sort of," Brooke admitted. "That and failing."

"First of all, you're not going to drop dead *or* fail," Jules insisted. "You're young, you don't smoke, you're female—that lowers your heart attack risk, you know—and besides, you were a track star once, remember? You'll pick it back up in no time. The hardest part is getting started."

"But will you still come with me?" Brooke pouted.

"Yes, I'll come with you," Jules told her. "A few times."

"I hate you," Brooke said.

"No, you don't," Jules told her. "Or at least, you won't forever."

"We'll see about that," Brooke said.

Brooke

~

Brooke flipped open her teacher's planner to the calendar. There was a huge red circle around the day's date. July fifteenth. She and her sisters were halfway to the deadline to get their inheritance. The problem was, they weren't halfway done with the work—far from it, in fact.

Brooke had tried to run; she really had. It was just so . . . *hard*. She'd nearly resigned herself to the fact that she was destined to be out of shape and poor for the rest of her life, until the night she'd overheard Jules and Shawn talking.

"I just don't think she's going to make it," Jules had said. Brooke assumed she was talking about Lexi.

"But she dumped Jake; that's a start," Shawn had replied. He didn't sound very hopeful.

"Dumping Jake wasn't exactly a Herculean feat. She's not just out of shape, Shawn, she's out of motivation. She's got no drive at all, and I don't know how to help her. I hate to say it, but I'm starting to think she's hopeless . . ." Jules trailed off here and Brooke had sat, stunned, realizing that the weight of the world—their world—had been dumped on her shoulders. She was hopeless?

No. She wasn't. She wouldn't be. She *couldn't* be. She owed it to her sisters, to Jules at least. That was all there was to it. It would be awful and painful and she might pick up a few new swear words along the way, but she was going to do this. She was going to run a godforsaken half-marathon, at twenty-eight-out-of-shape years old.

She said it out loud, for accountability, even though she was alone.

"I am going to run a half-marathon."

The dog-walking was going to help her kick off her training, she rationalized, and she was sure six months was still plenty of time to get in shape.

Brooke was buoyed by this newfound focus for about five minutes. Then she remembered that she had an entirely separate problem, at least as far as their inheritance was concerned: She didn't have a single prospect for a date on the horizon. It wasn't like Brooke was expecting or even hoping to meet her future husband before this charade was over; all she had to do was meet, and somehow engage, a decent-enough specimen of the opposite sex who might be willing to spend a few hours a week in her company.

How hard could it be? she wondered now. People met reasonably suitable potential partners every day of their lives, in every venue imaginable. They met in coffee shops and in bars, at weddings and in gyms, on cruise ships and airplanes and now, as often as not, online. Brooke even worked with another teacher at Little Me who'd met her husband at Chuck E. Cheese's. Lety had been very busy wrangling twenty four-year-olds at the annual end-of-the-year pizza party, and Jeremy was a part-time fix-it guy who'd been called in when the Skee-Ball machine had jammed up. Apparently it was love at first sight, even though Lety wasn't wearing a stitch of makeup and had just dripped pizza grease on her boob when her eyes locked with Jeremy's during Jasper T. Jowls's guitar solo. They'd been married for five years now and Lety had just had her first baby, a little boy they named Steven but called Skeeter, after the machine that brought them together. So obviously, you could find love pretty much anywhere. Brooke just had to get out there and start looking.

"What about Facebook?" Jules asked. She was chopping broccoli for a salad she'd promised Brooke was not only low-cal but delicious. Raw broccoli that wasn't drowning in blue cheese dressing and dusted with bacon bits? Brooke was skeptical, to say the least.

"I hate Facebook," Brooke said. "I had an account but I shut it down when I realized that it's basically a place for people to post pictures of their billion-dollar weddings and their Hawaiian vacations and their perfect children so that everyone else can feel like crap. I don't need that in my life."

"Oh, come on. It's harmless fun. You can check in with some of your old high school friends, see who's up to what, spy on Billy McCann . . ."

Brooke felt her face turn chili-pepper red at the mention of Billy's name.

"I can't believe you just pulled the name Billy McCann out of your butt," she said. Just saying his name after all these years made her knees turn to Jell-O.

"Are you kidding me? We all thought you'd marry Billy! I was ready to order you a Mrs. McCann T-shirt thirteen years ago."

"You were long gone by the time I was dating Billy," Brooke reminded her.

"I still came over and took you guys out for dinner and stuff. Don't you remember that?"

Brooke wasn't sure. She might recall grabbing a burger with Jules once or twice after she'd moved out, but that was about it.

"Well, yeah, of course," she said now, fearful of hurting Jules's feelings. "I just meant, we were kids. It was stupid. I'm surprised you paid attention, is all."

"What ever happened with Billy anyway?" Jules asked now.

"He was a year ahead of me, remember? He went into the Coast Guard after high school. Mom wouldn't let me call him—she said it was too expensive to call long distance, so I wrote him dozens of letters, but he never wrote back, not even once. Finally I stopped writing. I never heard from him again."

"Well, maybe he had a good reason; you never know," Jules said. "Besides, people change, they grow up. This is exactly what Facebook was made for. Let's look him up."

"I don't know—" Brooke started to protest, but Jules was already pecking away at her first-generation iPad that lived on the kitchen counter.

"Look! I think I found him! This is him, right?" Jules didn't wait for a response. "Wait for it," she said, scrolling through the About section. "Interested in . . . women! Relationship status . . . single! Bingo. I think we just found your suitable mate."

"Current city: Miami," Brooke read. "That's three thousand miles away."

"Big deal. Lots of relationships start out long distance," Jules insisted. "You guys have *history*. I'll bet he's tried to look you up a dozen times."

Brooke scanned his profile page. The banner photo was of

Paris at night, presumably taken by Billy, or why else would it be there? The smaller photo was of Billy and a little boy. They were on the beach and both of them were flexing and posing for the camera. Brooke took over the mouse and double-clicked the photo to enlarge it. "My little man," the caption read. The boy looked remarkably like him, and Billy hadn't changed one bit.

Brooke clicked the web browser closed.

"Why'd you do that?" Jules wanted to know.

"Did you get a good look at Billy?" Brooke demanded.

"I sure did. He's hot! What's the problem?"

"Have you taken a good look at *me* lately?"

"Brooke, you're beautiful," Jules said. "You have to see that. You don't have to have a protruding rib cage to fall in love. You know that, right?"

Brooke wasn't convinced.

"Look, he's on the opposite side of the country. You reach out to him, feel things out, see if it's even worth pursuing. And you're going to start running *tomorrow*, right? You'll lose weight naturally, and I'll help with the food. By the time you're ready to see Billy, you'll knock his socks off. It's actually perfect!"

"You realize you're basing this perfect-case scenario on the yet-to-be-confirmed fact that Billy is available and that he's been carrying a torch for me for the past dozen or so years and that he's got a thing for women who might actually weigh more than he does, right?"

"Mom died and left us thirty-seven million dollars," Jules reminded her. "Anything is possible."

Maybe Jules was right. Maybe it was worth a shot.

Lexi

~

"What can I get for you today, Officers?" Lexi said. She tried to sound casual and hide her excitement at seeing Rob, but she was sure it was written all over her face.

"I'll take the usual," Rob told her, giving her his big Colgate grin. "Extra nuts." The usual was a scoop of marshmallow swirl and a scoop of cookies-and-cream, and the "extra nuts" was their little private joke.

The first time he'd come to The Inside Scoop and ordered from Lexi, she'd burst out laughing.

"What's so funny?" Rob had wanted to know.

"That's the girliest ice cream order I've ever heard," she managed to say between laughing fits. "And you're a cop. You pack heat! You're killing me right now, Rob. You want some pink sprinkles on that?"

She'd fixed him the ice cream, and then dumped about a half cup of chopped peanuts on top.

"I didn't order nuts," he said when she handed it to him.

"I know," she said. "But I thought you could use some."

He'd taken a bite, proclaiming it even better with the unsolicited topping. "The salt and sweet together—" he'd started to say, but Lexi had cut him off.

"Stop, just stop," she'd howled. "Honest to God, you could lose your man card forever for talking like that."

"Just a scoop of vanilla today, please," his painfully shy partner Frank said now.

"For real?" Lexi wanted to know.

"Yeah, why?" Frank asked.

"Because vanilla is so . . . vanilla! We have pistachio and maple nut and rum raisin and mango and like twenty-five other flavors and you really want *vanilla*?"

Poor Frank didn't know what to say. "What's *your* favorite?" he asked her.

"Black raspberry chip with sour gummy worms on top," Lexi said without hesitation. "It's amazeballs." Rob raised his eyebrows. "Amazing. I meant it's amazing."

"I'll take that, then," Frank said. Lexi beamed at Rob, who shook his head, clearly impressed with her ability to turn grown men into mush.

"You might want to try not to make customers feel bad about their boring ice cream orders," Rob whispered when Frank went to the end of the counter for napkins and spoons.

"Vanilla? Seriously? He asked for it, Rob."

"Have you even tried the vanilla?" Rob wanted to know.

"I've had vanilla ice cream before," Lexi told him.

"Try it right now and tell me it's not delicious," Rob said.

She scooped some into one of the tiny taster cups.

"Can I at least put some pineapple or something on it?" she wanted to know.

"Nope. You need the pure, authentic vanilla experience."

She lifted the cup to her lips, feeling strangely self-conscious. Normally she enjoyed making guys squirm with her overt sexuality, but for some reason Rob was different. She wanted him to think she was classy, not just another whore he'd had to shuttle home from a dive bar. She wondered if he'd ever done that before, and tried to shake off the thought. Now she popped the ice cream into her mouth instead of sucking suggestively on the cup.

"Well?" Rob wanted to know. His mischievous grin was nearly more than she could take.

"Not bad," she said with a shrug, wiping her hands on a rag.

"Not bad?" Rob demanded.

"Fine, it's delicious," she laughed.

"You really shouldn't underestimate vanilla, Alexis," he said, winking at her.

Maybe I shouldn't, Lexi thought.

Jules

Jules had written just over thirty thousand words. It came out to one hundred and twenty double-spaced pages. They were good pages, too. The writing was solid and her thoughts organized, and the whole thing teemed with imagery and emotion. There were heart-wrenching parts because there had to be, but she'd peppered them with what she felt were perfectly placed bursts of comic relief, much like the incomparable "hit this" scene in *Steel Magnolias* that pulled viewers back from the brink of despair just when they needed it most.

The problem was, she was stuck. Completed memoirs ranged anywhere from sixty to a hundred-and-twenty thousand words; even on the low end of that scale she was barely halfway there. It wasn't the deadline anymore; she'd done the thirty thousand words in two months and had four months to go, give or take. The issue was that the story was told. She didn't know what else she could say. She'd even seen it through to the grand finale, when she and Lexi and Brooke received their inheritance. She'd had to be vague and ambiguous there, of course, because it hadn't technically happened. But she was sure she'd captured the emotions at least: the ecstasy, the pride, the relief.

Now she supposed it was simply a matter of going back through what she'd written and filling in with details and vignettes, and that thought overwhelmed her. She'd crafted her segues so carefully and paid such close attention to the balance of it all, she just wasn't sure that meddling around in there was a good idea. She needed to print it out, to see her words on actual paper with actual ink and not on a computer screen, she decided, before she could decide what to do next.

It turned out, one hundred and twenty printed pages was quite impressive. She fanned the stack back and forth in her hand and watched the words blur before her. *I wrote this. All of it. Those are my words, my stories.* She was torn between pride for what she'd accomplished already and trepidation about what she had yet to do.

"Is that your book?" Brooke asked excitedly, sweeping into the office.

"Jeez, you scared the hell out of me," Jules said. "When did you come home?"

"Just now, from walking the dogs," Brooke said. "I ran them today, too. Well, I ran and walked but mostly ran. Two miles!" Brooke had driven around the neighborhood and mapped out one- , two- , three- and five-mile loops. "And look," she added. She lifted her T-shirt to reveal the droopy waistband of her sweatpants. "They're practically falling off! They're a little stretched out because I haven't washed them in forever, but I still think I've lost at least a few pounds."

"That's fantastic, Brooke. You must feel so great."

"I wish I didn't have so far to go, but it's a start," Brooke said.

"I know what you mean," Jules said.

"Your book?"

"I've pretty much told the whole story, even the part about getting the money," she said.

"No way! That's amazing. You're done? Can I read it?"

Jules explained about the word-count business and how she basically needed to double what she'd written and she felt like she was right back where she'd been when she couldn't think of an idea at all.

"Maybe you need to take a break for a while, get some distance?" Brooke suggested. "I know when I'm grading the same papers over and over my brain starts to go numb. Sometimes if you just leave something alone for a while and come back to it, you can see things much more clearly."

"Maybe you're right," Jules said. What else could she do but take a break? It wasn't like you could force words out of your brain that weren't there. Jules had written enough to know that. She slipped the printed pages into a file folder in her desk drawer.

"Any progress on Project Billy?" she teased Brooke.

"Other than obsessively poring over his pictures and trying to piece together his life, not really. The kid's name is Alec, but I'm not even sure if Billy's the dad. It's hard to tell if he's ever even been married. I mean, it's not like people post pictures with captions like 'this is my awful ex-wife' or anything. But he went to grad school at the University of Miami and he's a marine biologist and he likes to surf and scuba dive and I think he has his own boat!"

"Wow, nice stalking, Nancy Drew." Jules high-fived her sister. "Have you contacted him?"

"Not yet," Brooke said. "I figured I should get my profile back up and get some photos up there and stuff before I do. Hey, do you know how to Photoshop?"

"No, why?"

"I was wondering if you could put my head on Angelina Jolie's body."

Jules laughed and shook her head.

"Too skinny? I thought you'd say that. How about Kate Winslet? Christina Hendricks? Mindy Kaling would be good, but you'd have to lighten up the skin. Ooh! How about Jessica Simpson when she was like four months pregnant the second time?"

"Brooke, you're being ridiculous. Why don't we go out and get you a nice outfit and take some really great pictures of your beautiful head on your actual body? Shawn has a pretty decent camera, and I've got mad shooting skills."

"I'm not spending one penny on an outfit that will fit me now. I'm going to get in shape and lose this weight. I ran six miles this week. Well, technically I jogged slowly, and not six miles in a row or anything. My farthest distance is two miles. But I did it three times!"

"That's fantastic!" Jules said, giving her another high five.

"It's a start, at least," Brooke said. "It's not about Mom's money even. I could probably run thirteen miserable miles once, knowing what's at stake. But I want to lose this weight. This isn't me, or it's not how I want to be, at least. I'm doing this."

Jules was blown away by Brooke's determination. She'd noticed her sister serving herself smaller portions when they ate together and passing up fattening side dishes in favor of extra veggies and lean protein. Brooke hadn't complained about walking the dogs since the first week; she'd even insisted on taking the route a few times when Jules was already dressed and ready to go. And now she was actually running, on her own even. Jules was nearly bursting with pride.

"How about this, then," she offered. "We go out and get you something crazy expensive and fabulous, and we don't take the tags off. We tuck the tags in and snap some pictures of you in it and then you return it and get your money back. No harm, no foul."

"I guess we could try. But will you come with me? I hate shopping. Absolutely hate it."

"Of course," Jules said.

"And will you let me read your book?"

"When it's finished."

If it's ever finished, she added in her head.

Brooke

❧

"That career fair is this Saturday if you're still interested," Brooke said. She had popped *Wedding Crashers* into the ancient DVD player and the three sisters were curled up on the couch together, waiting for it to cue up. Thursdays were Lexi's night off and somehow it had become movie night. Brooke was in charge of swinging by the library on her way home from work and checking out something for them to watch. She was the only one who hadn't seen this particular film yet, but since Lexi knew much of it by heart and quoted it often, Brooke was intimately familiar with most of the laugh-out-loud moments. Recently she'd said to the Little Me Preschool music teacher jokingly, "You shut your mouth when you're talking to me." It turned out, Mr. Walters hadn't seen the movie, either, so Brooke had had quite a bit of backpedaling to do.

"Oh shoot," Lexi said. "I forgot all about it. I have to work. Sorry, Brooke."

"Did you just say 'oh shoot'?" Jules asked, brows lifted.

"What's wrong with 'oh shoot'?" Lexi asked with feigned innocence.

"Not a thing," Jules said. Brooke was surprised when she decided to leave it at that.

Brooke munched on her raw carrots, thinking how nice this was, and how far she and her sisters had come in less than seven months. They'd practically been strangers when they'd been thrust together, and now she'd almost call them friends. She could barely remember the last time Lexi had called her Shamu or made a double-wide comment in reference to her behind; even Jules had seemed to mellow out and wasn't bossing everyone around all the time or grilling them each time they left the house. Brooke wondered if she was going to miss her sisters when she moved into her big fat mansion all alone.

"Well, you don't need a career fair now anyway," Brooke said to Lexi. "You've got a job. Besides, it'll probably just be a bunch of old guys in suits standing around handing out pens." Brooke had no idea if that was the case, but she didn't want Lexi to feel bad about skipping out on her. After all, she'd actually said she was sorry; that was huge for Lexi.

"People in suits give me the creeps," Lexi said.

"People in uniforms obviously don't," Jules teased. Lexi blushed beautifully and Brooke considered how unfair it was that Lexi was obviously falling in love when it wasn't even a condition of her inheritance.

"What about you, Brooke?" Jules asked, turning to her. "Any plans for the weekend?"

Brooke tried to look casual and not the slightest bit guilty, despite the fact that she felt the exact opposite of both of those things. The truth was, putting together Lexi's art portfolio had given her an idea. She was planning to spend any spare time she could find this weekend at the library researching literary agents for Jules. Her older sister had been so helpful and so supportive with her running and with Project Billy—which was on temporary hold until she buckled down with her running—that Brooke had wanted to return the favor. She'd gently suggested that Jules talk to their mother's attorney, Mr. Wiley, who supposedly had lots of contacts, but Jules had insisted she wasn't ready yet, so Brooke had begun researching how to get a book published. What she'd learned was that having an agent was key. Publishers wouldn't accept manuscripts that hadn't been previously vetted and approved by an agent, and Brooke was worried her self-critical sister would never take that first step. But what Jules didn't understand was that an agent could also help her hone what she did have and guide her in finishing it. Jules seemed to think the thing had to be polished and perfect before anyone could so much as take a peek at the first page.

But they didn't have forever.

She knew she shouldn't have, but Brooke had snuck into Jules's desk drawer when her sister was out walking her dogs and she'd read her memoir. Well, the first half at least; she'd run out of time, but she already knew how the story was going to end anyway. She'd been mesmerized by what she'd read and by her sister's ability to put her feelings—their feelings—down on paper so eloquently and powerfully. Her sister's writing was brilliant, but what did that matter if nobody ever saw it? Obviously, it was time to take matters into her own hands.

"Brooke?" Jules prodded. "Earth to Brooke?"

"Oh, sorry," Brooke stammered. "This weekend? Oh, I'm going to the career fair anyway. I told Pam I'd go with her, and you know, free pens! Plus, since Lexi will be working, it will be nice for you and Shawn to have the place to yourselves." She wiggled her eyebrows at Jules suggestively.

"As much as I'd love to hear all about the crazy monkey-sex you and Shawn plan to have this weekend, do you guys think you could zip it?" Lexi asked. "The movie is rolling and the best line is right in the beginning."

"You shut your mouth when you're talking to me," Jules and Brooke said in unison. Lexi just shook her head and laughed.

Lexi

~

"It's not that complicated," Rob insisted. "You get dressed, maybe in something sort of nice and not your Inside Scoop T-shirt or anything, and then I pick you up and I drive you to a restaurant and we eat a meal together. I'll pay for it and everything. What do you say?"

Lexi had never been on a real date. She'd never even gone to a homecoming dance or prom in high school. She'd pretended that she didn't want to and openly mocked the girls who got all googly-eyed about the whole thing, but secretly she had been dying to go. She wanted to get dressed up like a fucking fairy-tale princess, too, and have a cute, nervous boy pin a corsage to her dress. She wanted to wear sparkly pink lip gloss and delicate, pointy kitten-heel shoes and be swept around a dance floor so badly she could taste it. But she knew it could never happen. For one thing, she was pretty sure Juliana would have forbidden her from going because "boys only wanted one thing" (and Lexi wasn't about to tell her they'd already gotten it from her over and over by the time senior prom rolled around). And even if she miraculously had agreed to let her go, Juliana would have chosen her dress—probably something awful from a discount store—and mortified her in front of any boy who came to pick her up. Of course, there was another reason Lexi had pretended the whole scene nauseated the hell out of her: If she'd gushed and giggled over taffeta and tulle and blinking twinkle lights, her whole tough-chick image would have crumbled. And Lexi couldn't have that. That was how she had kept anyone from trying to get too close to her. But now she wanted to get close to Rob. She wanted to let down her guard and stop pretending her heart was made of steel and finally let someone in. Lexi was quite aware of the fact that she had seen a lot of scary shit in her day, but nothing she'd ever encountered terrified her more.

"Sure, I guess," she told Rob.

"Try not to hurt yourself with excitement." Rob laughed.

"It sounds great," Lexi said, smiling. Why did she always have to hide behind a veil of indifference? *Oh yeah,* she thought. *Because it's been your defense mechanism for the last twenty years.* She met Rob's gaze and held it, another gesture she found both unfamiliar and uncomfortable. "Really."

"What's your favorite kind of food?" he asked, returning her smile.

Lexi wanted to say something sarcastic—*the kind I don't have to skip out without paying for after I eat it or sell my soul to get in the first place*—but she stopped herself. Her favorite kind of food? She genuinely didn't know. She'd lived for so long on whatever scraps she could come by that it hadn't even occurred to her to develop a list of favorites or a preference for this over the other. The only thing she could think of was her mother's lasagna. Juliana had been an amazing cook, and if Lexi recalled correctly, her lasagna had been out of this world. All three girls would consistently request it as their "anything goes" birthday dinners, and their dad used to jokingly threaten to leak her recipe to the newspaper, just to get their mom all riled up. Jules actually was a pretty good cook, too, although she rarely made anything as decadent and delicious as a cheesy, meaty, home-made lasagna.

"I guess Italian," Lexi said.

"I was hoping you'd say that," Rob said. "Have you ever been to Il Tramonto?"

Il Tramonto had been around forever. It was, in fact, one of those fancy-schmancy places the giddy going-to-prom girls would always rave about, and if anyone had bothered to ask, Lexi would have said she was allergic to cheese, so she made a habit of purposely avoiding it. She'd never even set foot inside the place, but she'd passed the stunning stone castle–looking structure a million or more times over the years and wondered if it could ever be half as beautiful on the inside. She'd convinced herself that it couldn't.

"I'm not sure," she said now, intentionally vague.

"Well, if you haven't, you'll love it. They have the best lasagna I've ever tasted in my life. It takes a little longer than the other stuff because they make it in these little individual dishes, but it's totally worth the wait."

Lexi smiled. She could almost taste it.

"Sounds amazing," she said.

"Great. I'll make a reservation for seven thirty. Do you want me to pick you up here when you get off at six and I can drive you home to get changed?" Rob offered.

"That's okay," Lexi told him. "I'll ride my bike. Well, your bike. I can be ready at seven. Does that work?" Lexi had no idea what people wore to restaurants like Il Tramonto, and she knew she'd be scrambling through Jules's closet trying to unearth an appropriate outfit. The last thing she needed was Rob sitting on the couch making polite chitchat with her sisters while she flung various items of clothing around and cursed and pulled her hair out.

"Perfect," Rob said. "And Lexi? No stress, okay? This is supposed to be fun. It'll be casual, I promise."

"Why would I be stressed about dinner? I eat it every day, you know." Lexi knew that she sounded defensive, but she didn't want Rob to know what a big deal this was for her.

"Great, okay," Rob said, scooping the last of the crushed nuts from his cup.

"Nuts?" he asked, offering her the spoon.

"Yes, you are," she said, taking it from him and popping them into her mouth.

Jules

❦

"I'm excited for you," Shawn said, kissing her on the back of her neck. She stopped putting on her mascara and nuzzled into him.

"I feel so silly even going to this thing," Jules admitted. "It's like I'm pretending to be an actual author or something." The Southern California Writers' Conference had been Shawn's idea. He'd tried insisting that she attend the full five days, but the $400 ticket fee had seemed outrageous to her. Finally she'd agreed to the single-day pass, which still came with a hefty $150 price tag. Jules had prayed that forking over that much money would be motivating, but so far all it had done was make her feel guilty.

"Stop talking like that. You *are* an author. You're almost finished with your book. It may not be published yet, but it will be. I'll bet you the definition of author is 'someone who writes books,' not 'somebody who has written something that's been published.' Hang on."

Shawn buzzed out of the bathroom and came right back in, carrying her beat-up old *Oxford English Dictionary*. It had belonged to her dad and every once in a while she'd swear she could still smell his aftershave on it. Several years before he died, Jules had given it to him for his birthday or maybe Father's Day—she couldn't remember which—and it was one of her most cherished possessions. She hadn't asked Juliana if she could take it; she'd simply slipped it out of his bookshelf and into hers. She'd paid for it, after all, and her dad would have wanted her to have it, she was positive. She still used it to look up words and spellings, even though the Internet was faster and more convenient. Each time the OED announced a list of "new" words they were adding to the mix, like "bestie" and "wackadoodle" and "screenager," Jules would print it out and fold the page and stick it in the back, because it wasn't like she was ever going to replace the thing with an updated edition.

"Let's see, 'amateur,' 'anomaly,' 'aster,' 'austere' . . . here we go, 'author': 'a writer of a book, article or report.' Ha! See? You're already an author in that case. Oxford says so."

Jules took the book from him. "Definition number two: 'Someone who writes books as a profession.' I think that implies that I'm getting paid here."

Shawn took the book back from her. "Definition number three: 'An originator or creator of something, especially a plan or an idea.' So back to my original statement—ha! You're an author, Jules. Just face it. If anyone belongs at that conference today, it's you. I want you to walk in there and own the place, okay? If you do that, you'll knock them dead."

"Speaking of knocking . . . knock knock?" It was Brooke, standing outside the open bathroom door.

"Since when do you knock? The door's open, come on in," Jules said.

"Well, you're *both* in here," Brooke said, motioning to Shawn.

"When we have sex in the bathroom we almost always close the door," Jules told her sister. Brooke blushed furiously.

"Sorry. I just . . . I wanted to know if maybe you had a slip I could borrow. I just put on my old one but the elastic must have popped because it won't stay up. And the dress I was going to wear today definitely needs a slip. If you had one it would probably be tight but I might be able to squeeze into it."

"I don't think the elastic popped, you dingbat, I think you've lost a bunch of weight! Where are you headed anyway?" Jules hoped the question sounded curious and not prying.

"Wine tasting," Brooke said quickly.

"At eight o'clock in the morning?" Jules asked before she could stop herself. "Where? With who?"

"I'm driving up to Santa Ynez with some friends from work," Brooke explained. "There are supposed to be a lot of really beautiful wineries up there, so . . ." She trailed off with a shrug.

"I didn't even think you liked wine," Jules remarked.

"Oh, I'm just going for fun. I'm actually the designated driver. I don't need all those calories anyway." Brooke fidgeted with her watch, unbuckling and rebuckling the strap.

"Sounds like a good time. Let me just finish my makeup and I'll find you a slip." Jules met her sister's eyes in the mirror, and for a split second she hardly recognized her, and it was more than just the weight loss. She wanted to say how great it was that Brooke was getting out, trying new things and spending time with friends, but she didn't want to sound patronizing. Instead, she offered a simple truth. "I'm really proud of you, Brooke." Brooke smiled shyly, doing a lousy job of hiding her own pride.

"She *does* look great, doesn't she?" Shawn whispered after Brooke was out of earshot.

"Totally. She's been running every day, even on the weekends. When I told her she should take a day off every once in a while, she wouldn't even consider it. She's going to run that race no problem. Won't that be so great for her?"

"Um, yeah. And for us! God, Jules, it's going to happen, isn't it? I mean, Brooke is totally committed, and she already dumped Jake, and Lexi looks like she's taking this ice cream job pretty seriously—probably because her boss is Rob's brother-in-law, but who cares? She hasn't gotten into any trouble or caused any major drama in weeks. And you're practically finished with your book! It's going to happen. Goddamn it, it's really going to happen." Shawn squeezed her hard and Jules tried not to stiffen.

"Brooke still needs to meet a guy," Jules said.

"I thought she was flirting with her old high school boyfriend," Shawn said.

"She's thinking about considering whether or not she should contemplate the idea." Jules laughed.

"But still, that won't be hard. Brooke is beautiful, and even I can see she feels better about herself, more confident. If she just gets out every once in a while, she'll meet a guy. No problem."

"I'm just saying it's not a done deal, so don't go popping the champagne yet," Jules said.

"Whatever you say," Shawn said. "But when we do pop it, it's not going to be any of that Asti Spumante crap, do you hear me? We're drinking Dom Pérignon, damn it. Or whatever a good champagne is. I'm going to go look up really expensive champagnes."

After he'd left, Jules glared at herself in the mirror. *It looks like it's all up to you,* she said silently to her reflection. Who would have thought?

Brooke

〜

Brooke took the slip that Jules had found for her and went into
the bathroom to dress, replaying Jules's words in her head. *I'm
really proud of you,* her sister had said. Brooke was pretty sure
no human being had ever uttered those words to her before.
Even her dad, who'd been an affable, affectionate guy, had
never come out and said anything like it that she could recall.
It was astonishing to Brooke how good it felt to hear that
someone admired and respected you.

There was no question that the slip was tight, but she got it on
and it didn't seem like it would burst open or anything. She fit
into something of one of her supernaturally slim sister's? Unbe-
lievable. The dress she was wearing was one of the typical tent-
styles she always gravitated toward, but this one had little strings
sewn into the side seams that you could tie in the back. She gen-
erally tied them far too loosely and let the bow hang somewhere
above her butt, mostly so the ends wouldn't dip into the toilet
when she peed and because it had never occurred to her to cut

them off, but today she pulled the strings taut and gasped when she saw it: she had a waist. It wasn't tiny like either of her sisters', but it was definitely there and noticeable and without question smaller than her hips. Brooke could hardly contain her joy.

"Brooke, you look fantastic," Jules said when she saw her.

"I do look better, don't I?" Brooke asked. She felt better, too. Even a few weeks ago she'd have hemmed and hawed and insisted that it was the lighting or the dress or possibly even Jules's eyes playing tricks on her if for some otherwise impossible reason she might look a tiny bit good to anybody.

"For sure," Jules told her. "Hang on, wait here." Jules ran out of the room and came back with Shawn's camera.

"Really? Now?" Brooke said, smoothing her dress self-consciously.

"Sure, just for fun," Jules insisted. "If you hate them, we'll delete them immediately, okay? You really do look great."

"Fine," Brooke said. She posed awkwardly for a few shots and then she and Jules reviewed them together.

"That one's not bad," she admitted.

"Not bad? It's gorgeous, you dork."

"Well, I'd better be going," Brooke told her sister. "I'll be back around six . . . You know, so I can spy on Alexis getting ready for her date."

"I was planning the same thing." Jules laughed. "Hey, want to pick me up at the convention center on your way home, then? I heard parking was a nightmare so I was going to take the bus."

"Sure," Brooke said, collecting her purse and keys. "I'll text you when I'm on my way. Have fun today. I'm sure you'll knock them dead."

"I wish I was going wine tasting," Jules said.

Now that you mention it, so do I, Brooke thought, smiling weakly.

Brooke didn't like lying to Jules, but what choice did she have? She couldn't exactly tell her sister that she was off to the library to research literary agents and publishers for her. Jules would flip—especially today, when she was so nervous about the conference. Brooke was cautiously optimistic that her plan was going to work, but if it didn't, Jules would never have to know, never have to feel the sting of rejection. It was a perfect plan when she thought about it.

She whistled as she drove the twenty minutes to the Calabasas library. There were a half dozen closer branches, but she wanted to be sure she wouldn't run into anyone she knew—or more specifically, anyone Jules knew. As she walked up the wide entry steps, she had a flashback. Juliana had taken her and Lexi here once; she had no idea why, as it wasn't the branch near their house with the giant claw-foot reading tub that the girls loved. Maybe Juliana had been running an errand in the area? It was impossible to know. Lexi had been working on a school project and even though Brooke was fourteen, Juliana wouldn't dream of letting her stay home alone, so she'd been dragged along. She'd perused the shelves for a while before selecting Judy Blume's *Are You There God? It's Me, Margaret* and curling up in a big cushy chair.

"What are you reading?" Juliana demanded. Brooke hadn't heard her sneak up and she dropped the book in her lap. Before she could answer, her mother snatched the book out of her lap and opened to a random page. She began reading aloud.

"'All boys of fourteen are disgusting. They're only interested in two things—pictures of naked girls and dirty books.'" She lifted her brows at Brooke and continued riffling through the book, trailing the words with her finger. "'I took out a pair of socks and stuffed one sock into each side of the bra, to see if it really grew with me. It was too tight that way, but I liked the way it looked.'" She snapped the book shut, and the look on her face gave Brooke the shivers. "Your father would be *so* proud of your choice of reading material," she said finally, her words heavy with something close to venom. Then she turned and stalked away with the book clutched tight in her fist.

Brooke had been flooded with rage and shame. *Are You There God? It's Me, Margaret* was for babies, for crying out loud. She'd read the thing for the first time in the fifth grade! It was a beloved classic by a popular, bestselling author. But she knew better than to try to argue with Juliana, a move that was a losing battle at best and a bloody war at worst.

She tried to shake off the memory as she scanned the shelves for *Jeff Herman's Guide to Book Publishers, Editors & Literary Agents.* The Internet had insisted that if publishing were a religion, this was its bible. She located the tome, astonished by its size. The spine was at least three inches thick, fatter than any phone book or unabridged dictionary she'd ever seen. It was a good thing she'd told Jules she'd be gone all day, because clearly she was going to be here awhile.

Lexi

~

Lexi flipped the cone upside down and twirled it around in the sprinkles, expertly coating the ice cream tip with a layer of colorful confetti. Then she wrapped the cone part in a napkin and handed it to the little girl, who was waiting with as much patience as any kid who was about to be given a sugary handful of heaven ever could.

"Thank you," the golden-haired girl lisped, her face about to split open with her wide-eyed, gap-toothed grin. Lexi smiled despite herself. She truly had never felt any sort of affection for kids before this job, and she had been sure that waiting on them all day would make her like them even less. And certainly she'd had the displeasure of serving a half dozen or so kids who bore an unfortunate personality resemblance to Veruca Salt, the "I want a golden goose" girl from the Willy Wonka movie. But more often than not, the scrappy little tykes who came in for a scoop of this or that were undeniably adorable.

Yes, Lexi had grown to love her job, and no one was more

shocked by this fact than she was. It had turned out that Benji was totally cool, just like Rob had promised. After only a few weeks he'd presented her with her very own key so he wouldn't have to meet her there to open and close the place, and he was even training her on hiring practices. Summer was nearly over and they were going to lose their home-from-college crew, which meant they would need to hire two or three new employees and get them up to speed. Lexi couldn't believe that somebody was going to trust her with that kind of responsibility. She felt grown-up and capable and trustworthy. Still, this particular day had crawled by, probably because she was so excited about her date with Rob. Finally it was almost time to shut down for the night. She started in on her closing duties, praying no last-minute stragglers wandered in. She wanted to be out the door at six o'clock sharp.

It was with envy that Lexi watched the little girl and her mom, who seemed riveted by every word out of her daughter's mouth. She wondered what their life was like at home, if there was a dad in the picture or any other siblings. She hoped for the little girl's sake that her mom would always be like this, and would always make time to sit with her and listen to her and take her out for ice cream. The pair left the shop hand in hand and Lexi locked the front door behind them. All she had left to do was start the dishwasher and take out the trash.

She hummed her favorite Old Crow Medicine Show tune as she carried two huge garbage bags through the back office, then pushed the back door open and used her foot to move a mop bucket into the doorway to hold it open; she'd learned the hard way that if she didn't, it would shut and lock behind her. She set one of the bags on the ground and had just swung the other one over her shoulder, ready to launch it into the Dumpster, when she heard a voice.

"Well, well, well," he said. "Nice to see you again."

Lexi dropped the bag and spun around. She was face to face with a man—or was he a kid? It was hard to tell. He was rail thin and covered in tattoos and piercings, and Lexi thought he looked vaguely familiar, but she couldn't pinpoint where or how they'd met.

"Can I help you?" she said, taking a step backward. He smelled like booze and smoke, and his eyes were glazed and red and very, very angry.

"Yeah, you can," he said. In one swift move he grabbed her around the neck and put his other hand over her mouth. "You can pay me back the fucking money you stole from me, cunt."

Lexi tried to scream, but his hand was clamped down hard over her mouth. She looked frantically around the back alley, but it may as well have been a ghost town. The Inside Scoop stayed open later than any other shop in the little strip mall, and she was all alone. Her heart was pounding in her chest as he dragged her into the back office and kicked the bucket out of the way. The door slammed behind them.

He kept his hand over her mouth as he pushed her into a chair. When he did, she got a better look at his tattoos and piercings, and she realized who he was: the guy she'd taken a lousy sixty-five bucks from in that house the night she'd gone out with Brad and Ry. That seemed like another lifetime now, and she cringed at the knowledge that she'd probably fucked this disgusting guy, among other things. He put his face just inches from hers and stared at her with those wild eyes. When he did, she brought both knees up and tried to kick him in the balls, but he was amazingly strong for such a skinny guy. He caught her knees with his free hand and pinned her down.

"You fucking fight me and I will kill you," he hissed, spraying her face with spit. He grabbed both of her hands and yanked them behind her back, where he tied them to one of the slats of the chair with a rope he pulled from his back pocket. She was screaming but she knew it was useless; nobody would ever hear her in here. He grabbed a bandana out of another pocket and shoved it into her mouth, tying it behind her head. Then he pulled out a switchblade and flipped it open, waving it in front of her face. For a junkie, he was remarkably well prepared.

"Where's the fucking key to the cash register?"

"Wouldn't you like to know," Lexi said, her words muffled by the bandana. She braced herself for the blow she knew was coming. This wasn't her first rodeo.

At first she felt nothing; then a tingly numbness, then warmth. Blood.

"Let's try this again," he said, shaking the hand he'd just used to pound her face with. Lexi stared at the huge skull ring on it. "Where's the fucking key to the cash register?"

"Let me think," Lexi sputtered through the blood-soaked bandana. "Did you check your asshole?" This time when he hit her, she passed out.

Jules

❧

Jules was completely and totally overwhelmed, and her head was spinning. She had sat in on seminars on digital marketing and international rights, and attended workshops on blogging and self-publishing and writing children's books. All she could think of now was how true that old saying was: ignorance was bliss.

She would feel like a moron admitting it out loud, but until today Jules hadn't had the vaguest idea of all that went into producing a book and then actually getting it into someone's hands. She'd always considered writing a creative endeavor, a baring of the soul, and unequivocally something you did alone. Sure, she may have envisioned herself sitting behind a table stacked high with her books, meeting eager readers and signing their freshly purchased copies with a fancy pen and a beatific smile. She might even have allowed herself to imagine being interviewed on TV, chatting with the ladies on *The View* about her approach to the craft in general and her content in particular. But the harsh reality was, authors weren't just artists; they were also commodities. As such, they had to be packaged and promoted and, most important, sold. And Jules wasn't convinced anyone on the planet was going to want to buy what she was peddling.

She snaked her way through the crowded hallways, sizing up the other attendees. There were college-age guys with goatees wearing skinny jeans, and frumpy old ladies in faded housedresses; a man who looked like he had to be pushing ninety was creeping along in a wheelchair, chatting animatedly to the middle-age woman next to him decked out in designer yoga gear. *All of these people want to be writers, or actually are writers,* Jules thought. Instead of being buoyed by this realization—if them then why not her?—she felt overwhelmed, outnumbered and wholly out of place.

She walked slowly, wishing she had the courage to approach one of the groups of people, or even another lone straggler, and introduce herself. But since she'd come to understand how very little she even knew about the industry she so desperately wanted to be a part of, her courage had disintegrated. More than ever, she felt as if she didn't belong—not only at this conference but in this world.

Now Jules sat in the conference center's café, looking over the notes she'd taken in the various presentations. Her favorite by far had been the children's book workshop, to her great surprise. She had been positively riveted. Although Jules probably hadn't even held a picture book in more than twenty years, she'd found herself mesmerized by the colorful illustrations and the sing-songy lyrics. The workshop leader, a bestselling children's book author Jules had never heard of, had talked about the changing landscape of the industry, and about how hard it was to compete for a child's attention with all of the digital noise and electronic distractions in the world. Authors had to be ever more diligent in creating compelling characters and crafting fascinating story lines, she'd explained. The challenge was intriguing to Jules.

Her own childhood home had been overflowing with books, as one would expect of any family whose father wrote for a living. And yet Juliana would still regularly take Jules and her sisters to the library around the corner from their house, where they'd fight for the privilege of having the first turn in the reading tub—a claw-foot Victorian bathtub that was filled not with water but with cushiony pillows and a dozen or so velveteen blankets. The reading tub stood smack in the center of the children's section, and it was one of Jules's favorite places on earth. She wondered if that tub was still there. She hoped it was; she wanted to bring her own children there someday.

Her own children. The thought gave Jules chills. Would she really have children of her own one day? She couldn't even think about it until she finished her damned manuscript. What she needed was a mentor, she realized, a professional she could run her ideas and her words by and who could give her just the right blend of encouragement and constructive criticism. She needed her dad.

As Jules sat in the middle of the massive conference center surrounded by thousands of people who would relate to her and might even be able to help her, she had never felt more lost or alone. She sipped her iced tea and stared off into space, not sure who she was angrier with: herself or her dead mother.

Brooke

∾

Brooke looked at the fat stack of notes she'd taken and smiled. Five hours ago, she'd known next to nothing about the publishing process—heck, she still had a hard time remembering which one was fiction and which was nonfiction, because the terms had always seemed backward to her; shouldn't nonfiction be *not* true?—and now she practically felt like a professional. Well, maybe not a professional, but she knew that memoir was nonfiction and that Jules's manuscript fell into the "personal struggle" subcategory. (Did it ever.) She'd discovered that she couldn't just go mailing off unsolicited manuscripts, but would have to send a query letter first—and only to those agents who'd indicated that they were indeed accepting submissions—along with a brief introduction. She'd drafted a rough outline of her query letter with the help of the dozens of books she'd found on the subject, and compiled a list of almost forty agents she'd be contacting. She'd gone even further, ranking each one with an

A, B or C, based on their past successes selling similar books as well as the other sorts of works they represented. The agents who seemed to fancy things like humor or pop culture made the C list for obvious reasons; the ones who expressed a specific interest in women's issues, self-help or narratives sailed straight to the A list.

Brooke got up to stretch and looked at her watch. It was just after three o'clock and she had pretty much done all that she could do today. She still had several hours to kill before she picked up Jules, and she couldn't go back to the house because she was supposed to be in the Valley chauffeuring around a bunch of tipsy preschool teachers and she didn't know when Shawn would be home. Brooke wandered the library aisles aimlessly, pondering her options. She could go to the mall but she hated shopping even when she had someone fun to do it with. She'd gotten up early and gone for her run—three and a half miles, a personal best—so she crossed that off the list. Without really realizing it, she'd wound up in the young adult section. She scanned the spines for last names that began with B. There it was, looking exactly as she remembered it: *Are You There God? It's Me, Margaret.*

She returned to her table with the book, devouring the pages like a hungry kitten attacking a bowl of kibble. She cringed rereading the parts that had upset Juliana so, and felt pangs of jealousy when Margaret's mom took her bra shopping. Sure, the fictional character was mortified, but at least Margaret had a mother who would take her at all. Brooke had worn baggy T-shirts over layers of tank tops until she was fifteen and couldn't take it anymore; then she'd bought her own bra—just one, which she'd hand-wash at night to keep Juliana from discovering she'd gotten one behind her back. She wasn't sure *what* her mother would have said or done if she found out, but she hadn't been willing to risk finding out. Why couldn't she have had a mother like Margaret's? Or like Judy Blume? Or like pretty much anyone other than Juliana?

You're not being fair, the voice of her peacekeeping middle-child mind scolded her. *She did the best she could. She was grieving and scared and she had to raise us all alone. Try to cut her some slack.* Brooke knew all of this on an intellectual level, but on an emotional level, she couldn't help it; she felt as if she'd been robbed.

She finished the book with one eye on her watch the whole time, then packed up her things and texted Jules that she was on her way.

As Brooke made her way downtown, she busied herself by making up answers to the questions her sister would surely ask about her fake wine-tasting trip. Jules was waiting, of course, precisely where she'd told Brooke she would be.

"How was it?" Brooke asked, trying to keep her tone light.

"I don't want to talk about it," Jules said, slumping in her seat. She looked exhausted. They drove in uncomfortable silence for a while. Jules stared out the window.

"Well, did you meet any interesting people or—"

Jules cut her off. "I said I didn't want to talk about it," she snapped.

Jules rarely snapped at anyone, and the harshness in her tone stunned Brooke. She fought back tears and did her best to focus on navigating through the horrible L.A. traffic.

"Sorry," Brooke said. "I . . . I just . . ."

"No, I'm sorry," Jules said, softening. "It was awful. I mean, some of the seminars were interesting and everything, but I just felt . . . I don't know, out of place." She smiled warmly at Brooke. "It's fine. I'm new to this. I'll figure it out. How was wine tasting?"

"Oh, you know, it's beautiful up there, so that was nice. Hey, have you talked to Alexis? We're running a little late." She hoped the abrupt subject change didn't look too suspicious.

"I texted her a while ago but she didn't reply. She's probably digging through my closet and her phone is buried under a pile of my clothes. I told her she could borrow anything she wanted and that we'd be home a little after seven. I'm sure she'll be cool. She's changed so much since she met Rob and got that job, huh?"

"I've been afraid to even mention it," Brooke said, turning her car onto Jules's street. "I think she may have finally gotten her act together. How funny that Mom would have anything at all to do with that."

"Right?" Jules said. "Hey, there's Rob. Slow down." Rob's squad car was on the street in front of Jules's house and he was leaning against the front fender. He jumped up when he saw Brooke's car. Jules rolled down her window.

"Hey, Rob," Jules called out.

"Is she with you?" Rob demanded when they'd pulled up next to him.

"Alexis? No. She's at work. Well, she was supposed to be until six, and then she was going to ride her bike home. She's not here?"

"Not unless she's hiding or a dresser fell on top of her," Rob told them. "I've been out here calling her phone and banging on the door for twenty minutes."

Brooke's pulse began to race. She looked at Jules, who was trying her best to look calm and unruffled.

"She's probably just got her earphones on or is taking a bath and lost track of time," Jules said as she led Rob and Brooke to the front door. But Brooke knew better. Whatever the reason her sister wasn't ready and waiting for her cute cop boyfriend, it couldn't be good.

Lexi

~

Lexi had been floating in and out of consciousness for over an hour. Her arms and wrists ached and her face throbbed and she had a chunk of crusty, matted hair stuck to her face that she really wanted to wipe away. Rob would find her, wouldn't he? *Rob*. The thought of him showing up at Jules's house now and waiting and worrying or, worse, being furious at her, was far more painful than the ruthless beating she'd just endured.

How could she have let this happen? How could she have been so stupid? Lexi had practically grown up on the streets, and she'd learned to always watch her back. She'd let down her guard for five minutes, that's what had happened. She had no idea if this guy had gotten into the cash register, but if he had, there had to have been at least five hundred bucks in there. Benji would fire her for sure. Assuming somebody found her before her attacker came back for another round of beatings and finished the job.

After what felt like hours she heard rustling in the alley behind the shop, then banging on the door.

"ALEXIS! ARE YOU IN THERE?" It was Rob. He'd come for her. She was safe.

Lexi tried to yell but it came out a garbled croak. Her throat was parched and she still had the hardened, blood-soaked bandana in her mouth. She stomped her feet on the ground and shuffled the chair as hard as she could, hoping he would hear something and know that she was there and alive.

"Alexis?" It was Jules. "Alexis, please open the door if you're in there."

Lexi actually laughed at this, a tiny choked snicker. She knew she was a stupid fuckup, but did her sister actually think she was lounging in the back room waiting for her manicure to dry or enjoying a nice banana split? She prayed to a God she wasn't even sure she believed in that they'd insist on getting in there to look for themselves.

"Alexis, I'm going to shoot the doorknob to break the lock," Rob shouted. In the little snippets of anxious conversation she could make out, Lexi was pretty sure she heard sobbing, which would most likely be Brooke. "Kick something if you can hear me." Lexi pounded the floor with her feet.

"Okay, you're in there and you can hear me. Good. Kick again if it's safe for me to shoot at the doorknob," he yelled. Lexi scooted the chair until she was up against a far wall and not in the path of any imminent gunfire, she was almost positive. She kicked again.

There were four or five deafening pops and then the door flew open. Rob rushed to her first.

"Jesus Christ, Alexis, are you okay?" Rob tried to tug the bandana out of her mouth but the bastard junkie had knotted it good and tight, so he pulled a heavy-duty folded steel knife from his back pocket and snapped the thing off.

"My God, Lexi, what happened?" Jules cried. "Were you robbed?"

No, I'm practicing for my upcoming magic show, Lexi wanted to say. *Didn't I tell you about it?* It was the first time Jules had slipped and called her Lexi since the fateful day they'd heard about their inheritance, but Lexi wasn't about to point this out. Jules dropped to her knees in front of Lexi and grabbed her hands as Rob freed them. Her wrists were bloody and raw.

Brooke covered her eyes and sobbed. She was white and shaking.

"Hey, guys," Lexi said weakly. She pushed the crusty hair aside and she could see everyone trying to hide their horror. Her right eye was swollen shut, and she could feel that one of her front teeth was chipped. She lifted her hands to her face and felt the dried blood all over it. "Thanks for coming. Sorry I didn't have a chance to get cleaned up for you."

Just then Benji came blasting through the back door. He was wearing jeans and no shirt and his hair was wet and uncombed.

"Rob, I got your message . . . Oh my God, Alexis . . . What the hell?"

"We're trying to figure that out now," Rob said. Everyone looked at Lexi.

"A guy jumped me when I went to take the trash out." She shrugged.

"And then what?" Rob demanded.

"He wanted the key to the cash register."

"And?" Rob said.

"I wouldn't give it to him."

"So he beat the shit out of you." Rob finished her sentence. Brooke let out a gasp; Jules buried her face in her sister's lap.

"I was sort of unconscious, so I don't even know if he got anything," Lexi told them apologetically.

"Jesus," Rob said again, shaking his head.

"I'm fired, aren't I?" Lexi asked Benji.

"You're kidding me, right?" Benji said. "Even if he took every penny we had, the fact that you tried to stop him blows my mind. We didn't really cover that when I hired you, but for future reference, if anybody ever threatens you in any way, you're welcome to let him clear the place out."

"Really?" Lexi asked, shocked. She still found it hard to believe that there were people this good in the world, people who might even value her safety over a few hundred bucks.

"Really," Benji insisted.

"Was it just one guy? Did you get a good look at him?" Rob wanted to know.

Lexi shook her head. "It was just one guy, but that's all I know. It all happened so fast, and when he was hitting me my eyes were closed. And then I passed out." She couldn't tell Rob the truth; that she knew the guy and had fucked him and then stolen his money. She just couldn't.

"It's okay," Jules soothed. "You were amazing, Alexis. You *are* amazing. Do you want to try to stand up? Do you think we should take you to the hospital? That eye looks pretty bad. You might need some stitches."

"Are you worrying about my modeling career again?" Lexi asked, grinning. Then she turned to Rob. "I'll bet you want to kiss me really badly right now," she said, looking up at him and batting her eyelashes. Between the tooth and the eye and that crazy, bloody hair, she was quite a sight. Jules couldn't help it; she laughed. Benji chuckled, too. Even Brooke was smiling now.

"You have no idea," Rob said. He pulled her to her feet and kissed her tenderly. Lexi swooned a little bit when he did. She'd have blamed the standing-up part if anybody had asked, but she was pretty sure it was the kiss that was responsible.

Jules

~

Jules was ashamed of herself. She'd been worried sick about Lexi before they found her, and she'd nearly vomited when she first got a glimpse of her sister's battered, bloody face. She wanted to hunt down the animal that would brutally beat any woman like that and cut off his testicles with a dull, rusty butter knife, and then watch him die a slow, painful death. But as soon as they'd found Lexi alive and they knew she'd be okay, Jules's very first thought had filled her with self-loathing: *This would make a great scene in my book.*

She pulled up her manuscript and found the place where it would fit in—right there, toward the end, just when everything was looking up and they were heading into the home stretch. As she re-created the gruesome scene in her head and then on her computer screen, Jules couldn't shake the sinking feeling that her ending was a joke. She had Brooke finishing her race and falling in love with Billy McCann because she was going to do everything in her power to make sure both of those things happened, and now that Lexi wasn't going to get fired she was all taken care of—assuming they could keep her out of trouble for the next few months, which Jules now realized was a pretty big "if." The biggest problem was that in her story, she'd completed her book and they'd all gotten their inheritance. But she hadn't, so they couldn't. It was that simple. And if she didn't finish it, there'd be no money, no happy ending. It wasn't a book without a happy ending, was it? Jules just didn't know.

For the hundredth time, she kicked herself for the missed opportunity at that writers' conference. If she could rewind the clock and go back in time, she'd just suck it up and do it. She'd march right up to at least a handful of strangers and introduce herself, maybe see if she could find a few people interested in starting a critique group. She'd sign up for a seventy-five-dollar hour of coaching and collect business cards and force herself to approach some of the authors who had been there. But she'd blown it, big time. Maybe it was time to reach out to the super-connected Jefferson Wiley, Esq. As much as she didn't want to rely on even peripheral help from her mother, she was fresh out of options.

She closed the manuscript file and wrote Mr. Wiley a quick email—she didn't have the nerve to pick up the phone and call him—before she had a chance to lose her courage. She simply told him that her manuscript was nearly complete and asked if he could introduce her to an agent, as her mother had mentioned in her letter. It was mostly true at least. She hit Send and turned her attention to Project Billy.

Without Brooke's consent or even knowledge, Jules had created a new-and-improved Facebook profile for her sister. She'd posted a few of the pictures she took the day of the conference as well as some funny jokes that reminded her of Brooke. She was careful to keep it clean and family friendly. Brooke was, after all, a preschool teacher; the last thing Jules wanted was to get her in trouble. She had racked her brain to come up with the names of some of Brooke's high school friends and then friended them; from there, she'd searched *their* friend lists for names that sounded familiar. Brooke now had 154 connections and a smattering of posts from other people on her page; enough, Jules figured, to make her not look like a total loser when she reached out to Billy McCann.

She pulled up Billy's profile page and could see that he was online right now. She clicked the message button and typed quickly. "Hey, Billy, it's great to see your face again. Hope you've been well. I'd love to catch up sometime . . ." She put a little smiley face at the end, because she supposed that's what Brooke would do. A line at the bottom of the box said: *Your message will go to Billy's Other folder because you aren't connected to him on Facebook.* So be it. She hit Send.

Now what? It could be days, weeks, even months until Billy saw that note. And he may get it and not even respond. Jules hated waiting; even more, she hated not having any control. She refreshed her email and saw she had a reply from Jefferson Wiley. She scanned it hurriedly: some pleasantries about how he hoped that she and her sisters were well, congratulations for making such headway on her manuscript, and then a name: Derek Stanford, literary agent. A phone number and email address were included. Mr. Wiley ended his email with, "Derek is a lovely man and a good friend. Do tell him that I sent you."

Now she had no excuse. She opened a new email and addressed it to Derek Stanford; in the subject line she put "Referred by Jefferson Wiley, Esq." She figured it couldn't hurt.

"Dear Mr. Stanford," she started. "My name is Jules Richardson and I'm—"

She couldn't do it. She couldn't write *author*, no matter what Shawn said. She was contemplating the perfect wording when her computer made the familiar you-have-a-Facebook-message bleep.

It couldn't be; not this quickly. But it was. Billy.

Jules hovered her curser over the unopened message guiltily, wondering if this had been such a great idea after all. Now she was pretending to be Brooke and talking to the one great love of her sister's life. She prayed his note wasn't too personal or, God forbid, didn't include a picture of his penis. Figuring she'd better finish what she started, Jules clicked the message open. She hovered her cursor over the little escape-to-close X in the corner, just in case.

Brooke! I couldn't believe it when I saw your name in my inbox. I thought after you sent me that letter at the Coast Guard Training Center telling me not to write to you that I'd never see you again. I can't tell you how many times over the years I've wondered about you and where you wound up and, honestly, what I even did to make you write me off the way you did. I'm sure you had your reasons, though. I settled in Miami after grad school—I didn't feel like I had much to come back to SoCal for, if you want the truth. I was married for two years but that didn't work out. Long story, but I've got a great kid. His name's Alec and you'd love him—he's hilarious. Tell me about your life. It's really great to hear from you. You look fantastic, by the way. Hope to hear from you soon . . .

No penis picture, phew. But what was he talking about? Jules wondered. Brooke had said that after Billy left for the Coast

Guard, she'd written him dozens of letters but he hadn't written her back. And now he was saying she'd told him not to write to her at all? With a heavy heart, Jules realized it must have been Juliana. What other explanation could there be? But why? Jealousy, possibly. Control, probably.

Jules shook her head as if it were an Etch A Sketch she was trying to clear. The motive didn't matter now. That was all in the past, and Jules was tired of trying to rewrite that. But she *could* affect the future. Buoyed by that thought, she pulled her focus back to the present.

She reread Billy's note and decided that despite dropping that little bomb, the rest of it was great news. He was obviously thrilled to hear from Brooke, so to speak; he hadn't sent her anything X-rated; and, most important, it appeared he was indeed single and interested in reconnecting. Jules knew she should probably hand things over to her sister now, but she was worried. What if Brooke was furious at her for meddling, or said she needed to lose more weight first? What if she was just too scared to pick up the ball and run with it? Jules decided she would nudge things with Billy along a bit, gently, just for a little while. Brooke would thank her when she told her eventually; she was sure of it.

Brooke

~

Brooke had taken to carrying her cell phone in her pocket at school, even though it was frowned upon. She didn't like breaking rules, but she was ninety-five percent sure that one was for the teachers who had a habit of surfing social media or texting their boyfriends during the day. She, on the other hand, was worried about her sister, plain and simple. She'd never been a caretaker before, at least not in her family; that role had always belonged to Jules. But after Lexi's run-in with that thug, Brooke had the feeling that one mere parent figure wasn't enough for her capricious baby sister. She wanted to be available if Lexi—or Jules or Rob, on Lexi's behalf—needed to reach her.

It was nine a.m. sharp when her phone vibrated in her pocket. Brooke pulled it out and looked at the screen anxiously: unknown local number. Well, that wasn't very helpful. It could be the hospital or the police station or a wrong number; it could be the shoe repair place calling to tell her that her heels were fixed, or her dentist reminding her it was time for a cleaning, or Lexi on the side of the road. She had to take it.

Her students were very busy cutting out construction-paper circles for their Kandinsky trees, so Brooke walked casually across the room—no sense even alerting them to the fact that she was going anywhere—and stepped right outside the door. She could still see each little head clearly through the door's small window.

"Hello?" she croaked into the receiver.

"Jules Richardson, please," the woman on the other end of the line said.

"I'm sorry . . . I . . . May I ask who's calling?" Brooke stuttered.

"This is Allison Zachary with the Kaplan Literary Agency," the woman replied. Brooke had mailed her queries to her A-list agents only last week; she hadn't expected to hear from anyone this quickly. And truth be told, the name Allison Zachary wasn't ringing a bell, but the Kaplan Literary Agency had definitely been on her list. Brooke's heart began to throb in her chest and her hands felt suddenly clammy.

"Do I have the correct number?" the woman prodded.

"Oh, yes, sorry. Yes, this is Jules. How can I help you?" She hoped she wasn't going to hell for this.

"Jules, hello! Nice to meet you. I received your query letter and I have to say, I'm intrigued. I'm calling to request the full manuscript."

"Oh! That's great! Really great! I could drop it by this afternoon? Wait, are you in Los Angeles?" She'd sent several queries to agents in New York and even one in Miami. She wondered if the question was a gaffe, but Allison laughed.

"Actually I *am* in L.A., but you can just email it to me. I presume you have my email address? It seemed as if you'd done your research."

Of course she could email it. At least she'd done *something* right.

"Absolutely, then. I'll shoot it over this evening," she promised, hoping she could pull that off without Jules finding out, as she'd have to send it from Jules's account. *Oh, what a tangled web we weave,* she thought.

"Terrific," Allison said. Brooke could hear the smile in her voice. "I'll be in touch within a week, if not sooner. I'm sure you'll be getting other calls." And then she was gone.

Brooke was trembling with nerves and excitement and the most overwhelming urge she had ever felt; unfortunately, it was the urge to call Jules, which she clearly couldn't do. Ever since that writers' conference, Jules's confidence was more fragile than ever. Brooke needed to get this ball rolling on her own. That way, if this Allison Zachary rejected the manuscript after reading it, Jules would never have to know. Because if that was how this went down, Brooke knew it would be the beginning of the end. *That's not going to happen,* she told herself now. She had a feeling about Allison Zachary and the Kaplan Literary Agency. A very good feeling.

The days seemed to crawl by. Five, six, seven, eight. On day nine, Brooke did what she'd been trying with all of her might *not* to do: She emailed Allison, again from Jules's account. The email bounced back immediately. She deleted the bounce notification and tried again. *Bounce.* What on earth? She could call the agency, but what would she say? "Did you like it?" Maybe agents didn't take things like "within a week" literally? She hadn't heard from another single agent, and she didn't have the luxury of time on her side. In a burst of inspiration, Brooke had an idea: A gift! She'd just swing by the agency after work—it was only a few miles away—and drop off a little thanks-for-your-time note and maybe a candle or a pretty little potted plant. She would insist she was *just in the neighborhood, certainly not stalking*, and wanted to pop by. It was a stretch for sure, but it was all she had.

The Kaplan Literary Agency was in an ugly strip mall in Van Nuys. Brooke pulled open the massive glass door with a trembling hand, clutching tight to her succulent. The door had a giant cowbell tied to the handle, and a clanking sound echoed through the cavernous space. Brooke saw a few heads peek up through nearby doorways as she made her way to the receptionist's desk, where a frazzled-looking woman sat in front of a phone that was a sea of blinking lights. She held up one finger to Brooke.

"Kaplan Literary Agency, can you hold? Kaplan Literary Agency, please hold. Kaplan Literary Agency, may I help you?"

Brooke stood there, willing her body not to break out in a sweat. Each time the woman looked as if she might be able to help her, another line lit up. Minutes became days.

"Maybe I can help you?" said a deep, husky voice from behind her. She jumped, and the man laughed.

"Sorry to startle you, I just thought you might be standing here a long time. We're a little shorthanded, as you can see. I'm George Kaplan. What can we do for you?" He had the bluest eyes she'd ever seen and just the lightest smattering of gray at his temples. He looked more like a movie star than a literary agent, if you asked Brooke.

"Oh, I just wanted to drop this off for Allison Zachary," Brooke said, trying to sound breezy and holding up her plant as if it were Exhibit A.

"That's a lovely gesture, but unfortunately Miss Zachary is no longer with the agency," George said. "Is there something I can help you with, Miss . . . ?" He trailed off here, and Brooke gulped.

"Richardson," she croaked. "Jules Richardson. I sent a query to Allison and she requested the full manuscript. I just wanted to bring her a little token of my appreciation for her time and interest." Brooke could barely hear her own words over the thrumming of her heart, but she had to admit she thought she was handling this rather nicely.

"I see," George said, his blue eyes twinkling. "Well, today might just be your lucky day. I don't normally answer cold calls or attend to walk-ins—it's my agency, after all—but since Lucy here is all tied up"—he gestured to the receptionist, who grimaced and mouthed the words "thank you"—"why don't you give me the elevator pitch?"

"The what?" Brooke asked, saucer eyed and feeling fifty shades of stupid. George just laughed.

"Pitch me," he said. "Sell me on your book in thirty seconds or less, you know, like we're in an elevator. If you can't do that, you can't sell me in an hour. And whatever you do"—he raised his eyebrows mischievously and lowered his voice to a near whisper—"*don't* say 'you have to read it.'"

To say that Brooke wasn't prepared for this would be like saying the *Titanic* had sprung a little leak. Did this man really expect her to stand here in the lobby of his strip-mall office with a dozen pairs of eyes watching and sell him on the concept of a book she hadn't even written? *Be cool*, she told herself. *This is for Jules, and for all of you. You can do this. You have to do this.*

Sensing her hesitation, he nodded. "Follow me."

He led her to his office, where he motioned to one of the chairs across from his big desk. Instead of taking the giant, executive-looking chair across from her, he sat in the cushy club chair next to her and looked at her expectantly.

"Well, it's a memoir," she began, and she thought she saw George wince just a little bit. She tried to ignore the deafening sound of her heartbeat in her ears. "It's the story of my two sisters and me, and how our dad died when we were little and our mom checked out when he did. Then *she* died and left us thirty-seven million dollars we didn't even know she had, but we had to meet all of these crazy conditions and work together to get it, even though we weren't even speaking when she died. It's not just about the money, of course. It's about us and our individual journeys. I'm much more articulate in print." She managed a nervous laugh.

George's ears had perked up at the mention of thirty-seven million dollars. Now he looked at her with his mouth agape. "This is a true story?" he asked.

Brooke nodded.

"It's *your* story?" he demanded.

Brooke nodded again.

"I'd like to see the manuscript," he said. Brooke fought the urge to throw her arms around him and kiss him passionately. Instead, she told him she'd email it to him that evening.

"I can't wait to read it," he said, rising from his chair and leading her back toward the front door.

"It's short but it's pretty clean, I think," she said, thankful that she could say this because it wasn't her own work.

"I'll be the judge of that," George replied. His words were ominous but his tone was light. She extended her hand and when he shook it, a tiny jolt of electricity shot up her arm.

"Thanks in advance, Mr. Kaplan," she said, desperate to maintain her composure. "Truly."

"Jules, please. Call me George."

Jules.

"George." She forced her lips into a trembling smile and then raced out the door to her Kia before she could do or say anything (else) she might regret.

Lexi

〜

Benji had given Lexi two weeks off with full pay to recover from the vicious attack. She was a week into it and bored out of her mind. She'd found a dentist and gotten her tooth fixed temporarily; a permanent implant cost thousands of dollars, so that would have to wait until she'd gotten her inheritance. The temp fix had cost her most of her savings but at least they'd done a pretty good job; Rob swore he had to be three inches from it to even tell. And even though she'd refused to get stitches despite great protesting from her sisters and Rob, her eye seemed to be healing nicely. She was pretty sure that if she did have a scar, it wouldn't be gruesome or anything. Besides, scars gave people character. Lexi didn't think she'd mind hers at all.

She grabbed her backpack and poked her head into the office, where Jules was working. Well, she'd said she was in there working, but Lexi was almost positive she'd just busted her surfing Facebook. Oh well, everyone needed breaks once in a while.

"I'm going for a bike ride," she told Jules.

"Now? Really? It'll be dark in less than an hour," Jules said. She quickly minimized the browser page and turned around to face Lexi. She looked awfully guilty; maybe she was watching porn and not surfing Facebook like she'd thought. *It would probably do her some good,* Lexi mused.

"Rob's coming with me," she lied.

"What time will you guys be back?" Jules asked, looking concerned.

"Couple hours," she said. Lexi could see the little vein in her sister's forehead pulsing, the one that liked to pop out when she was anxious. "I won't be late," she promised. "How about if I'm going to be any later than ten o'clock I'll call you, okay?"

"Okay, yeah, great. Have fun and be careful." She managed a smile, and Lexi could tell she was reluctant to end the conversation.

"I will," Lexi said. "See you in a bit."

She pedaled the familiar route to The Inside Scoop, grateful for the solitude. Jules had been fawning nervously over her day and night since the assault at the shop, and Lexi wasn't really comfortable with that level of attention. Besides, the four of them living in that tiny, cramped house could get stifling. She just needed a little space.

Lexi cruised contentedly through the neighborhood and then tucked into the alley behind the strip mall that housed The Inside Scoop. Her shop key was on a chain around her neck, which she pulled out now to unlock the back door. She hadn't been back since that awful night and a chill ran up her neck. *He won't come back,* she told herself. *He got what he wanted.* Quietly she let herself in, then pulled her bike inside for safekeeping. The door slammed behind her, but she checked anyway to make sure it was locked.

Satisfied, she turned on the desk light and pulled her cell phone from her backpack. She took a picture of Benji's desk so that she could re-create the order of things when she was finished, and then carefully stacked his papers and put them aside. Smiling, she spread out her things and went to work.

When the door burst open behind her, Lexi let out a yelp and her pencil went flying. She jumped up instinctively and spun around with her hands protecting her face; when she did, she sent pages scattering to the floor.

"Alexis, what the fuck are you *doing*?" Rob demanded. He was red faced and flustered and had his hand on his hip, on his gun.

"Rob . . . I . . . What are you doing here?" Lexi asked. Her heart was pounding in her chest and her face was a picture of guilt.

"I was about to ask you the same question," Rob said. His hand didn't move.

"But . . . how did you know I was here?" She wanted to know.

"Benji had security cameras installed after the attack. He was worried about you, Alexis. At least until he saw you letting yourself in tonight. He called me instead of calling 911, so you'd better have a good explanation. Are you robbing the place? Was that attack some sort of setup? What the fuck, Alexis?"

Lexi hung her head in shame. She really hadn't thought she was doing anything all that bad.

She bent down now and scooped up a handful of the papers on the floor and handed them to Rob.

"What are these? I don't understand."

"I drew them," Lexi said.

Rob raised his brows, skeptical. Lexi nodded.

"They're fucking incredible," he said, shuffling through the stack. He kneeled down and carefully picked up the rest of the pages; there were dozens of them. "I had no idea . . . But what do they have to do with anything? Why are you here?"

"I just wanted to be alone," she said simply. "Jules and Brooke are hovering over me twenty-four-seven, and I can't work in a coffee shop without creepers trying to talk to me or offering to buy me a fucking pastry. I wasn't going to take anything or hurt anything, I swear. I guess I should have asked Benji, huh?"

"Um, yeah, you should have asked Benji. Otherwise it's called trespassing, which is a misdemeanor. Unless you have a weapon; then it's a felony."

"No weapon," Lexi said, holding up both hands and grinning. "Please don't shoot."

"Damn it, Alexis, I had no idea what I was going to find when I came down here. I certainly didn't expect to find you quietly working on your latest art installment." He shook his head and laughed, palpably relieved. Lexi saw the tension leave his shoulders as he held his arms out to her; when he did, she fell into them. Immediately she could feel Rob's erection pressing into her, and she desperately wanted to rip both of their clothes off. She'd decided early on that she wanted things to be different with Rob, because they were. She hadn't slept with him yet, and he'd told her that was just fine, that she could have as much time as she needed. Well, time wasn't what she needed anymore. She pulled him even closer.

"I want you so badly," she whispered.

"Security cameras," he whispered back, his face buried in her neck.

"Then let's get out of here."

Rob pulled away from her. "I need to call Benji and let him know that everything is cool, and that it was just a little misunderstanding. And then I'd love nothing more than to have you elaborate on that thought."

"Is he going to fire me?" Lexi asked, biting her lip, her passion waning just a tiny bit.

"I don't know," Rob admitted. "It might help if you called him yourself tomorrow and apologized and promised it would never happen again."

"I can do that," Lexi said. "And Rob?"

"Yeah?" he asked.

"I'm sorry. I really am." Lexi had never meant anything more in her life, except maybe the part about how badly she wanted him.

Jules

Jules was ecstatic for Lexi; she really was. Her dangerously deviant baby sister had made a serious one-eighty ever since she met Rob, and the transformation was astonishing. The other day, she'd complimented Jules on her hair, and last night she'd come home from work with a pint each of her and Shawn's favorite ice cream flavors, as well as a low-fat frozen yogurt for Brooke. She was rarely surly or sulky; in fact, Jules had grown to genuinely enjoy her company. She wondered if Juliana would be proud, and she decided that she would. She'd have to be.

Jules marveled at the fact that of the three sisters, Lexi was the only one who'd satisfied their mother's demands. She'd been promoted to assistant manager at The Inside Scoop and Benji had even offered to split the cost of health care coverage with her. And she'd achieved all of this with time to spare, to boot. Who would have thought?

Still, Jules couldn't help feeling that eventually her sister would get antsy in that environment, performing the same mindless tasks day in and day out. People like Lexi were different; anyone could see that. Jules might have inherited some of her father's writing talent, but Lexi was a creative genius. Jules had to struggle to get words on paper; Lexi's talent was effortless, as if it was always there, just below the surface of her skin, aching to be set free. Without excitement and stimulation and an outlet for self-expression, Jules feared those urges wouldn't just bubble to the surface but explode. She was terrified of what the aftermath of that would look like.

She'd tried to broach the subject of Lexi's artwork several times, but Lexi had brushed her off.

"You just think my crap's good because you're my sister," Lexi had insisted. "It's like how moms always think their ugly babies are beautiful because they can't see what everyone else sees."

"I'm not that nice," Jules replied. "And until fairly recently, I wasn't even sure if I liked you. So I'm pretty sure you're wrong about my alleged familial bias."

"Whatever," Lexi said, brushing off the backhanded compliment. "Maybe with some lessons or something I could be halfway decent, but I've never even taken a single drawing class. I'm an amateur; I'd be mortified if a real artist ever saw my stuff. And besides, like I said, I just do it for fun."

"But the fact that you've never had a single art class is what makes you so remarkable," Jules had argued. "We could make you some promo cards and take them out to some galleries or artists' agencies, and just see if you get any bites." But Lexi was having none of it and Jules was at a loss. It wasn't like she could go showing her sister's work around without her permission. Besides, Lexi was taken care of. It was herself she needed to worry about.

Ever since that awful writers' conference, she couldn't shake the idea of writing a book for children. She had pages of notes now, something she realized was probably a diversion, a way to occupy her time and distract her mind from the more pressing task at hand: finding an agent for the manuscript she already had, the one she desperately needed to finish—and at least make an effort to sell.

Jules had spent hours writing and rewriting her email to Derek Stanford, Mr. Wiley's literary agent friend, and she was mostly pleased with the latest incarnation, which was sitting in her drafts folder. She'd pored over the Query Letter sections of her many writing books, and crafted what she felt was a well-written, compelling sales pitch. She'd given a concise overview of her story, briefly mentioned her dad and his work (it couldn't hurt to have a published author for a father, she supposed) and then explained that she was looking for an agent who could help her hone and sell her manuscript. But she just couldn't bring herself to send it. What if there was a typo in it she'd missed? What if this Mr. Stanford laughed at her when he read the sample chapters she planned to attach? What if she never heard from him at all?

But time was running out. A good plan today was better than a perfect plan tomorrow. There were other agents if this one passed. She couldn't afford to put it off any longer. Jules pulled up her draft and scanned it one final time, touching each word on the screen with her finger as she did, to make sure they were actually there. When she was finished, she attached the sample chapters and hit Send before she could change her mind.

Now Jules took a deep breath. The moment felt terribly anticlimactic. She hadn't expected anyone to shout *YOU DID IT* or for her computer to explode with a soundtrack of bells and whistles, but she thought she'd feel . . . something. Sweet relief or gut-churning anxiety or anything, really. *You sent a lousy email; big deal,* she chided herself. *You'll feel something when something actually happens to you.*

That much settled, she could get back to the other pressing item on her to-do list: Project Billy. She'd written him back—as Brooke, of course—and explained that she'd never written that letter at all; that, unfortunately, it must have been Juliana. Billy had responded, horrified, and apologized for believing even for a minute that she would write him off like that. He should have known better, he said. Jules had insisted that she forgave him, on Brooke's unknowing behalf. Things were moving along perfectly, except for the fact that he was three thousand miles away. Maybe it was time to invite Billy for a little visit.

Brooke

~

Brooke had added the Kaplan Literary Agency to her phone's contact list after her fortuitous meeting with George, and she'd been holding her breath ever since. It was snack time at Little Mc Preschool when she saw the call coming in. She told the assistant teacher she needed to run to the bathroom and dashed out, ducking into the nearby art room for privacy. She left the door propped open because that was the rule ever since the huge scandal last year when two of the teachers had been caught doing it in the computer lab. In the middle of the day! Brooke wasn't sure having an open-door policy would have stopped those two, but what else could they do?

"This is Jules," she said. The words felt strange coming out of her mouth.

"Jules, George Kaplan," he said, and she could picture his smile when he said it.

"Oh, hello, George," she said, hoping she sounded casual and confident. "What can I do for you?"

"Well," George said, drawing out the word. "I was just calling to tell you how disappointed I was when I read your manuscript."

Brooke didn't know what to say. What a jerk! Really, he had so much time on his hands that he felt the need to call her and tell her how disappointing her manuscript was? Well, how disappointing Jules's manuscript was, but whatever. Wouldn't a polite not-my-thing note or even just no follow-up at all have sufficed? She was so glad she'd done this behind Jules's back. What an awful call to have to get if you were in reality the author.

"Okay, then, thanks for letting me know—"

"May I finish?" George asked.

"Oh gosh, I'm sorry, please do," Brooke stammered, angry at herself for being so polite to this guy.

"I was disappointed reading your manuscript to find out that you're married, *Mrs.* Richardson. Because frankly, I was hoping that you weren't."

Brooke couldn't think of a single thing to say. Fortunately, George rescued her swiftly.

"But alas, I'm in the business of finding new and fabulous talent, not meeting eligible women," he said. "And I'm not about to let the little fact of your romantic unavailability stand in the way of a relationship. A working relationship, that is."

"Do you mean . . . Are you saying . . . you liked the manuscript?" Brooke actually crossed her fingers when she asked this.

"It's wonderful, Jules, truly. Oh, it needs some work, don't get me wrong, but I'd like to be the one to help you shape it. You're an incredibly talented writer, and I don't have to tell you that your story is, well, one in a million. I'd love to represent you. What do you say?"

What else could she say? What would *Jules* say? Brooke channeled her older sister. "That's fantastic, George," she gushed on

Jules's behalf. "I accept." She felt like she'd just won the lottery. Jules's head was going to explode with excitement—wasn't it?

"I'll have my office send you our agency agreement. It basically just says I have the right to shop this around to various publishers and that you're not working with any other agents. Boilerplate stuff, although it can take a while to put together. In the meantime, I think we should meet for a drink to celebrate. Bring your husband, of course. I'd love to meet him. Sounds like a top-notch guy, from what I read."

"You're right, Shawn is wonderful and I'm sure he'll be eager to meet you as well," Brooke said with a newfound confidence. "The problem is that he actually works nights so it could be tough to coordinate with him. But I'm sure he wouldn't mind if I met you alone. Especially after I tell him why we're meeting. Besides, he's not the jealous type." She was flirting with a man— a successful, good-looking man, if she recalled correctly—who had just told her that he found her attractive? Brooke wondered if maybe pretending you were somebody else was the unknown secret to dating.

"How about tonight, then?" George asked. "I had a client meeting that just canceled. Are you by any chance free? I could meet you at six."

"It just so happens that I am," Brooke purred, surprising herself at how bold and sexy she sounded as Jules Richardson, author extraordinaire. Tiny pangs of guilt were dancing around her brain, but she pushed them away. She wasn't doing anything *wrong*, she was certain. She was doing her due diligence, for her sister's sake. She was only meeting this guy so she could get some more information about his plans for Jules's manuscript. And fine, she wanted to see him again. But first and foremost, it was a reconnaissance mission. When she had all of the information she needed, and she'd gotten to know George a little bit better and knew she could trust him, then she'd come clean. To both of them.

"Plow and Kettle, six o'clock?" he asked now.

"See you then," she said.

The Plow and Kettle was a newish, upscale farm-to-table-type bistro just a few blocks from Little Me Preschool. Brooke had plenty of time to run home and freshen up after work—she was officially off the clock at three thirty—but she didn't need Jules asking her a million questions about where she was going or why she was getting all dolled up, so instead she texted her sister that she'd be at a staff meeting until late and went to the mall. She slowly perused the various makeup counters in Macy's, stealthily checking out the salesgirls. Brooke couldn't understand why most of them looked like either a scary Halloween witch or a drag queen. Did this actually help them sell makeup? It was mind-boggling.

"Are you familiar with Shameless?" asked a pretty, fresh-faced young girl behind the counter Brooke was ogling. The products and the packaging were beautiful—soft earth tones in simple, elegant tubes, with just a touch of shimmer here or there. She was spellbound by the display.

"Pardon me?" Brooke said, blushing. Was she familiar with *shameless*? Was she ever, considering where she was headed after this. But how did this woman know that?

"We're totally vegan; one hundred percent organic; and also cruelty-, gluten- and chemical-free. Nothing we make has BHA, BHT, coal tar, formaldehyde, perfume, parabens or petrolatum. All of our formulas are mineral-based and there's not a product in our collection that has more than nine ingredients. Oh, and we use seventy percent recycled materials in our packaging. Would you like to try something?"

Brooke tried to process all of this information. She'd never even heard of half of these words, and had this woman said *gluten-free, vegan makeup*? What on earth did that mean? Did her dollar-store lip gloss and her crusty, trusty tube of drug-store mascara—the one she knew she should replace every few months but was probably two years old at least—have flour and beef and all of those scary chemicals in them?

"Oh, I was just looking . . ." Brooke trailed off. She didn't even want to let herself imagine how much a PETA-approved lipstick in a recycled Coke can might cost.

"We give free makeovers—not that you need one of course!— and there's no pressure to buy anything, ever. We just want customers to experience the brand. Plus, you're already beautiful, so it makes my job that much easier. My name is Summer, by the way. What's yours?" She smiled warmly at Brooke.

Brooke looked around nervously. Just because this woman didn't look like a hooker didn't mean she wouldn't make Brooke up to look like one.

"It's Brooke, and thank you, but I don't wear much makeup," Brooke said. "I really prefer a natural look."

"Oh my gosh, me too!" Summer leaned over the counter and spoke in a conspiratorial voice. "I promise I won't make you look like one of these clowns I work with."

Forty minutes and a hundred and sixty dollars later, Brooke was a department-store makeup convert. She knew that was an obscene amount of money to spend on makeup, but she could justify it a million ways to the moon. She rarely splurged on herself. She never ate out. She worked hard. She was living rent-free for the moment and had paid down a good chunk of her once massive debt. Oh yeah, and she was this-close to being a millionaire. Brooke hoped this little overindulgence wasn't a sign that she was going to be wasteful and irresponsible with her inheritance. She made a mental promise to herself that the very first check she wrote from her seven-figure bank account would be to charity.

"Seriously, what did you *do* to me?" she asked Summer. "I mean, it doesn't even look like I'm wearing makeup, so why do I look so much better? Not to brag or anything, but I look amazing! Look at my cheekbones!" Brooke turned from side to side in the mirror, mesmerized by her own reflection.

Summer laughed. "That's what makeup is *supposed* to do. Some people don't seem to get that." She shifted her eyes from side to side, silently indicating her overly made-up coworkers at neighboring counters, and then winked at Brooke. Brooke thanked her profusely and gathered her purchases. She still had an hour to kill, and was meandering through the store when she spotted a familiar-looking woman. *She'd be cute if she wasn't wearing a tablecloth as a dress,* was her first thought. Then she realized she was looking in a mirror.

Another two hundred dollars in the hole, Brooke left Macy's wearing a brand-new black sheath dress and hot-pink heels. The dress was elegant and fitted and showed off her surprisingly toned arms beautifully. She'd closed her eyes when she'd handed over her credit card and prayed that it wouldn't be declined, and miraculously it wasn't. When she got outside, she shoved her wadded-up tablecloth dress into the first trash can she passed.

Brooke knew for a fact that she had never looked better—at least not in the last decade. Still, as she walked into The Plow and Kettle, her heart was pounding in her chest so hard that she was positive it was both visible and audible. She wasn't sure if it was because she knew George had been attracted to her, or because she was a big, fat liar.

"Wow, Jules. Just . . . wow," George said when he saw her. He'd been waiting just inside the door for her, and she was grateful that he was prompt and that he'd recognized her immediately. Brooke tended to have the sort of social anxiety that caused her to forget the names of even her closest friends and to introduce herself to seeming strangers only to be told that they had actually met dozens of times. George was beaming at her now, clearly pleased to see her.

"Hi, George," she said, blushing. "It's nice to see you again." She held out her hand to shake his, but he laughed and put his arm around her instead, pulling her into a friendly hug. George was tall, at least six feet if not a few inches taller, and she could feel his taut back muscles straining beneath his crisp blue business shirt. She felt almost petite in his arms.

"If we're going to be working together, we can't have any of that hand-shaking formality," he said. "And I hope you don't take this the wrong way—because I accept and respect the fact that you are happily married—but you're even more beautiful than I remembered."

It was at that moment that the maître d' appeared to take them to their table. Brooke trotted behind him on wobbly legs, conscious of George's eyes on her back.

"So," George said after they'd been seated. "Awkward almost-advances aside, I'm certainly glad you wandered into our offices looking for Ms. Zachary." His eyes were dancing again and Brooke felt a flush creeping up her cheeks.

"I'm glad I did, too," she said, sipping her ice water.

"Allison wasn't even an agent," George explained. "She was an assistant, and a terrible one at that. She'd been given several notices—it's the protocol before you fire someone, as you probably know—and in her last week, out of spite I suppose, she contacted every single person who'd submitted a query and requested a full manuscript. That's why poor Lucy, our receptionist, was so frazzled the day you came in."

"I guess I got lucky," Brooke said, smiling nervously.

"You have no idea. I have to tell you, I find very few promising new authors in what we call the slush pile, and even fewer who waltz through the front door trying to endear themselves to a fired employee. So kudos to you, Jules. Your writing is fabulous, and your timing is just as good."

This would be the perfect time to tell George who she was and what she'd done. "Well, the truth is," she could have said, "I'm not in fact the author of that manuscript. It's actually my sister—my married sister. And for the record, I am *very* single, Mr. Kaplan, and by the way, my name is Brooke."

But she couldn't do it. Not yet. For one thing, she didn't know George Kaplan from George Clooney; she certainly didn't know him well enough to be sure he wouldn't try to have her charged with plagiarism—which is essentially what she was guilty of, and a plagiarism claim could be an excellent publicity stunt for his agency. For another thing, he was part of the literati; he was probably attracted to her because he believed she had this incredible writing talent and he found that impossibly captivating. She would bet that he would never have given Brooke-the-glorified-babysitter the time of day. Plus, she needed to tell Jules first so that she could immediately pass the baton before George got angry or lost interest. Most of all, she was rather enjoying pretending to be a wildly gifted aspiring author. She felt confident and brave and a tiny bit reckless in her alter ego, and she definitely wasn't ready to go back to being boring old Brooke Alexander. At least, not yet. When their server came, she ordered a glass of pinot noir. She had no idea what that was, but it sounded sexy, like something an up-and-coming new author would sip.

George talked about his agency and their philosophies and Brooke wanted to melt into a puddle at the sound of his voice. She knew she should be taking notes or at least paying attention, but right now all she wanted was to enjoy this moment, to bask in the glow of the attention of a man who thought she was talented and interesting and fabulous. She hardly even noticed when the server brought their wine.

"To a wildly successful partnership," George said, lifting his glass.

Brooke batted her mascara-coated lashes and clinked his glass, toasting to an entirely different partnership than the one George obviously had in mind.

Lexi

∽

"I'm not trying to be nice or anything, but you look really great," Lexi told Brooke. Brooke had asked her if she wanted to come along on one of her dog-walks—which were becoming definitive *runs*—and Lexi figured it was better than sitting around the house watching reality TV or fantasizing about how she was going to spend her millions. Lexi didn't like to admit it, but it turned out she was really bad at imagining what being obscenely wealthy would look like. She tried not to beat herself up about it, though; there'd be plenty of time to learn the rich-girl ropes.

Brooke laughed. "Oh, well, as long as you're not trying to be nice, then thanks." She twisted one of her leashes, deftly thwarting a schnauzer who was trying to dart through her legs.

"Seriously, you've probably lost like a hundred pounds," Lexi said. "Have you weighed yourself?"

"No," Brooke admitted. "I hate the stupid scale. Anyway, I ran five miles yesterday. Five miles, can you believe it? That's like from here to Braemar Country Club. These are Jules's sweatpants." Brooke beamed with pride when she pointed this out. The pants were skintight, but she'd gotten them on without even busting any of the seams, as far as Lexi could see.

"Well, that's one hurdle we can almost scratch off the list," Lexi said, tugging on a boxer's leash to slow him down. "Any hot dating prospects? We're getting down to the wire here, you know." Lexi still couldn't believe that she was the single success story among her sisters so far. It felt so good not to be the fuckup that she was more determined than ever to prove herself at the shop. Benji had forgiven her little trespassing episode and even thanked her for the courtesy of apologizing directly. Lexi was sure it was because he was Rob's family and friend, but still she had promised him it would never, ever happen again. In a show of forgiveness and confidence, he'd given her free rein to hire and train two new employees, and she couldn't be happier with her choices. Amanda and Jordan were both college students with far more impressive résumés than Lexi had, yet they both seemed to admire and respect her. The high she got from that was better than any drug she'd ever snorted, smoked or jabbed into a hungry vein. She almost couldn't believe it herself.

"Well, I sort of did meet someone, but it probably won't work out," Brooke said.

"Why would you say that?" Lexi demanded. "You're turning into a pretty hot piece of ass over there. Don't sell yourself short. Hey, can we turn around? Rob's coming by at five. We're going to go grab a burger. Want to come with us? They have salads where we're going, too. My treat." The truth was, she had no idea where they were going, but lots of places had burgers and salads. It wasn't technically a lie.

"Me? Really? You want me to come on your date with Rob?

And you want to pay for me?" Brooke looked as if Lexi had suggested they film themselves having a three-way or something.

"Frank might come, too, but whatever, if you have other plans just forget it," Lexi said. She knew Brooke would think she was throwing up her protective shell like a shield, but she had different reasons for wanting to play it cool.

"No, I'll go, I'd love to go," Brooke insisted. She'd glossed right over the Frank part, just as Lexi had hoped she would.

"Well, then pick up your pace there, runner girl. They'll be at the house in less than an hour," Lexi said.

"Oh, okay," Brooke said, pumping her free arm vigorously. "What should I wear? I don't have much that fits me right now."

"What about that hot little black dress I saw you slink in wearing the other night?" Lexi said, trying to sound casual. Brooke really did look like a million bucks in that thing; Lexi almost hadn't recognized her. "And maybe some of your new makeup? You know, since you have it and everything."

"Isn't that dress a little fancy for grabbing a burger?" Brooke asked.

"Nah, wear it with flip-flops and it'll be perfect," Lexi insisted. She wondered if Rob had told Frank about the setup or if he was playing it the same way she was. At the thought of her might-be boyfriend, Lexi's stomach turned a tiny somersault. A thousand times a day she wanted to pinch herself to make sure she was really awake and not imagining that she'd met a sweet, hot cop who seemed to adore her. One she'd been intimate with in the truest sense of the word, and in a way she'd never known was possible. Lexi almost understood now why people used that awful, clichéd, cloying phrase: making love. Oh, she'd never in a million years use it herself, and she still didn't even like admitting it, but when she was with Rob, that's exactly what it felt like.

She'd opened herself up to him and let him see the parts of her she'd kept hidden from, well, everyone. They were as close as two people could be, with one exception: She still hadn't told Rob about her mother's money. Lexi was pretty sure he liked her for who she was, but she also didn't want the fact that she was an almost-millionaire to taint his opinion of her, for better or for worse. As long as she was just little Lexi-the-imp-turned-shopgirl, she would never have to question his motives or affection. Sure, those days were definitely numbered, but she'd just have to cross that bridge when she came to it.

Jules

❦

Jules's finger ached from hitting the Refresh button on her computer. It had been exactly seven days and she hadn't heard a peep from Derek Stanford about her query. She cursed the person who invented email in the first place. If she'd snail-mailed that thing, she damn well would have paid the buck extra for a return receipt. Now she was left to torture herself, wondering whether he never got it at all or got it and just plain hated it. Jules knew that the path to a published book was paved with rejection letters, and that she'd be best off casting the widest net possible. She told herself that was exactly what she would do, just as soon as she had Mr. Stanford's feedback, good or bad. Or in a week. Whichever came first.

The clock was definitely ticking—in more ways than one. Brooke still hadn't gone on a single date, and it wasn't like Jules could go out and meet eligible men on her sister's behalf. Part of the problem was that every spare minute Brooke had these days she spent running. Jules was beyond proud of her sister's dedication and determination, but enough was enough. It was time to ramp up Project Billy.

Jules hadn't responded to his last note yet, because both of her sisters never seemed to be gone at the same time, and she needed to be stealthy. But now she had a window, so she logged in to Facebook as Brooke. She felt terrible each time she did, but she tried to convince herself that the cause justified the crime. She knew that if she overthought it she'd chicken out, so she dashed off a quick note:

> Hey, Billy . . . Just wondering if you might like to
> come out to California for a visit. Would be so great
> to see you again in person. Let me know if you have
> any travel plans that might bring you this way . . .
> XOXO

Well, it was technically all true; it *would* be great to see Billy. She hit Send before she could change her mind, congratulating herself on the XOXO at the end. She certainly wasn't the hugs-and-kisses type herself, but she thought it was probably something Brooke would do.

That much accomplished, Jules paced around the empty house, marveling at how alone she felt when her sisters were gone. When had that happened? She had felt anxious and claustrophobic when they'd first moved in, and yearned to have her space to herself again. Jules liked things the way she liked them: the pillows plumped, the dishes washed and put away, the afghan on the back of the couch folded just so. At first, the chaos and disarray that came with her siblings had driven her nuts, and she'd found herself biting her tongue a hundred times a day to keep from mentioning this dirty coffee mug or that pair of mislaid shoes. But now, with Lexi and Brooke out walking the dogs and Shawn off at work, the silence was almost deafening to her. She needed to get out of the house.

She left a note on the counter—*Going to run some errands, back in a bit!*—and grabbed her keys and her phone. She drove aimlessly and without even thinking, so even Jules was surprised when she found herself smack in front of the Garden Villas apartment complex. She hadn't driven to this part of town since she'd come back to clean out her mother's things, and a wave of sadness hit her by surprise. It wasn't that she missed Juliana, exactly; her regular visits had been painful and strained, and more often than not she'd barely make it to her car before she broke down in tears afterward. The sadness she felt now was more *for* Juliana than about her. Jules tried to imagine her future family, happy and whole, and then Shawn suddenly being taken away from them. Would she become a totally different person the way Juliana had? Would she turn controlling and bitter and angry and emotionally abandon her children, *Shawn's* children? Jules desperately wanted to believe that she wouldn't. But how could she be certain?

Jules was so lost in her thoughts that she didn't see Judith Steinman until her face was inches from her own, separated only by the front windshield. Jules let out a terrified squeak. Mrs. Steinman laughed and motioned for Jules to roll down her window.

"Julia! Shabbat Shalom! Did you have that baby yet? Is he with you? What's his name? Roll down that window and let me get a peek! I can't stand the suspense!"

Jules was flustered for a split second and then she remembered her encounter with Rita Berkovitz at Motherhood Maternity. Obviously Mrs. Berkovitz had ignored her request to keep her fake pregnancy under wraps and had told the entire complex the joyous news. What was she going to do now? Judith was frantically motioning at the window, so Jules lowered the glass and tried to wipe the guilty expression from her face.

"Hi, Mrs. Steinman," she said. Children addressing their elders by their first names had been one of Juliana's big "things," of which there were many. At almost thirty-three, Jules felt she'd earned the right to be on a first-name basis with other adults; at the same time, she couldn't imagine calling this woman Judith, ever.

"Where is he? I don't see him in there. Is he with a babysitter? Or that handsome husband of yours? Back in my day we'd never have *dreamed* of leaving the babies alone with the fathers, but you kids are much more progressive than we were. I even know a lady whose son married another man and they adopted a baby together. Can you imagine? Two men raising a baby? Wait, wasn't that a movie?" Mrs. Steinman chatted a mile a minute as she craned her neck trying to see into the backseat. When that proved fruitless, she bent over and pressed her face to the back window of the Honda, cupping her hands around her plump cheeks for a better look. She straightened back up and looked at Jules, confused. Jules had to stifle a laugh; the woman was obsessed with an imaginary baby—one that she'd predetermined was a boy, no less.

"I'm sorry, Mrs. Steinman, I'm not sure what you're talking about," Jules said sweetly. She felt bad throwing Mrs. Berkovitz under the bus, but the woman had said she'd keep her lips zipped. Turnabout was fair play, even if it meant adding fuel to the biggest fire the Garden Villas would likely ever see.

"But Rita said . . . I mean, I thought I heard . . . I guess I was mistaken . . ." Mrs. Steinman's face was beet-red, although

Jules couldn't be sure if it was from anger, embarrassment or exertion. Probably a combination of all three. She was too flustered to even ask Jules why she was sitting in the shade of one of the giant magnolia trees that flanked the Garden Villas sign, her car engine still running.

"Well, don't tell anyone," Jules said conspiratorially. "But we're trying."

At this secret revelation—or perhaps the thought of passionate, baby-making sex—Mrs. Steinman brightened considerably.

"Mum's the word," she said, pressing her finger to her lips. "B'sha'ah tovah."

"I'm sorry?" Jules said.

"When the time is right, my dear," Mrs. Steinman explained.

"Right, well, I'd better be going," Jules told her. "Will you say hello to Mrs. Berkovitz for me? She's such a dear woman."

Mrs. Steinman's face flushed again at the sound of her nemesis's name. Jules waved as she drove away, trying to imagine the catfight that was about to go down at what she was pretty sure was the old-lady Melrose Place of the Valley.

Brooke

❧

Brooke shuffled out of the bathroom in the black dress and flip-flops with a smirk on her face, her arms dangling limply by her sides.

"I look *ridiculous* wearing this dress to go out for a burger," she told Lexi.

"No, you look ridiculous when you walk like a sad, pathetic duck whose ankles are tied together," Lexi said. "The dress looks great."

"Are you wearing that?" Brooke asked, pointing at Lexi's jeans and plain white T-shirt. It was the most basic outfit ever created or even conceived—what a construction worker would wear on the job or a soccer mom would sport to her kid's game—and yet on Lexi the combo looked like haute couture, the picture of casual chicness. Brooke thought her baby sister couldn't possibly look more beautiful in an evening gown.

"You want me to change?" Lexi asked with what Brooke considered uncharacteristic thoughtfulness.

"Sort of," Brooke admitted. "But nothing too . . . fancy or sexy. Just something a little dressier so I don't look so stupid. Would you mind?"

"You should really ask Jules since I'll be borrowing something of hers," Lexi said, sauntering toward Jules and Shawn's bedroom. Brooke followed her, curious to see what she'd choose and envious that no matter what it was, she'd undoubtedly look like a supermodel in it.

Lexi gently pried a few hangers apart, careful not to crush or wrinkle any of the surrounding clothes as she did. Brooke marveled at the change in Lexi. Seven months ago her reckless little sister wouldn't have noticed—or cared—if she knocked half of Jules's things to the floor in her hunt to find something she deemed suitable to wear. Brooke smiled but said nothing.

"This okay?" Lexi asked, holding up a heather-gray T-shirt dress. It was slouchy and had a high neck and it wasn't even short.

"Are you serious?" Brooke asked. "You'd wear that for me?"

"What do I care?" Lexi said, pulling her T-shirt over her head without an ounce of self-consciousness and replacing it with the dress. She still looked stunning, but at least Brooke wouldn't feel like a pig in a wig next to her.

"Thanks, Alexis," Brooke said sheepishly. She wanted to say something more, but she was still apprehensive around Lexi. She couldn't help it; she'd bared her heart to her sister and gotten battery acid poured on it in return too many times not to be.

"I didn't do anything," Lexi insisted, brushing off the gesture. "I changed my clothes. No big deal. Oh, I think they're here." Her face lit up when she said this, and when it did, Brooke realized that this was what love looked like. She ached to feel what Lexi was feeling.

"Put on some makeup," Lexi whispered as she hustled out the door. "I mean, if you want to!"

Brooke dutifully took out her makeup bag and heard Lexi invite Rob and Frank into the living room.

"You clean up pretty well," Rob was saying to Lexi. Even her sister's laugh was beautiful. Sometimes life really wasn't fair.

Brooke drew a faint line of purple across each eyelid and smudged it with her finger. The lady at the Shameless counter in Macy's had told her this would really bring out the green in her hazel eyes, and Brooke had to admit she was right. She added some pale sparkly gloss to her lips and fluffed her naturally wavy hair with her fingers.

Not half bad, she thought, smiling at her reflection and secretly wishing it was George Kaplan waiting for her in the living room. Even thinking George's name made her feel lightheaded, and she regretted the slip. Their meeting at The Plow and Kettle had been bordering on magical, if you didn't count the part where he kept calling her Jules and she kept going along with it. The evening had ended with him saying he'd be sharing her manuscript with some colleagues while he was waiting for the paperwork to be processed, and promising to be in touch. He'd warned her it could take a few weeks, and she'd been thinking about him nonstop since then.

He thinks you're someone else, she scolded herself now. *Not exactly the best way to kick off a relationship. Let that one go. You blew it. It's time to try to meet another guy. Maybe you'll meet someone interesting tonight even. Stranger things have happened.* She squared her shoulders and flipped off the light.

"Hey, Rob; hey, Frank," she said, sweeping into the living room and wondering why Frank looked all fidgety.

"Hi, Brooke," Rob said. He gave Frank a not-so-gentle nudge.

"Oh, right, yeah, hi," Frank stammered. Brooke gave them each a friendly peck on the cheek. The guys often stopped by during their patrols, so they'd made plenty of polite small talk before. Both Frank and Rob were so sweet and easygoing, and Brooke liked to think of them as the brothers she never had. Maybe Rob would even be her brother-in-law someday. Brooke sure hoped she'd have a date to bring to the wedding.

"You lovely ladies ready to go?" Rob asked, slinging his arm around Lexi's shoulder. Brooke was waiting for one of her sister's famous replies, like, *Does a bear shit in the woods?* but Lexi just nodded demurely, so Brooke did the same.

"So where are we going?" Brooke asked as they walked out to Frank's gigantic Ford truck.

"Where would *you* like to go?" Frank asked her.

Brooke turned and raised her eyebrows at Lexi. "I thought you guys had some burger joint in mind," she said. *Was this some sort of setup or something?*

"Oh, right, Rob and I were talking about going to Roger's," Lexi said. "I guess Frank didn't get the memo."

"Roger's sound okay to you, Brooke?" Frank asked politely.

"Sure, I'm easy," Brooke said. Then she blushed furiously at the innuendo. Even if this *was* a setup, she certainly had no intention of putting out. It had been ages, and Brooke didn't care about that whole like-riding-a-bicycle thing. She didn't even know Frank's last name! No, she was definitely not getting naked with Frank tonight.

Lexi

∽

Lexi was so proud of herself she wanted to pound her chest while swinging from a chandelier. To say that Brooke and Frank had really hit it off would be an understatement, unless Brooke had actually gone home with him after dinner to help him write some lame-ass report like they claimed. She'd seen the sparks flying between them, she was sure of it. Besides, Brooke taught *preschool*, not college English. Her students didn't even know how to write their names! Lexi would bet her last push-up bra that her sister was riding that pig like a rodeo queen right now and not drafting up a rap sheet on some drug dealer or gang-banger. The thought made her beam in the darkness.

"So, if you don't have plans for Thanksgiving," she said, high on post-sex bonding hormones, "Jules is planning this ridiculous spread at the house, and you're welcome to come. I mean, you know, if you don't have any better offers." They were in Rob's gigantic California king bed, their limbs entwined like the roots of a tree. Lexi still couldn't get over how different

Rob was from every other man she'd ever been with—and not just because she was sober now, either. She felt so close, so connected to him, that it alternately overwhelmed and terrified her.

"Oh, wow, that's really sweet," Rob said. Lexi thought she heard some hesitation in his voice. "But actually I have a fishing trip planned that week. Some of the guys from my unit go every year."

"I didn't know you liked to fish," Lexi said, trying to hide her disappointment.

"Yeah, well, it's a once-a-year thing," he replied.

Lexi felt like she'd been punched in the gut. Sweet? It was *sweet* of her to want to spend a holiday with him? It hadn't even occurred to her that he might say no. They were a couple, weren't they? Thirty seconds ago she would have said that they absolutely were, but now she wasn't sure.

"Where do you guys go?" she asked.

"Catalina," he said. Lexi had never been to Catalina Island. She'd never even been on a boat.

"That'll be fun," she said coolly. It took every ounce of strength she had not to ask about his friends, who they were and why she hadn't met them yet. The only thing that mattered was that he would rather spend Thanksgiving with them than with her. Or was that even what was going on here? Maybe it was all a big lie. Maybe he just needed a break from her, or maybe there was another woman in the picture. Why hadn't he mentioned this little trip—or these friends—before? It certainly seemed like something that would have come up. And if she hadn't asked him about Thanksgiving today, was he going to tell her at all? Lexi felt like everything she knew about him, and their entire relationship, was suddenly questionable.

It was her own fault, too. She'd gotten soft, complacent. She'd rolled over like a dog and exposed her soft, vulnerable underbelly and, in doing so, allowed herself to forget one of the most basic tenets of the human condition: Other people only looked out for themselves. Well, two could play at that game.

"We can celebrate Christmas together," Rob said now, pulling her in for a hug. He was obviously trying to change the subject, to deflect, and Lexi could feel her heart hardening. "Hey, what do you want for Christmas? Do you like picking out your own presents or being surprised? Wait, why did I even ask you that? I'm surprising you; you don't get a choice. I know exactly what I'm getting you, too. At least, I know one thing."

Rob was blabbing on and on, but Lexi wasn't listening anymore. It was all a distraction tactic anyway, his way of diverting her attention away from the fact that she wasn't important enough to spend a holiday with. Lexi let out a gentle, fake snort.

"Alexis?" Rob whispered. She didn't reply. He stroked her hair tenderly and Lexi fought back tears of anger and shame. How could she have been so stupid? She should have known that nothing this good could ever last, at least for someone like her.

Jules

❦

"Do you have the day off?" Jules asked Lexi. She was curled up on the couch with an unopened magazine in her lap, staring off into space.

"I'm going in at eleven," Lexi said in a monotone.

"Want any breakfast?" Jules asked, trying her best to sound casual.

"I'm fine," Lexi said.

"Well, there's some fresh fruit in the fridge and Shawn brought home some bagels yesterday if you get hungry."

Lexi said nothing.

"You sure you're okay?" Jules asked again. Lexi had been unusually quiet for several days and downright curt when she did speak. Jules was worried that it had something to do with Rob, but she knew better than to come out and ask. She was hoping Lexi would snap out of it, because she really needed to talk to someone about Billy McCann. She had just gotten an email from him saying he was planning a Thanksgiving visit, and now she *had* to tell Brooke. She wouldn't mind having some reinforcements around when she dropped that little bomb, but it didn't look like that backup was going to come in the form of her testy little sister anytime soon.

"I said I'm fine," Lexi said angrily. "You want me to learn how to say it in a different language or tattoo it onto my forehead or something?" Jules's heart ached for her sister, but she had no idea how to help her.

Her phone rang just then. She didn't recognize the number so she let it go to her voice mail.

"I'm going to go walk the dogs," she told Lexi brightly. "You want to come?"

"No, thanks," Lexi said. Jules sighed, grabbed her keys and phone, and headed outside.

It was a brisk fall day, sunny and clear. Jules slid her sunglasses from the top of her head to the bridge of her nose with one hand as she dialed her voice mail with the other. She was expecting a telemarketer or even a wrong number—only a handful of people had her cell phone number—so she was only partially paying attention as a man's voice began to speak.

"I'm calling for Jules Richardson. The name's George Kaplan. My colleague Derek Stanford forwarded the query for your book. I'd love to speak with you about it. Please give me a call at your earliest convenience. Thanks." He left his number at the end.

It was a three-block walk to the first dog's house but Jules couldn't even think straight. She plopped down right where she was, on the curb four houses down from her own, and tried to quiet her pounding heart with the deep breathing she'd learned in yoga. It was a fruitless exercise.

She was shaking as she replayed the message. This George

person hadn't said he was interested in the manuscript, but why else would he be calling? Probably not to tell her that he *wasn't* interested, she thought. She felt like a tourist who'd been dropped down in an unfamiliar country where she didn't speak the language or know the customs. Should she call him back right away? Would that look desperate? *You are desperate,* she reminded herself. She took a deep breath through her nose and slowly exhaled as she dialed Mr. Kaplan's number.

"Hi, this is Jules Richardson calling for Mr. George Kaplan," she said, willing her voice not to shake.

"One minute please," a woman said.

"George Kaplan."

"Oh, hello, Mr. Kaplan, this is Jules Richardson. I just got your message about my manuscript and I'm returning your call." *Short, professional, to the point; nailed it.*

"Ah, Jules," he said in a booming voice. "May I call you Jules? After reading your manuscript I feel as if I know you so well, it's almost as if we've met. But of course we haven't . . . Isn't that right?"

"Not that I'm aware of," Jules replied. *What a strange question to ask,* she thought.

"Well, Jules, in any case I'll cut right to the chase. I'm extremely interested in meeting with you to discuss your manuscript. I don't always insist on an in-person meeting right away, but in your case I feel I must. When would be a good time to get together? I usually take new client meetings in the evenings and save nine-to-five for my existing clients. Would that be okay?"

New client meetings? Was he offering to represent her? Jules was so wound up by that possibility that it didn't even occur to her to question the suggested meeting time. Heck, if he'd suggested they meet at the midnight showing of *The Rocky Horror Picture Show*, Jules would have convinced herself that this was how all "new client meetings" went down.

"I'm free most evenings," Jules told him. "You pick, please. I'll work around your schedule."

"Well, next week is Thanksgiving and I'd love to get this all hammered out before then, so how about tomorrow or Thursday? I'll have my assistant Laurel check my calendar and call you back with a time and place. Sound good?"

"It sounds great, Mr. Kaplan," she said. "I'll wait for Laurel's call, then."

"Please, call me George," he said.

"Okay, George," Jules said. "I look forward to meeting you."

"Likewise," George said. And then he was gone.

She dialed Shawn's work line with trembling fingers and told him about the call.

"So did he offer to represent you?" Shawn whispered.

"I think so!" Jules squealed. "Shawn, I was so nervous I'm not even sure what he said at all. His assistant is going to call me with a meeting time, that's the only part I remember clearly. But I know he said something about wanting to wrap it up— or something like that—before Thanksgiving, and that's *next week*! You don't think he means finish the manuscript, do you?"

"Of course not, honey," Shawn said. "He wants you to sign his contract or agreement by then, that's all. Oh, Jules, I'm so proud of you! I mean it. Can we celebrate tonight? I'll take you out anywhere you want to go. I mean it, anywhere. Even the Thai place I hate."

Jules laughed. "Let's celebrate when something is signed," she said. "And, Shawn, don't say anything about this to my sisters yet, okay? I don't want to jinx it."

"You know I don't believe in that crap, but my lips are sealed until you give me the green light," Shawn promised.

"I love you," she said. It came out a croak because of the gigantic lump in her throat.

"I love you more," he said. She could hear him smiling when he said it.

The sidewalk felt like a bed of clouds beneath her feet as Jules led her dogs around the neighborhood, lost in thoughts of maybe actually becoming a bona fide, published author.

Brooke

～

"She says she's just not feeling well," Brooke whispered into the phone. Lexi was still asleep in the office, and Brooke didn't want to wake her.

Brooke had been surprised when Rob called her at first, but now she was downright worried. She'd noticed Lexi acting sullen and withdrawn, of course, but she hadn't realized Rob was getting the silent treatment, too.

"Well, she's blown me off all week," Rob said. "I offered to stop by with chicken soup or even to take her to the doctor, but she said she just wants to be alone. Will you call me if there's anything I can do?"

"Of course," Brooke assured him.

"Thanks, Brooke," Rob said. "Oh, Frank said to say hello."

"Tell him I said hello, too," Brooke said.

Frank. What was she going to do about him? He was certainly a nice enough guy, and not bad looking, although he was a little short for her tastes. It was just that there wasn't a single spark between them. Zero. Maybe it was because he was so quiet, Brooke thought. She certainly wasn't the chattiest gal on the planet herself, and she thought she probably needed someone . . . bigger than her, someone with a little more spunk. Maybe that was why there was no chemistry between her and Frank: It was like going on a date with herself.

But still . . . she was positive that Jules and Lexi would consider him a *suitable man*, and wasn't that really all she needed at the moment? The inheritance deadline was only two months away, and it wasn't like she had any other prospects on the horizon. He seemed to like her, but Brooke didn't think it was right to play with his emotions like that. Even for millions of dollars. She hadn't done it consciously, but she had put Project Billy on hold ever since she'd met George. Oh, if only—

The ringing of the phone cut into her thoughts. She looked at the screen: George Kaplan. It wasn't even work hours yet! Her heart skipped a beat.

"Hello?" she said, trying to sound her sexiest.

"Jules, George Kaplan, how are you?" *Right. You're Jules. Try not to forget that.*

"I'm wonderful, George, thanks," she said. "You?" The familiar feelings of guilt began to bubble to the surface, but Brooke tried to push them away. She was doing this for Jules, to spare her the humiliation if George passed on her manuscript. That and because she had a massive crush on the guy, but she knew that was pointless, not to mention beyond her control, so she refused to let that part weigh too heavily on her conscience.

"Exactly the same," George boomed. "And I'm calling to see if we might be able to discuss how wonderful we both are this evening, in person? If it's not too last-minute, that is."

"Of course not," she lied. "I mean, of course it's not too last-minute. I'd love to see you this evening."

"Great," he said. "How about seven o'clock at Kushiyu? Bring Shawn, of course."

"Shawn's working again tonight, but I'll be there," Brooke told him.

"Great," he said. "Looking forward to it."

She checked her watch; if she called in sick right now, she might be able to leave a message and not have to talk to the Little Me director personally.

"Hi, Marcy, this is Brooke Alexander," she croaked after the beep. "I seem to have caught that bug that's been going around, so I'm going to stay home today and get some rest. Hopefully I'll be back tomorrow, but I'll let you know either way. Thanks."

It was a thirty-minute drive to Burbank Town Center, but she couldn't risk running into any of the preschool parents if she shopped in the neighborhood or even nearby Woodland Hills or Sherman Oaks. And she needed to shop; even the perfect little black dress was big on her now, and besides, she'd worn that the last time she'd seen George. She needed at least one other weapon in her arsenal.

She brought four dresses into the first fitting room and was shocked to find that she felt—and looked—fantastic in all of them. What an incredible luxury it was to be able to try on clothes and actually like what you saw in the mirror. Brooke made a vow never to take that for granted again. She settled on a royal blue sweaterdress that hugged in all the right places and would look fantastic with her knee-high brown boots.

Now all she had to do was show up and find a way to tell this guy she was wildly interested in that she wasn't who he thought she was at all. Piece of cake.

Lexi

~

"Did you invite Rob for Thanksgiving?" Jules asked. She was pouring a cup of coffee at the counter, her back to Lexi sitting on the couch, and Lexi was glad her sister couldn't see the pain she was sure was painted all over her face. Her heart ached at the sound of Rob's name.

"He's got other plans," Lexi said. The words crashed out of her mouth on an angry wave. Jules turned and looked at her, then turned back around, busying herself with stirring her coffee.

"Oh," Jules said brightly. "Well, we'll have fun anyway."

Yeah, Lexi thought. Stuffing herself sick and trying to hide a broken heart was a regular old barrel of monkeys.

Brooke bustled into the kitchen. "Guess who ran ten miles this morning? Come on, guess!"

"Brooke, that's amazing," Jules said. Brooke beamed. Lexi tried to arrange her face into something resembling a smile.

"It wasn't even hard," Brooke said. "I mean, the beginning

part was hard—it always is—but honestly, I think I could have even kept going today. I could hardly believe it myself."

"You're awfully dolled up," Lexi pointed out. Brooke was dressed in a sweaterdress that was bordering on sexy, and she was actually wearing makeup.

"Oh, I have a little work thing tonight," Brooke said, smoothing down her dress. "Do I look okay?"

"Fabulous," said Jules. "Really great. And actually I have a thing tonight, too—" Jules was cut off by three sharp knocks on the front door. "Expecting anyone?" she asked her sisters.

Brooke and Lexi shook their heads.

"I'll get it," Brooke said. She swung open the front door.

"Hi, I'm sorry to bother you, but I'm looking for Alexis Alexander?" Lexi didn't recognize the voice and couldn't see the face it belonged to. She slowly got up from the couch as Brooke tried to step outside with the woman. What could this be about?

"I'm Alexis Alexander," she said, trying to edge around Brooke, who was blocking the doorway. The woman was wearing a pale blue dress that had QUALITY CLEANING sewn onto the pocket. She held out a large, flat black suitcase with handles.

"I work at The Perk sometimes, and I found this out by one of the Dumpsters," she said. "It had your name on it and, I don't know, I just thought you might want it back. Seemed like you put a lot of work into it and it was probably pretty expensive. I've actually had it for a while. I threw it in the back of my car and I was going to call you, but I forgot about it until I saw it in there this morning."

"I'm sorry," Lexi said, edging into the doorway next to Brooke. "I've never set foot in The Perk and I've never seen that thing before in my life. Is this some sort of a scam? What do you want?" She planted her hands on her hips, ready for a fight.

"She's probably got the wrong house," Brooke said, trying to pull the door shut. Lexi stopped it with her hand.

"Then how does she know my name?" Lexi demanded. "Can I see that?" she asked the very confused-looking woman.

"Look," the woman said, handing over the case, "I was doing my job and it was going to get thrown away. I thought I was doing something nice by returning your sketches. Sorry I bothered you." She turned and rushed down the front path, shaking her head. Lexi brought the case to the couch and sat down, shaking.

"Alexis, wait—" Brooke started, but Lexi was already unzipping the portfolio. She gasped when she saw the picture she'd drawn of the three girls and the woman. She flipped through the book, which was filled with page after page of her private drawings, each slipped into its own protective sleeve.

"You made copies of my sketches, and you did what with them exactly?" Lexi asked, glaring back and forth between her sisters.

"I brought them to The Perk. It's just a coffee shop, but they have a rotating art installment and a lot of really big artists have been discovered there." Brooke hung her head.

"I had nothing to do with this," Jules said, raising both hands as if someone were pointing a gun at her. Lexi thought she looked awfully guilty if that was indeed true.

"I just thought—" Brooke tried, but Lexi cut her off.

"What did you think?" Lexi shouted. "That some talent scout would see my pathetic excuse for art in the local fucking coffee shop and hire me to illustrate some stupid book? Or make me into the next Picasso? Is that what you thought?" She could feel her blood boiling with rage.

"Well, actually, yes—" Brooke stammered.

"How did that work out for you?" Lexi screamed. "Do you think the janitor lady liked my stuff? Because I didn't get a chance to ask her." Lexi wasn't sure if she was more angry or humiliated, not that it mattered.

"Alexis, Brooke was just trying to help," Jules said, coming over to sit by Lexi. She pulled away from her sister.

"I don't want her help, and I don't *need* her help," Lexi said, jumping up. "I told you both that those sketches were private. How would you like it if I took your manuscript and started shopping it around to see if anybody thought it was any good? Huh? Would you like that, Jules?" She brushed past her sisters toward the office.

"I'm sorry, I really am," Brooke said, following her. She was crying softly, but Lexi had no urge to comfort her. She did this to herself. Lexi slammed the office door in her face.

First Rob, and now this. How much humiliation was she supposed to take?

"Alexis, please," Brooke was whimpering through the door. "Please come out and talk to me. I should have asked you first, okay? But I knew you'd say no and the thing is, you're a really good artist. No, that's not even true; you're an *amazing* artist. I'm sorry that I didn't get it to the right person, but now you have a portfolio. It's all together, and you could send it out to agents or magazine editors or . . . someone. I'll help you figure out who to send it to if you want. Alexis? Please come out."

Lexi put the portfolio down on Jules's desk, then laid her head on it. *Goddamn her,* Lexi thought. *Goddamn her for trying to make me think I have some sort of talent, and for putting all of that pressure on me to do something with it.* Now Lexi hadn't just let herself down, she'd let Brooke down, too. She wanted nothing more than to fall into Rob's arms and weep, and to have him tell her everything would be okay. But of course that was never going to happen, because she'd blown that, too.

Jules

~

"That was really sweet of you to do, and I'm guessing that portfolio cost a fortune," Jules said, rubbing Brooke's back. "But you probably should have asked her first."

Brooke heaved a giant, snotty sigh. "I know," she said. "Obviously I hoped it would turn out a little differently." She managed a weak smile.

"She'll come around," Jules said, even though she wasn't convinced of this herself. She tried switching gears. "So what's your work thing tonight?"

"Oh, just some of the teachers are going out," Brooke said. "Group birthday celebration for a few of them."

Jules had her meeting with George Kaplan tonight and Shawn had class, so Lexi would be alone. Jules wasn't sure if this was a good thing or a bad thing.

"Sounds fun," Jules said distractedly. "You look great, by the way."

Brooke snorted. "Really? I do? I look great with big puffy red eyes and snot hanging out of my nose?"

"Well, you *looked* great." Jules laughed. "And you'll clean up okay. I'm positive." She gave Brooke a hug. She was glad she wouldn't have to explain where she was going tonight, since she almost never went out, at least not without Shawn.

When Brooke was gone, Jules thought about what she had tried to do for Lexi. It really was a sweet, generous gesture—and it wasn't like it had anything to do with their inheritance, either. It was completely selfless, a gift, really. Why couldn't Lexi see it that way, and thank Brooke for the effort? Jules shook her head. For a while there, it had looked like she and her sisters were coming together, forming genuine bonds and becoming a family again. And Lexi, damaged little Lexi, had made the greatest strides of all. She'd become what Jules would almost call warm and might dare to consider happy. The worst part was, Jules had no idea what had happened—and despite her repeated reconnaissance attempts, Lexi was showing no signs of clueing her in.

Jules tried to shake off the feelings of despair. She was meeting with an agent tonight—a hotshot L.A. agent at that. She'd Googled this Kaplan guy, whom the *Los Angeles Times* called "a tenacious and talented miner of literary talent," and had nearly fainted when she saw who some of his other clients were: famous actors and acclaimed doctors and global thought leaders and political luminaries. There were several names she didn't recognize on his author list, and she'd looked each of them up in turn, hoping at least a handful were nobodies like her. But they weren't. The lowliest name on the list was a syndicated advice columnist. Jules wanted so badly to stay hopeful and optimistic, but her spirits were beginning to sink.

An author is someone who writes, she told herself as she pulled out her vintage *Sunset Holiday Cookbook*, conjuring Shawn's words. She was an author. An unpublished author with a manuscript in serious need of help, but an author nonetheless. At least, until George Kaplan told her otherwise.

And what if he did? She couldn't go there. She just couldn't, not yet. Her sisters' fates—and futures—depended entirely on her. In this whole crazy inheritance scheme, she was the holdout. How had she let that happen?

Between anticipating her meeting and worrying about Lexi, this day was going to be endless. Jules pulled out a fresh sheet of notebook paper to start her Thanksgiving shopping list, mostly to distract herself. She flipped through the tattered cookbook—*the person who wrote this book probably considers herself an author,* she mused—dog-earring the familiar recipes. There was the baked sweet potato casserole she'd helped her mom make as a child; the apple and sausage stuffing she'd suffered through alone when Juliana had been unwilling to participate in the meal prep; the pull-apart rolls she'd proudly produced for her first Thanksgiving as Shawn's wife. Jules thought about all of those meals now, and the time that had passed and where she was today. She had a great husband, a roof over her head and more than enough money to put on an elaborate holiday spread. She had her health, and after so much heartache she had her sisters back in her life, for better or for worse. *No matter what happens at this meeting tonight, I have a lot to be thankful for,* she reminded herself. She prayed she would never forget that.

Brooke

~

Brooke had tried to put Lexi's art portfolio fiasco out of her mind all day, but it refused to budge. She hated having anyone be mad at her, for one thing, and for another, why couldn't Lexi see that she'd just been trying to help? Brooke was frustrated beyond words, and now she was on her way to meet with George Kaplan. She was going to have to tell him the truth, and she was positive it wasn't going to go well. There was really no way that it could.

When she arrived at Kushiyu, George was already there waiting for her, just as last time.

"Jules," he said warmly, his face brightening when he saw her. "Again, you continue to look lovelier each time we meet. How is that even possible?" He kissed her on each cheek, European-style, and Brooke breathed in the heady scent of his aftershave. It smelled of moss and oak and fresh-cut grass, and she wondered if that was what heaven smelled like. She hoped it did, even though they probably didn't let in liars like her.

"It's nice to see you, George," she said sheepishly, high on fumes and forgetting for a split second why she was there.

"And nice to be seen," George said. "I hope you like sushi. I don't think I even asked you."

"I love sushi!" Brooke gushed, even though she'd never technically had it. At least, not the raw-fish kind. But she did like teriyaki sauce, so she felt like this was probably true.

"Fantastic," George said, steering her toward the hostess station.

"Do you have a reservation?" a pretty young girl dressed in a kimono asked.

"We do," George told her. "The name's Kaplan."

"For three?" she asked, putting a fat red grease-pencil check on her laminated sheet before George even had a chance to answer her.

George nodded and Brooke raised her eyebrows at him. "A colleague may be joining us," he explained. "Another author, actually." She smiled in response, a wave of nerves crashing over her. She had no idea what that meant. They followed the hostess to a table that had been elegantly laid out with three place settings. She sat and pulled her napkin into her lap timidly.

"So, Jules," George said when they'd been seated. "First of all, let me say how much my associates and I have enjoyed discussing your manuscript." His eyes had that unnervingly mischievous twinkle again.

Brooke opened her mouth to say something, but George continued.

"It's not every day we see such promising writing from a mysterious and unknown author."

"Well, thank you, George, that's sweet of you to say—"
George cut her off.

"And the fact that it's a true story—and you've assured me

that yours is indeed a true story?" He paused here, looking at Brooke expectantly. She nodded dumbly. Well, it was indeed a true story.

"Well, then that makes it even more extraordinary," George continued.

"George, I wanted—"

A sommelier appeared seemingly out of nowhere. "Your Kenbishi, Mr. Kaplan," he said, holding out a bottle with Japanese lettering on it. George nodded at him and the sommelier bowed back and opened the bottle swiftly. George swirled the small pour he'd been given thoughtfully, tasted it and nodded again. "Lovely, Masato." Masato filled both of their glasses and backed away from the table with another bow.

"I'm sorry, Jules," George said. "You were about to say something. But first, a toast: to you and your incredible story." He lifted his sake glass toward her, and Brooke had no choice but to clink her glass against his. Then she lifted her glass to her lips and took a small sip, a fusion of sweet, slightly nutty flavors dancing on her tongue. She closed her eyes to savor the incredible tastes.

"Brooke?"

Brooke's eyes flew open and she nearly choked. Her brain couldn't process what was happening. Jules—her sister Jules, the woman she was at this very moment pretending to be— was standing beside her table. She looked wildly from Jules to George and back again, utterly unable to speak.

Jules looked at the hostess, who nodded in George's direction.

"Mr. Kaplan," she said, bowing deeply.

"George Kaplan?" Jules asked, visibly confused.

George nodded and extended his hand.

"Then you must be . . ." George began; Brooke let out a tiny, barely audible yelp.

"Jules Richardson," Jules said, shaking his hand firmly. "But how . . . I mean, I didn't know that you knew . . ." She looked pleadingly at Brooke, whose face had turned the color of an overripe Roma tomato.

"George," Brooke croaked. "This is Jules. She's . . . She actually wrote my book. Well, obviously it isn't my book—but it *is* my story, too. I'm her sister. Brooke. From the book. The book I didn't write. There, I said it." Brooke slumped down in her chair, trembling with a mixture of relief and mortification.

"Where are my manners?" George asked, thumping himself on the forehead with the heel of his hand. "Jules, please have a seat." He stood and pulled the third chair back for Jules. She sank into it, her eyes saucer-wide. George sat back down, looking not the least bit flustered.

"Brooke, would you mind telling me what's going on?" Jules said. To an outsider, she sounded almost warm and friendly, but Brooke could see the clench of her jaw and the vein pulsing in her forehead.

"I think I can explain, if that's okay, Brooke?" George raised his eyebrows at Brooke, and she hesitated before nodding ever so slightly.

"Your lovely and loving sister sent your manuscript to an associate of mine, and I was fortunate enough to intercept it," George said. "I've surmised that she pretended to be you because she was shopping your material, as we say, without your knowledge or consent. What she didn't take into account, however, was that I might actually *read* the thing and hastily discern, thanks to your detailed descriptions of your characters, that she was not the author, Jules Richardson, but her eager and well-meaning middle sister, Brooke Alexander."

Jules just stared at Brooke, her mouth agape. George looked

from one sister to the other, and when he did, Brooke would have sworn she saw traces of a smile fighting their way to his lips.

"Well? How'd I do?" He directed this question at Brooke.

"You pretty much nailed it," she admitted. She turned to Jules. "Wait, why are you even here?"

"He invited me!" Jules said loudly, pointing at George. Several heads turned in their direction. "Oh, sorry for pointing. And shouting. I sent my manuscript to Mr. Wiley's friend Derek Stanford, and he passed it along to George, who called me and said he wanted to meet with me. But obviously he only wanted to meet with me to humiliate me. Well, *us*. So thanks for your time, Mr. Kaplan. I'll be going now." She pushed herself back from the table and stood up so quickly that her chair fell over backward, clipping the one behind it on its way down. The deafening crash that followed got the attention of the half dozen or so tables who weren't already watching the drama unfold.

George stood and placed his hand gently but firmly on Jules's arm. "Please, Jules, wait," he said calmly. Her eyes were brimming with tears and Brooke had never felt more helpless. A server swept in and righted the chairs.

"Is there more humiliation to come, Mr. Kaplan?" Jules asked. "Because I'd rather not—"

George put both of his hands on Jules's shoulders. "I invited you here this evening to ask you if you would allow me the pleasure of representing you as your literary agent," he said, speaking slowly and over-enunciating each syllable.

"You did?" Jules and Brooke asked at the exact same minute. George beamed and nodded.

"I did," he insisted. Jules sat back down tentatively.

"But what . . . I mean why . . ." Brooke couldn't even formulate a coherent question.

"Well," George began, pausing to take a healthy swig of sake and directing his reply at Brooke. "I made it clear that I was intrigued by your story and also attracted to you when I met you, she-who-called-herself-Jules. So when I read the manuscript and realized you weren't who you said you were, I was planning to see how that played out, you know, how and when you were going to come clean. But then my colleague Derek started telling me about this fabulous manuscript he'd read, and it took me a while but I started to put two and two together. Oh, fine, it wasn't nice to spring this on you two ladies the way I did tonight, but I'll be honest. It's going to make one hell of a scene for that book." He sat back in his chair, the picture of smug satisfaction.

"Are you serious?" Jules asked finally. "You actually want to represent me, and you think you can sell my manuscript to a publisher?"

Brooke was too busy relishing the fact that George had declared, in front of Jules, that he was attracted to her to think about anything else he'd said.

"Dead serious," George said. "About all of it. But I have to know: Where are you in terms of your mother's deadline?"

The sisters exchanged nervous glances.

"About eight weeks away," Jules admitted.

"That's cutting it close," George said. Jules looked forlorn. "Although, technically you've already made the requisite concerted effort. Still, since lawyers can be a prickly bunch, it can't hurt that I've already mentioned it to two editor friends and they're both interested. One asked for an exclusive read."

Jules's jaw dropped. "Are you serious?" she whispered.

"I've already marked up the manuscript with notes on where I think you can expand," George said, "and I'll be working very closely with you to see that it gets wrapped up in time. But we've literally not a minute to waste."

Jules nodded eagerly.

"And, Brooke," he said, turning to face her. "Since your sister will be so busy writing, I'm afraid you're going to have to find someone else to spend your free evenings with. I'd like to suggest myself."

Brooke blushed furiously. "I think that can be arranged," she said demurely.

"Excellent," George said, lifting his glass. "I'll have the agency agreement and my notes sent over tomorrow. In the meantime, cheers! Jules, welcome to the agency, and Brooke, it's lovely to remeet you."

"Would you like to join us for Thanksgiving dinner?" Jules blurted out.

Brooke's eyes nearly popped out of her head. "I'm sure George already has plans," she said, desperate to save him—or herself, she wasn't sure which.

"Actually, that sounds wonderful," George said with a wink in Brooke's direction. "What can I bring?"

Lexi

~

Lexi checked her phone for the billionth time. No message from Rob. Not even a "Happy Thanksgiving." Her heart sank even lower, something she hadn't even thought could be possible. How in the bloody hell was she going to get through this day, surrounded by two disgustingly lovey-dovey couples? She was sure Jules was already pissed at her because she wasn't helping her cook, but Lexi didn't care. She'd just as soon eat a bowl of Lucky Charms alone in the office anyway, so Jules could kiss her ass.

She was flipping through her phone, looking for a distraction and trying to block out the happy holiday chatter in the next room, when she saw it: Find My Friends. When Rob had told her that he wanted to install the app on her phone, she had been insulted and angered.

"Why don't you just put one of those tracker thingies on my ankle like parolees wear, huh?" she'd scoffed.

"It's not because I don't trust you, it's because I *care* about you, Alexis," he'd insisted. "You're a beautiful woman, and I've seen some unholy things happen to beautiful women. I'll just feel better if I know I can find you if I need to. Do it for me, please?"

She'd hemmed and hawed and finally acquiesced, but only on the condition that she had the same ability to track him.

"So you can come rescue me if some gangbangers kidnap me?" he'd laughed.

"Something like that," she'd replied.

Now she clicked on the app. Rob Cooper's was the only phone she'd registered, and she clicked on his name. A map popped up instantly.

Malibu. Rob was in Malibu.

He'd lied to her. She'd known he was lying even as the words were coming out of his mouth—years of living on the streets had honed her instincts to a fine point—but seeing the proof in her hand was like a blow. What was he doing in Malibu? Did he have another girlfriend there? Wait. His parents were divorced, and they both lived in Malibu. His mom was remarried with a new family that Rob didn't seem to care for, and he'd never said much of anything about his dad, now that she thought about it. Would he have gone to see one of them? It *was* a holiday after all. But if he had, why would he lie about it?

Oh.

In a painful flash it was all starting to make sense. Malibu was the home of the richest of the rich, business tycoons and billionaires and mega-celebrities like Mel Gibson and Goldie Hawn and Robert Redford. Obviously, Rob's parents were loaded—at least one of them, probably his father, Lexi thought; hence the radio silence—and even more obviously, Rob was embarrassed of his poor, working-class girlfriend and her highly questionable past. Even though Rob was a cop, or maybe because of it, they probably wanted him to hook up with some blue blood, or at least the daughter of one of their famous neighbors.

Lexi wondered briefly if she was being ridiculous. Surely there were *some* blue-collar types in Malibu, fast-food fry guys and grocery store checkout girls and the folks who worked at the quaint little newsstand down by the beach. His parents could be those, couldn't they? But no, she realized. Those people schlepped in from the Valley; they didn't *live* in Malibu. Obviously, he was ashamed of her.

I'm going to be rich soon, too, she shouted at him in her head, but she knew that wasn't the point. It wasn't about money; it was bigger than that. Money couldn't buy class, everyone knew it. Even if she already had her millions, she wouldn't be good enough for him. She was street trash; an embarrassment.

Well, fuck him. If that was how he felt, she'd give him something to be ashamed of.

Jules

~

Jules had gotten up before the crack of dawn to start slicing and dicing and mixing all manner of decadent, once-a-year treats. Brooke was by her side, breaking away only for her obligatory run and to clean up afterward. Now the sweet and savory smells of Thanksgiving filled the house, and Jules's mouth was already beginning to water. George had arrived bearing flowers and wine and a scrumptious-looking pumpkin pie from Hygge Bakery in L.A., and he and Shawn were chatting amiably, some football game or other on mute in the background. A fire crackled in the small fireplace and Jules's iPad was playing a festive holiday soundtrack. The two couples were dressed in holiday-appropriate style, and Jules was positive she'd never seen Brooke look lovelier. The day would have been bordering on perfect—if it hadn't been for Lexi.

Jules had made several attempts to coerce her out of the office, but Lexi had deflected each one with increasing animosity. Should she try to force her to join them for supper? Jules was pretty sure that would backfire miserably, but how could she enjoy her own meal knowing her sister was locked up in a desolate prison of her own making?

"Everything smells amazing," George was saying. Jules had worried that her impulsive invitation had been a mistake; he and Brooke barely knew each other, and she wasn't exactly versed in the proper ways to act around your agent. She and Brooke had discussed it and agreed that since George had had an exclusive peek into the most private and sacred parts of their lives, putting on any sort of airs would be a futile exercise. He liked them both; that much was evident. They were what they were and he was there anyway. *It's a Thanksgiving miracle,* Jules thought wryly.

"Thanks, George," she said now, topping off his wineglass. She settled on the couch next to Shawn.

"Do you think Alexis is going to eat with us?" Brooke wondered aloud. She had put the two extra leaves into the kitchen table and was setting it with their parents' wedding china.

"Set her a place," Jules said. "I'll try her one more time when we're ready to sit down."

Just then, Lexi came bursting out of the office. She was wearing the yoga pants she'd been wearing for days on end and a thin white T-shirt. At least she was wearing a bra, Jules was relieved to note.

"Happy Thanksgiving, Alexis!" Shawn said brightly. Jules stood.

"Alexis, this is George Kaplan, my literary agent and Brooke's . . . friend." Jules tried not to grin like an idiot when she said the "literary agent" part.

George stood and extended his hand.

"Wonderful to meet you, Alexis," he said, smiling broadly.

"Pleasure," Lexi said, brushing him off and turning to Jules. "I need to borrow your car."

"Where are you going?" Jules asked.

"Out," Lexi said. "Can I have your keys? Please." Her eyes were wild, and a wave of worry washed over Jules. Was she doing drugs again? Or about to?

"You're not on our insurance—" Jules started, but Lexi cut her off.

"Spare me the liability lecture," Lexi huffed. She turned to her other sister. "Brooke? Can I take your minivan?"

"I need to know where you're going," Brooke said. Jules was surprised at how forceful she sounded.

"For fuck's sake, Brooke, *please*." Lexi looked desperate.

"Alexis, it's Thanksgiving," Jules pleaded. "Nothing is open except the grocery store. Can't it wait?"

"No, it can't," Lexi insisted. "Brooke?"

"You can't take my car," Brooke answered, "but I'll drive you wherever it is you so urgently need to go." She looked at George apologetically. He nodded, signaling, *It's okay. Do what you have to do.*

"Well, then I'm going, too," Jules said. Lexi rolled her eyes.

"You three are not going anywhere without me," Shawn said. "Not after the TV debacle."

"Jesus Christ, you guys, please just let me do this alone," Lexi fumed.

"Nope," Brooke said.

"Not a chance," Jules said.

"I'm with them," Shawn said.

"Fuck it, fine, then let's go," Lexi said with a dramatic growl. "But everyone shuts the fuck up and no questions, okay? I mean it."

Jules cringed; she couldn't believe this was happening at all, let alone in front of her *literary agent*.

"Are we going to get into any trouble?" Brooke asked timidly. Jules waited for Lexi to jump down her throat for ignoring the no-questions command, but apparently Lexi had no time for such trivialities.

"I hope not," Lexi said.

"I'll get my keys," Brooke sighed.

"I guess I'll turn the oven off," Jules said, hoping this little diversion wouldn't ruin the meal she'd been working on for three days. "Will we be back for dinner?"

"Can't really say," Lexi said impatiently.

"I get to come, too, right?" George asked.

Brooke shrugged. "If you want to," she said, turning pink. "That would be great. I mean, I think."

"This is fucking perfect," Lexi said, shaking her head before storming out the front door toward Brooke's powder-blue minivan. Jules waited until everyone else had followed her and then locked the door, wondering where in the hell this spontaneous mystery journey was going to take them.

Brooke

❧

Well, this isn't exactly the most ideal first date, Brooke thought as she swiped some lip gloss across her lips. But what was she going to do? Thanks to Jules and her manuscript, George already knew all about her crazy family. If he wasn't scared off before today, this wouldn't necessarily be a deal breaker. Of course, she had no idea where they were going or why, so she thought she probably shouldn't go making any overly optimistic predictions, especially since Lexi was at the helm of this ship.

"Everyone buckled up?" Brooke asked after she fired up the engine. Lexi had taken the front seat—of course—and Jules, George and Shawn sat in the middle row.

"Yes, Mom," Lexi said with forced patience. "Any day now."

"Which way am I going?" Brooke asked as she put the mini-van into reverse.

"North on the 101," Lexi said. Brooke glanced at her nervously. She hadn't planned on a road trip. She hadn't even brought a bottled water or any almonds, and she'd run twelve miles this morning. She hoped Lexi would at least let them stop for some snacks. She had a feeling it was going to be a long day.

As she started backing up, a taxi pulled up directly behind her Kia and stopped, completely blocking her path.

"What are you *doing*?" Lexi shouted at her.

"There's a cab behind me, Alexis," Brooke said, summoning her patience. Lexi reached for her door handle but Brooke grabbed her arm.

"I've got this," she said. The last thing she needed was Lexi getting into a fistfight in their driveway. She put the minivan back into park and got out.

"Excuse me?" she called to the taxi driver. He was talking to a man by the trunk. "Um, you're sort of blocking my—" Brooke stopped cold. The taxi driver wasn't talking to a man. He was talking to *Billy McCann*.

"Brooke!" Billy shouted. "Hey!" He was ruggedly handsome in jeans and a button-up shirt, and her heart began pounding in her chest. He had a suitcase in his hand and the world's biggest grin was plastered all over his face. The cab pulled away behind him.

"Billy?" Brooke said. He set the suitcase down and began running toward her, as if he were going to tackle her. She didn't know what else to do, so she closed her eyes and braced herself. Then his arms were around her and he had picked her up and was spinning her around, and either a brain aneurism was exploding in her head or someone was laying on a car's horn.

"Brooke, what the *fuck*?" It was Lexi, who'd gotten out of the minivan and was oblivious to the unfolding Billy situation. "We have to go!" Brooke looked back and forth from her sister to Billy.

"Billy *McCann*?" Lexi asked.

"Billy!" shouted Jules, who had jumped out of the Kia. "It's so great to see you! Wow. You look great. Really great. Doesn't he look great, you guys?" By this point, Shawn and George had gotten out of the car, too. Shawn looked confused, George amused.

"He does, you do," Brooke said, turning to Billy. "But . . . what are you doing here?"

Billy's smile fell. "You invited me. I mean, I thought you invited me. Didn't you invite me?"

"I'm serious, you guys," Lexi interrupted. "We have to go, like, *now*. Can we please enjoy this little high school reunion in the car? You two will have plenty of time to catch up." She stalked back to the minivan, got in the passenger seat and slammed the door. Jules slunk away after her, dragging Shawn with her.

Brooke smiled nervously. "Um, Billy, this is my friend George Kaplan. George, this is Billy McCann, my . . . high school boyfriend." The two men shook hands uncertainly. "I guess we're going for a drive," Brooke told Billy.

"Oh, okay, sure," Billy replied with a bewildered shrug.

"This just keeps getting better and better," George mused. They shuffled back to the Kia. Shawn had crawled into the far back—where Brooke would very much like to be right now, except she had to drive—and now it was Jules, George and Billy in the middle row.

Brooke was very busy concentrating on driving, so Jules spoke first. "Brooke, I sort of have a confession," she said. Their eyes met in the rearview mirror; Jules was cowering in her seat.

"Okay," Brooke said, drawing out the word. "Shoot."

"I invited Billy to visit," she said, turning to Billy. "That was me. On Facebook. Pretending to be Brooke. The whole time. She didn't know anything about it. I was going to tell her and then, well, the past few weeks have been crazy—actually, the past *year* has been crazy—and I completely forgot. I'm so, so sorry to you both. Really. Like, beyond sorry."

"Wait, you pretended to be *me*?" Brooke said, aghast.

"Well, in my defense, you were pretending to be *me* when you met George, so we're sort of even," Jules said.

"She has a point," George agreed.

"This is awesome," Lexi chimed in. Brooke looked at her sister in disbelief; Lexi was smirking. It was the first time Brooke had seen her look anything close to happy in weeks, so she reluctantly let it go.

"So, Brooke," Billy said, struggling to piece the puzzle together. "You didn't want me to come?"

"Razor sharp there, Billy, razor sharp," Lexi muttered.

Brooke could see his face in the mirror and he looked crushed. She felt awful.

"I didn't *not* want you to come, I just didn't know about it!" she insisted.

"And your friend here," Billy said, pointing to George. "Is he a friend-friend or more than a friend?"

Brooke felt the blood rushing up her neck to her face in a fast-paced fury. What could she say?

"More than a friend, if I have a say in the matter," George replied for her. "Sorry, buddy."

An awkward silence filled the car.

"Get in the right lane," Lexi instructed. "You're going to get off at Las Virgenes."

"Where are we going?" Brooke asked.

"Malibu," Lexi told her.

"What's in Malibu?" Brooke asked.

"That's exactly what we're going to find out," Lexi said.

Brooke didn't like the sound of that one bit.

Lexi

❧

Lexi looked out the passenger window, oblivious to both the beauty of the canyon and the tension in the car. Her stomach was churning, a discomfort that still didn't distract from the ache in her heart. She was losing Rob, had probably already lost him. Is this how Juliana had felt when her husband dropped dead? For the first time that she could recall, Lexi was overwhelmed with something that could only be described as compassion for her mother. She'd always thought of her dad's death as something that had happened to her and her sisters; Juliana could go out and get another husband, after all, but they only had one father. Now she realized that just like her, Juliana had lost something she loved deeply and wholly, something she probably never would have let herself imagine living without, because even the fleeting hypothetical thought would be excruciating. Lexi had been too young to fully grasp the enormity of *forever* the first time it sucker-punched her, but now she understood on a visceral level. Her head spun with a mixture of her own grief mingling with a newfound sympathy for her mother, the whole mess wrapped in a web of regret and sorrow.

Stop it, she chided, angry at herself. *Don't feel sorry for her. Shitty things happen in life. She had a choice, and she chose to push you away. You can forgive her, but don't ever forget that.*

"So, uh, where are we headed?" Billy asked tentatively. His words slicing through her thoughts were a welcome distraction.

"It's sort of a surprise," Jules responded. "For all of us. Only Alexis knows. And we're not allowed to ask any questions. It's . . . complicated."

"You can say that again," Brooke said with a grimace.

"I would have been more than happy to come by myself," Lexi said, but it was a knee-jerk reaction, a lie. The uncomfortable truth was, she was glad that she wasn't alone. She hated to admit it even to herself, but these past few months at Jules's house had been some of the happiest of her life, a truth she hadn't even recognized until this minute. She was almost compelled to say something, to thank them maybe, or just acknowledge their being there with her and for her, but she couldn't bring herself to do it. She wanted to blame Juliana for this—that had always been her default, after all—but Jules and Brooke hadn't shut down the way she did under the same circumstances, so the problem must be her.

Lexi thought now about the aftermath of that tragic fork in the path of their lives: how Jules had jumped in and taken over the parenting when their mom checked out, and how Brooke had taken up running with a near vengeance. And what had she done? Gone in the polar opposite direction, deciding that she didn't need anyone or anything but herself. The root of all three reactions, she could see now, was a need for some sense of control. Juliana had wanted the exact same thing that they all did: to create an illusion of power where none actually existed. And in her own weird Juliana way, she'd managed to give Lexi the greatest gift she could imagine, one she hadn't even known how desperately she wanted or needed: her sisters back in her life. If nothing else, Lexi had Jules and Brooke, which was more than she'd had for most of her life. She might be about to cost them their inheritance—Rob was her connection to Benji, after all, and without Benji she had no job—but they would forgive her, and they would continue to love her. It was a mind-blowing thought, and just the one that would give her the courage and the strength to do what she was about to do. She didn't need Rob to prove she was lovable; she didn't need Rob for anything. Unwittingly, the Gloria Gaynor song "I Will Survive" popped into her head, and she actually snorted. It was the cheesiest song ever written—except when her gay friends sang it; then it was epic—and she'd danced on countless bars over the years, belting out the lyrics only to mock them. But she wasn't going to crumble *or* lay down and die, at least not for Rob to see. She wouldn't give him the satisfaction. She would survive, damn it. She might not be good at a lot of things, but *that* she'd mastered.

Jules

As Brooke steered the minivan carefully through the winding canyon roads, the silence in the car was starting to give Jules a migraine.

"So, Billy, tell us about Alec," she suggested, rubbing her temples.

"Oh, right. Alec's my son. He's two and a half. He's awesome," Billy said.

"Wow, that's great," Brooke said, a little too brightly. "So you're divorced?"

"Unfortunately, yes," Billy said.

"Anyway, Billy, you should tell Brooke about the letter," Jules urged. Under any other circumstances, she wouldn't be prying the lid off a can of poisonous worms in front of her sister's date, but George was an exception. He already knew everything. In fact, the ending of her manuscript currently had Brooke doing the happily-ever-after dance with Billy! How on earth could she have forgotten about inviting him to visit? She considered herself lucky that nobody was threatening to inflict serious bodily harm on her. She wasn't sure she'd have been so gracious.

"She doesn't know?" Billy asked. Jules shook her head.

"I got a letter from you—at least, I *thought* it was from you, I mean it said it was from you—telling me not to write to you or contact you ever again. No explanation. You said . . . I mean, Jules said she thinks . . ." He trailed off here, obviously not wanting to disparage their dead mother.

"I never wrote that!" Brooke cried. "I don't even understand. I wrote you dozens of letters, maybe hundreds! I gave them all to Mom and she mailed . . . Oh my gosh." Disbelief washed over her face.

"Mom must have written it," Jules said softly. "And then she never sent any of your other letters."

"But *why*? Why would she do that?" Brooke demanded.

"Maybe she couldn't stand to see you having what she'd lost," Shawn offered.

"Or maybe she was afraid she was going to lose you, too," Jules added, putting her hand gently on Brooke's shoulder and giving it a soft squeeze.

Everyone paused to consider this.

"Or maybe she was just miserable," Lexi added finally. "Misery loves company, right?"

"I suppose," Brooke said. "That could explain living the way she did, too."

"You mean like a welfare case? Hey, speaking of, does Billy know about the money?"

"You'd have to ask Jules," Brooke said sarcastically, giving her older sister a backward glance. Jules cringed.

"I didn't mention it yet," Jules said.

"Mention what?" Billy wanted to know.

"Oh, just that our mom died filthy stinking rich—we had no idea she had a penny, by the way—and left us millions of dollars but made it so we couldn't have any of it unless we could *all* meet these fucked-up conditions she came up with," Lexi explained. "One of them was that Brooke had to be dating an upstanding guy. So you should feel honored. Jules obviously thought you fit the bill."

"For real?" Billy wanted to know. *"Millions?"*

"It's crazy, I know," Brooke told him.

"Go left on PCH," Lexi said, looking at her phone. Las Virgenes had become Malibu Canyon Road, and they were approaching the spot where it dead-ended into the famed Pacific Coast Highway.

"Anyway," Brooke said. "We all had to do this stuff our mom insisted on in order to get her inheritance, and we're almost there. Alexis was actually the first one to the finish line, believe it or not."

"I've always been an overachiever," Lexi said, turning toward them with a grin. Jules was so relieved to see a smile on her sister's face that she wanted to weep.

"What do you have to do, Brooke?" Billy wanted to know.

"Run a half-marathon," Brooke said.

"That's really . . . weird," Billy said.

"I know. Mom was like that," Brooke said.

"And?" Billy asked.

"It's in three weeks. I'm ready. I've got this." Brooke nodded for emphasis.

"I had to get an actual job," Lexi said. "I'm managing an ice cream shop now. I get benefits and everything."

"That's great, Lexi," Billy said sincerely.

"ALEXIS," the three girls shouted in unison.

"Sorry," Jules said. "That was another of her conditions—she has to go by Alexis now, all the time, forever. No more Lexi. And I had to write a book. That's how we met George. He's my agent." The words still felt foreign in her mouth, but she loved the sound of them more than the Internet loved memes.

"What's your book about?" Billy asked politely. Everyone else cracked up.

"This," Jules shouted. "Us. Our crazy story. All of it."

"Am I in there?" Billy wanted to know.

"You are now!" Jules said.

"Cool," Billy said. He looked genuinely pleased.

They can be mad all they want, Jules thought smugly. *Even if nothing comes of it, Billy was a great call on my part.*

Brooke

⌒

Brooke knew she shouldn't be this blissful at the moment, but she couldn't help it. She felt like a million bucks, and it had nothing whatsoever to do with money. As wacky as this day was—as her whole existence had become, in fact—she hadn't had this much fun in, well, ever. She had not one but two guys interested in her, and she'd managed to get into the best physical shape she'd been in since high school. Jules had a manuscript and an agent, and even though something was clearly going on with Lexi, Brooke had watched her morph into an entirely new person over the last few months. Surely whatever the current drama was, Lexi would get through it. She had Brooke and Jules now to help her. The thought jolted her back to the mystery mission at hand.

"Are we getting close?" she asked Lexi. She was starting to get hungry and desperately needed to pee.

"Yup," Lexi said, studying her phone. Brooke waited for her to elaborate, but she didn't.

"Anyone else have to go to the bathroom?" she asked. She peered into the rearview mirror, where several hands shot up.

"Can I pull into that Starbucks?" she asked Lexi, pointing to a shopping center on her right.

"If the alternative is pissing yourself, I guess we have no choice," Lexi huffed.

There was a parking space right up front and Brooke eased into it, between a gigantic Cadillac Escalade and an even bigger Chevy Suburban. They looked like they could eat her Kia for lunch. *It must cost more than a hundred dollars to fill those tanks,* Brooke mused, wondering if she'd ever be able to stop having thoughts like that when she was rich. *When she was rich!*

"Coming in or should I leave it running?" she asked Lexi.

"If you leave the keys with me, I guarantee you this car won't be here when you get back," Lexi insisted.

"Fair enough," Brooke said, killing the engine. "Want anything, then?"

"You're actually going to order something?" Lexi asked.

"I could use a coffee," Jules said, rescuing her. "I'll wait in line while Brooke goes to the bathroom."

"Fine," Lexi said. "Get me a vanilla latte."

"Vanilla?" Brooke asked, surprised. Lexi ignored her.

"I'd love a pumpkin spice latte," Billy added from the backseat.

"There's really such a thing?" Shawn asked.

"Yeah, it's seasonal, though," Billy explained. "They only have them around the holidays. They're amazing. They really taste like actual—"

"ARE YOU PEOPLE KIDDING ME RIGHT NOW?" Lexi shouted. Billy blushed furiously.

"Sorry, Lexi."

"ALEXIS!" the three sisters bellowed again. Billy's face was bordering on purple.

"Right, Alexis, sorry. We'll hurry." Billy scrambled out the side door; Jules and Shawn crawled out after him. Brooke glanced back at George.

"George? Get you anything?" Brooke asked.

"Seeing as I need *Alexis's* enthusiastic blessing to be dating you, I think I'm good," George said with a smile. "But I think I'll use the restroom, too." Brooke felt her cheeks burning as he followed her into Starbucks, his hand resting gently on the small of her back. *Life sure is crazy sometimes,* she thought. *Crazy, but good.*

Lexi

~

"Take a right on Webb," Lexi instructed Brooke. "Then an immediate right onto Malibu Road. Holy shit, you guys. He's actually *on* Malibu Road."

"Who is?" Brooke asked.

"Really?" Jules asked. "You don't know what we're doing, Brooke? We're looking for Rob. Obviously."

Lexi ignored her, too busy gaping at the mansions all around her. They were cruising along the exclusive frontage road in Malibu, the one that housed only a handful of homes, all of them sitting smack on the ocean's edge. Lexi couldn't even begin to hazard a guess as to what these homes might cost. Three million? Thirty? She had no earthly idea.

"That's it, the gray and mirrored one," she whispered. Brooke's eyes bugged out of her head. Shawn let out a whistle. Billy and George exchanged looks but said nothing.

"Rob's in *there*?" Brooke asked with disbelief. She was idling in the bike lane just before the driveway.

Lexi held up her phone so Brooke could see the Find My Friends app. A little red pin said ROB COOPER on the spot right where they were sitting.

Brooke pulled into the circular drive. It was lined with fancy cars—a Rolls-Royce and a Bentley and two Range Rovers—plus Frank's truck. *Bingo.* Lexi thought the house itself was awful—a giant gray cement frame with a million mirrored windows on every side. If she had three or thirty million bucks, she'd bet at least half of them that she could find a better-looking house than this one, but to each his own she supposed.

"Now what?" Brooke asked. "Should I shut off the car? Are you getting out? Are you going *in*?"

Lexi tried to ignore the pounding in her chest.

"I'm just going to go up and say hello," she said, unbuckling her seat belt.

"Whose house is this?" Jules asked.

"No idea," Lexi admitted.

"I'm coming with you," Jules said.

"Me, too," Brooke said.

"Can I come?" George asked. "I really don't want to miss this."

"I guess I should come, too," Shawn said.

"You can all come; I don't give a shit," Lexi said. She got out of the car and slammed the door extra hard for good measure before stomping up to the front door, her entourage hot on her heels.

Lexi banged her fist on the giant metal door three times as hard as she could. Her hand stung from the blows.

"Or you could ring the doorbell," Jules said, depressing the button, setting off what sounded like a goddamned symphony to Lexi.

A man in a black suit opened the door, presumably a butler. Lexi sucked in her breath. All of those mirrors might be god-awful looking from the outside, but inside was a different story entirely. She could see straight through the white-on-white floor-to-ceiling marble-and-chrome house straight to the ocean. There were a handful of people mingling on a back deck, but she'd bet they couldn't see in—and why would they want to? The view was the other way. Everywhere she turned, in every direction from every angle, there was nothing but sand and sky and ocean. It was breathtaking.

"May I help you?" asked the butler. Until this moment, Lexi had thought butlers were just a made-up thing on TV—like Smurfs or unicorns. She didn't know they actually existed in the world.

"Sure thing, Jeeves," Lexi said, dusting off her nearly forgotten tough-chick persona. "I'm looking for a guy named Robert Cooper. He's a cop. Tall, dark, handsome; you know the drill. Ring any bells?" If the butler was taken aback by her brazenness, he had one of the best poker faces Lexi had ever seen.

"May I ask who's calling?" He took in the whole group when he asked this.

"Just some friends," Lexi said. "It's sort of a surprise."

"As you wish," he said with a subtle bow. "You may wait in here." Their footsteps echoed around the cavernous foyer as the motley crew filed their way in. There were white tufted-leather ottoman-style benches along the stark white walls. The benches didn't look like they'd ever been sat on, and no one sat on them now.

Lexi saw feet beginning to descend a massive iron spiral staircase and looked up. Her eyes locked with Rob's.

"Alexis!" he called out. Lexi was taken aback; he seemed

genuinely pleased to see her. She smiled evenly but said nothing. "What are you *doing* here? I mean, how did you find me?" His own smile fell when he said this, and Lexi knew he realized he was busted. He paused midway down the stairs.

"Hey, Jules, Brooke, Shawn," he said, lifting a shy hand in greeting. "And, I'm sorry, I don't believe I've met your friends."

"George Kaplan," George said, lifting his own hand as if he were expecting to be called on.

"Billy McCann," Billy said. He mimicked George's hand gesture.

"Nice to meet you guys," Rob said with a nod. "Robert Cooper." He continued down the stairs.

"Catching anything good?" Lexi asked, folding her arms over her chest. She had no interest in watching the guys strike up a bromance right now. She was here to make a point and get out. Period.

"Huh?" Rob said. He looked confused and guilty, *as he should*, thought Lexi.

"You told me you were going fishing with some buddies in Catalina," she spat, her voice rising. "You fucking *lied* to me, Rob. And I know why you did, too. Because you were too embarrassed to invite your second-class girlfriend into your richy-rich world. Who'd blame you? Look at this place. I'm guessing your friends aren't entertaining a lot of poor white trash like me on a regular basis." Her voice had risen to an uncomfortable pitch, and she couldn't possibly care less.

"Alexis, please," Rob said. He was standing in front of her now and he reached for her, and when he did she smacked his hands away. People were beginning to trickle into the room from the back patio, but Lexi was on fire and blinded by indignation. She didn't care who saw this.

"Don't touch me; you might get some of my nasty street-girl germs on you," she hissed at Rob.

Jules tried to put her arm around Lexi, but she brushed that off, too.

"Alexis, you've got it all wrong," Rob said sternly.

"Do I, Rob? Really? I don't think I do," Lexi fumed. "Tell me one good reason why you lied to me about where you were going, and one good reason why you didn't invite me here with you. Did you meet a newer, better whore? Is that it? Is she here?" She looked around wildly, scanning the strange faces for her replacement. When she did, she spotted Frank and Benji and Susie. Great. Now she was out of a job *and* a boyfriend. So much for her inheritance.

"I'm the reason." The crowd parted and a man in a wheelchair rolled through the gap, coming to a stop directly in front of her. He looked too healthy to be in a wheelchair and too much like Rob for her comfort.

"I'm Robert Maxwell Cooper," the man said, holding out his hand. "Rob's father. Most people know me as Robert Maxwell. Yes, *that* Robert Maxwell." Lexi shook his surprisingly strong, tan hand reluctantly.

"The artist?" Jules asked from somewhere behind Lexi, and then it clicked. The name wouldn't have even rung a faint bell before she'd moved in with Jules, but now she knew exactly who he was: Robert Maxwell was the J. D. Salinger of the modern-day art world, a brilliant but reclusive painter whose work hung in galleries around the world and who was rarely, if ever, seen in public. Jules had read a book about him and been so intrigued she'd gone out and bought one of his prints. It was hanging in her bathroom, and one day Lexi had made the mistake of asking about it. Jules had gone on and on about the guy, and Lexi hadn't even bothered to pretend to be interested. But his work was phenomenal; that much she knew.

"Yeah, there was another Robert Cooper churning out some lousy shit back when I was just getting started," Rob's father explained with a good-natured grin. "I took to going by Maxwell, even though I was way better than that sonofabitch. Asshole drank himself to death at thirty-eight, too, so I could have been Cooper all along." He chuckled softly at this and winked at Lexi. "But then again, going by Maxwell helps with the whole douchebag-recluse thing."

Lexi couldn't help it; she smiled.

"So now you've met Pop, the famously eloquent Robert Maxwell," Rob interjected, blushing.

"But I don't get it," Lexi said, looking back and forth from father to son before settling her gaze on Rob. "Why are you here? Why did you lie to me?"

"You might have noticed that Pop is a little feisty," Rob said. His dad snorted proudly. "He's only got a handful of people he likes to have around, and I came down here to tell him about you and try to convince him to add you to the list. I've been talking about you for two days straight. Ask him. Really."

The senior Cooper nodded in agreement. "Couldn't get him to shut the fuck up about you, is more like it," he said. "But he did mention you were a firecracker, and that you were a fine-looking broad, and from what I can see he was pretty spot-on, on both counts. You're a hell of a talent, too. And I'm not talking about in the sack, just so you know. I don't ask my kids about that crap."

Lexi's heart skipped a beat. She looked at Rob.

"I might have taken some pictures of your sketches and showed him?" Rob said, phrasing it as a question.

"You didn't," she whispered, humiliated.

"He sure did, and like I said, you've got some serious chops," Robert insisted. "You're not gonna be pissed off at him for that, are you? 'Cause I hate seeing pretty girls looking pissed off. It's such a waste of good eye candy."

Lexi blushed and returned his smile, then turned back to Rob. "But why didn't you just tell me who your dad was?" she asked, still struggling to take all of this information in.

"I don't know, I thought maybe you'd get scared away or think differently about me if you knew," Rob said, his dark eyes filling with tears. "I shouldn't have lied to you, Alexis—that was a bonehead move. If you give me another chance, I swear to you I'll make it up to you." He searched her face pleadingly for a response.

"The kid's telling you the truth," Robert interjected. "And if you're the reason I see my goddamned cop son cry, I'm going to run you over with this chair. Fucker's heavy, too. No shit." He said this with a mischievous smirk, though, and Lexi managed a grin in return.

"I'm sorry," she whispered, letting Rob wrap his arms around her and burying her face in his chest. He squeezed her until she thought she might pass out. "I'm . . . just so sorry."

Rob pulled away from her, his hands on her shoulders. "I love you, Alexis Alexander. With all of my heart. I'd never hurt you on purpose. In fact, I'll make it my life's purpose to protect you from getting hurt. If you'll let me."

"Please say yes before I have to hear any more of this blubbery pussy-boy shit," Robert pleaded, holding his hands in a prayer pose. Everyone laughed.

"Anyone need to take a shit or anything—sorry, use the shitter—before we eat?" Robert added, spinning his wheelchair until it was facing the direction he'd come from. "I presume you and your friends will join us for a little Thanksgiving dinner, Alexis? Chef made pot brownies for dessert. They're out of this world."

"You do know I'm a cop, right, Pop?" Rob asked with a laugh. Then he squeezed Lexi again. "Will you stay? Please?" Lexi looked at her ragtag group of family and friends; they all nodded enthusiastically. It wasn't like any of them got the chance to share a holiday meal with a world-famous artist in his Malibu mansion every day.

"This is fantastic, *fantastic*," Lexi heard George say as they followed Robert to the magnificent dining room.

"Oh shit," Lexi whispered to Rob. "Brooke's technically here with *two* dates—long story, I'll tell you later. Is that going to be awkward for Frank?"

"You ready for this?" Rob whispered back. "Frank's gay. Came out to me in the car on the way down here. Obviously don't say anything, but I *was* wondering how I was going to break it to you that we tried to set your sister up with a guy who's batting for the other team. It looks like that crisis has been averted."

"That and a few others," Lexi pointed out.

"I guess we can add that to our list of things to be thankful for today," Rob said, kissing the tip of her nose.

Lexi closed her eyes and said a silent prayer. *If I'm dreaming*, she begged, *please don't ever let me wake up.*

Jules

～

Jules was holding her breath, watching George read the last few pages of her revised manuscript. With his helpful guidance, she'd been writing around the clock for three weeks straight, and she was cautiously pleased with the results. Finally, George took off his reading glasses and set them aside. He exhaled deeply.

"Well?" Jules asked breathlessly.

"It's . . . not good," he said after a painful pause.

"It's not," Jules echoed. It wasn't a question. She felt like a balloon that had been stabbed with a butcher's knife.

"No," George said. "It's not."

"Oh," Jules said. What else was there to say? She stared at the nameplate on his desk.

"It's absolutely brilliant," George said. She glanced up to see his face lit up like a starlet's makeup mirror.

"Wait, what?" Jules said, terrified she'd heard him wrong this time.

"Jules, it's perfect. You nailed it, all of it. The emotion, the drama, the suspense . . . It's a masterpiece. And I particularly like the new ending." George was referring, of course, to the part where Brooke wound up with him—and not Billy McCann.

"You *do*?" she screamed, jumping out of her chair and throwing her arms around George. She probably wouldn't have done such a thing if he was just her agent, but now he felt practically like family.

"I do," George told her. "Let's hope my editor friends agree. It's a fickle business we're in, you know."

A fickle business we're in. We're in the publishing business. I'm *in the publishing business.* Jules's brain couldn't quite process the thought. She nodded in agreement.

"So what's next?" she asked tentatively.

"I do have a few tiny edit suggestions—you can probably wrap them up in a couple days—and then we send it out and cross our fingers. I'm not going to tell you to get the champagne chilling yet, but you should be really proud, Jules." He rose from his chair and walked around his desk to give her a warm hug.

She'd done it. She'd written a book, and her *agent* just called it brilliant. She was going to be rich, and possibly even famous. Usually when anything good *or* bad happened, her immediate urge was to call Shawn. But this time, for some strange reason, her very first involuntary thought was *I can't wait to tell Mom.* The realization that she couldn't—and that she was still just a little girl who wanted her mother's approval and recognition— brought tears to her eyes.

"Jules?" George asked. "Are you okay?"

Jules nodded and swiped at a tear that had escaped and was winding its way down her cheek. She hated it that she always cried in situations like this, but it was just how she was built. She cried when she was sad and when she was happy and when she was tired and when anybody sang the National Anthem, even the time Christina Aguilera butchered it at the Super Bowl. It was a curse.

"It's overwhelming, I'm sure," George said soothingly. He handed her a box of Kleenex from the credenza behind his desk. "You must be feeling a million different things, most of them good, I hope."

Jules nodded again. She wasn't ready to speak.

"I assume you'll be at the race on Saturday?" he asked now, graciously trying to change the subject. Brooke's half-marathon was just five days away, the last hurdle on this long and crazy journey of theirs. Jules couldn't believe nearly a year had gone by, and how drastically all of their lives had changed—and all because of Juliana. She smiled wistfully at the irony.

"Of course," Jules sniffed, dabbing her eyes. "I'm planning a little celebration at the house afterward. Will you come?"

"I wouldn't miss it for the world," George promised. "I'll bring a case of champagne."

Jules went home and looked at his edit suggestions; they were indeed tiny. A segue change here, a word-replacement suggestion there. She had it wrapped up within two hours and sent it back to George with trembling fingers.

Now all she could do was wait. She tried to picture some fancy New York editors reading her manuscript, but she couldn't. Would they read it on their iPads in bed, like Jules did, or would they have the pages printed and bound so they could make old-school notes in pen? Would they read it all in one sitting, or spread it out over the course of a week or several? Jules had read an interview with a top literary agent who'd said that he only ever allowed himself to read the first ten pages of any manuscript on first sitting; the next day, if he wasn't absolutely dying to pick it back up, it went into the trash. The thought made her stomach churn.

Her mother had only demanded that she write the book and "make a concerted effort to sell it." Technically, Jules had completed the task she'd been given. Presuming Brooke didn't break her ankle in the next five days or pass out during the race, they were home free. Millionaires. Jules wouldn't have believed it a year ago, but right this minute, that wasn't enough. Not even close. She wanted to see her published book on a bookstore shelf a thousand times more than she wanted to be rich. If this first round of editors passed, she wouldn't give up, she promised herself. If twenty editors passed, she still wouldn't give up. If every editor on the planet passed, she'd publish the damned thing herself. People did that all the time—and some of them were even bestsellers, like Hugh Howey and Allison Winn Scotch and even E. L. James. There was no way she was going to let this dream die. Not ever.

Her phone rang; it was Brooke.

"George said you finished and that it's brilliant and that he's sending it out this week and *oh my gosh, Jules, we did it!* Well, I still have to run on Saturday, but that's so going to happen and then it's all over and we get all of that money, are you *kidding me* right now?" Her sister was breathless and giddy on the other end of the line.

"I've gotta tell you, it sure feels good not to have all of the pressure on me anymore," Jules laughed.

"Thanks a lot," Brooke said, a touch of mock sarcasm in her voice.

"You know what I mean," Jules insisted. "I was seriously terrified for a while there, Brooke. I never had any doubts about you finishing. Well, maybe at first. But I'm so proud of you! A year ago, would you have even thought any of this was possible?"

"A year ago, I was fat, miserable and living with that slime-ball Jake," Brooke laughed. "I've got to hand it to Mom. She sure knew how to make us turn things around. I'm actually sort of sad that she's not alive to see us now."

"Me, too," Jules said. "She'd be really proud. Oh, she wouldn't show it, and she certainly wouldn't come out and say it, but I'm pretty sure she'd feel it."

"Well, anyway, I've got to get back to work," Brooke said. "Gigi needs me to rub her back or she can't fall asleep."

"Those kids are so lucky to have you," Jules said.

"And I'm lucky to have *you*," Brooke told her. "Thanks for everything, Jules. I mean it."

"It was nothing," Jules said.

"It was everything," Brooke insisted.

Brooke

⁓

Everyone had told her that the race would be different from her training runs, but beyond that, Brooke hadn't really known what to expect. She'd arrived forty-five minutes before registration even opened, because this was Los Angeles, after all, and traffic could be a nightmare even at six thirty on a Saturday morning. Her race bib was pinned in place and her timing chip was clipped securely to her shoelace and she'd already hit the port-a-potty twice. She reviewed the course map for the twentieth time, memorizing every twist and turn.

As she waited for her wave to be called, Brooke went over her mental checklist. *Stay hydrated, even if you don't feel thirsty. Pace yourself; you don't need to win or even place, you've just got to finish. Remember to look around, take it all in and enjoy the experience. Visualize yourself crossing the finish line, strong and proud. And whatever you do, don't trip!*

The energy was electrifying. She wasn't sure how, but she

was positive that the two thousand amped-up bodies getting ready to run could power all of Los Angeles for at least a week.

She saw someone holding a sign: "Run for the money." The race had a fund-raising component, and that was obviously what the sign referred to. In a way, that was what she was doing, too, but deep down, Brooke knew that wasn't the only reason she was here today. She'd gotten strong and fit and had set a goal for herself that she was about to meet. Maybe her mom had lit the fire, but it was Brooke who'd put in the training time to make this happen; Brooke who'd endured the aches and pains and blisters and shin splints and freezing cold early morning runs, when every breath felt like a knife to her lungs. Everything in life really was a choice, she realized. And it was Juliana, of all people, who had helped her to see that. Juliana, who'd chosen to be bitter and distant and die alone and estranged from all three of her daughters, yet almost subconsciously determined to bring them back together. It was a bittersweet acknowledgment, and a motive she knew she'd never understand.

The starting gun roared and Brooke took off cautiously. She'd been following a dozen or more marathon-training blogs, and every one of them made a point of mentioning all the trip hazards at the start. That was when everyone was clustered together and elbowing for space, discarding sweatshirts and water bottles thoughtlessly in their competitors' paths. Brooke held back just enough to find her comfortable pace and a little room to breathe, and then she went into the zone.

It was like being swept along a river. She could barely even feel her feet beneath her, she was so enthralled with the chanting crowds and blaring music. All along the sidewalks people were holding up signs that said "Run like you just robbed a liquor store" and "Hurry up, Mom, we're hungry" and "Even if you feel like crap you look great" and "13.1 miles because you're only HALF crazy." She smiled and laughed and waved back at the spectators who screamed and yelled and told her she was amazing. She was a runner. A true, legitimate athlete. Her wonderful, sweet, amazing boyfriend was waiting for her at the finish line, and she was about to have more money than she could ever possibly spend. Brooke couldn't believe this was actually her life.

By the tenth mile, she had a stitch in her side and could feel blisters forming between her toes, and her nipples felt as if they'd been rubbed with sandpaper, but these things that would normally demand immediate attention were like tiny annoyances in the back of her mind, a gnat buzzing around her head at a campfire or a car alarm wailing down the street. She'd learned from her training that running was as much mental as it was physical. Yes, it hurt. Absolutely, it was hard. But could she push through the pain and keep going? That wasn't up to her body—it was up to her mind. And at this point, her mind wouldn't let her stop if she was running barefoot on broken glass and vomiting blood.

When Brooke caught sight of the finish line in the distance, she picked up her pace. Not because she was trying to beat or impress anyone, but because she was determined to give it everything she had. She pumped her strong, muscled arms as hard as she could, throwing them high into the air as she hit the finisher's shoot. She kept them there until she crossed the actual finish line, where she heard an announcer call her name—*Brooke Alexander from Reseda, finishing strong.*

She hadn't just finished, she'd finished *strong*. She was overwhelmed with emotions: pride and relief and accomplishment, and a bottomless joy she'd never felt before. If she could bottle this feeling and sell it, she'd be the richest woman on the planet.

"Brooke! Brooke Alexander! Over here!" She scanned the crowd and saw them: Jules and Shawn and Lexi and Rob and George. They were waving frantically from behind an orange-netted safety fence, and Jules was crying and holding up a sign that said "YOU ARE MY HERO." Lexi was holding a sign, too; hers said "If your feet hurt it's because you just KICKED ASS." George was carrying a bouquet of what looked like three dozen roses, maybe more. Shawn was snapping photos and beaming. Brooke laughed and waved and hobbled over to them.

"That was sick," Lexi said, high-fiving her. "In a good way, I mean."

"You're amazing," George told her. He kissed her sweaty cheek and tucked a stray strand of hair behind her ear.

"How do you feel?" Jules asked, wiping away a tear and hugging her over the fencing.

"Like about six million bucks," Brooke said, a smile the size of downtown L.A. lighting up her face.

Lexi

❧

"What?" Rob asked, putting down his beer.

"Nothing," Lexi said. She took a sip of her lemonade. They'd just watched *The Princess Bride*—Rob had been horrified that she'd never seen it and insisted they rectify that immediately—and were curled up on his distressed leather couch. Lexi loved that couch; it was solid and relaxed and smelled delicious, just like Rob.

"You started to say something," Rob pointed out. "What was it?"

"Fine, I was going to ask you about Christmas, but the last time I asked you about a holiday it didn't end so well, so I decided not to." Lexi crossed her arms over her chest.

"You're doing it," Rob pointed out.

She rolled her eyes and immediately uncrossed her arms.

"You did it again," Rob said. Lexi pretended to look innocent and he raised his brows.

"Anyway," Lexi said. "That was what I was going to say."

"Alexis, will you do me the great honor of spending Christmas with me?" Rob asked, taking her hands in his.

"I don't know," she said, trying to sound petulant. "Depends on what you want to do, I guess."

"Well, Pop wants me—actually, *us*; he invited you specifically—to spend the day with him, but I told him you might want to be with Jules and Brooke."

"What, he doesn't want all of us?" Lexi asked, feigning surprise. Rob laughed.

"Funny you should say that, because he *did* offer that," he said. "You've got that man wrapped around your little finger, whether that was your intention or not. My dad hasn't wanted to socialize with anyone outside of the family, with the single exception of Frank for some strange reason, for more than a decade. Hell, at this point I wouldn't be surprised if he offered to throw a New Year's Eve party for a thousand of your closest friends. You're good for him, Alexis. I guess I'm going to have to keep you around." It was exactly what she wanted to hear.

Their Thanksgiving dinner had been one for the books. Robert had insisted that Lexi sit directly next to him and had shot questions at her like machine-gun fire all night. Lexi had never met a boyfriend's father before, let alone a famous, reclusive one with a potty mouth as bad as hers. But for some reason—maybe because of their shared affinity for both Rob and profanity—she felt completely at ease around him. She had sensed Rob watching her all evening; he told her later that he had never, not once in his entire life, seen Robert Maxwell Cooper look so genuinely interested in anyone or anything that wasn't a canvas. Lexi thought her heart might actually explode, it felt so full.

"Well, I like him, too," Lexi said now, smiling at Rob. *I almost threw all of this away,* she realized. She shuddered at the thought.

"That's not all he said," Rob said. He polished off the last of his beer and set down the bottle on the trunk-style coffee table. "I don't know if you know this, but it's practically impossible to get your work into an art gallery in this town. There's this whole unwritten protocol for up-and-coming artists, where you have to do this many small shows and be invited to that many openings and be seen at so many events before anyone will even consider showing your work, and even then you're lucky to get it up in a coffee shop."

"Okay," Lexi said slowly. "So what's your point?"

"Well, there's one exception to everything I just said: If the one and only Robert Maxwell offers to show some of his previously unseen works alongside an unknown artist."

Lexi's mouth fell open. "What are you saying?"

"My dad wants to do a show with you," Rob said. He looked as excited as any kid waiting in line to sit on Santa's lap and unload his six-page wish list ever did. "He wanted to ask you himself but I told him you might freak out, so I wanted to be the one to present the idea. He doesn't have all of the exact details worked out yet, but he's working on that part as we speak. But you'll do it, right?"

"But, Rob, all I have is a big, sloppy pile of sketches!" Lexi cried. "Nothing is matted or framed or anything. I'm not a professional artist. I have no training at all. I'm nobody. I'll humiliate him!"

He squeezed her hand. "Close your eyes and come with me." Lexi did as she was told, walking carefully on trembling feet.

"Open," Rob instructed. Lexi gasped. The walls of Rob's entire spare bedroom, floor to ceiling on all four sides, were a patchwork of her sketches, each one beautifully matted and expertly framed. She had to admit; the collective effect was stunning.

"It'll look better under the spotlights and everything," Rob said bashfully. "And these are just the copies—Brooke lent me the portfolio she made. I didn't have them seal the backs, because we'll have to use the originals and you'll need to sign them and all, but . . . what do you think?"

Alexis Alexander didn't cry. Not as a child, not even when she watched them lower her father's body into the ground, and not as an adult when any of seven million horrible, heartbreaking things had happened to her. When she was hurt or sad or embarrassed, she bit the inside of her cheek until she could taste the salty blood, but she never, ever cried.

"I . . . I . . . can't . . ." She shook her head from side to side, her hands covering her mouth.

"Do you hate it? Are you mad? Alexis, please don't be mad. I only thought—" Seeing Rob so distraught sent Lexi careening over an unfamiliar edge.

The tears came hard and fast, as if someone had turned on an old faucet that had been gathering pressure for years. She heaved and sobbed and Rob had his arms around her, rocking her gently.

"You don't have to do this, Alexis," he was saying. "I didn't mean to push you. It's just, my dad got me so worked up, and he really thinks you can be a huge, famous artist—and not like when you're dead, but *now*, in this lifetime, in our lifetime. But if it's not what you want, we can forget this ever happened. Okay? Alexis? Talk to me, please."

She pulled away from him. Her eyes were wet and red and her lips were quivering.

"I've never been good at anything," she whispered. "Ever."

"Not true," Rob said.

"Blow jobs don't count," Lexi said, smiling despite herself.

"Actually, you've probably always been good at lots of things, but nobody ever told you that you were," Rob said, holding her face in both of his hands. A fresh tear slipped down her cheek; he wiped it away with his thumb and tilted her chin up toward his face. "Or maybe they told you but you didn't believe them. But I want you to listen to me now: You, Alexis Alexander, are the most incredible woman I have ever met. You're smart and beautiful and funny and fierce and have balls the size of Texas and more talent in your pinkie toe than an army of artists has in all of their bodies combined. And you do, in fact, give the world's best blow job."

Lexi melted into his arms, wondering why in the hell nobody had ever told her that a good cry felt better than any drug ever created.

The Sisters

~

Jules had called Mr. Wiley the Monday after Brooke's race and told him the news: They hadn't merely met their mother's conditions in turn, but they'd beaten their deadline by more than three weeks. Alexis had a job, Jules had an agent and her manuscript was making the publishing house rounds, and Brooke had a shiny half-marathon finisher's medal and a handsome new boyfriend that everyone adored. Mr. Wiley had been speechless. Then he'd apologized and explained that he was at that moment en route to LAX and would be gone through the holidays. They made an appointment for January fourth. Jules assured him that they could wait.

"I heard from Billy today," Jules said. The girls were in her Honda, driving to their meeting with Mr. Wiley. Jules hadn't changed much in a year, at least outwardly, but Brooke and Lexi looked like entirely different women. Jules couldn't wait to see Mr. Wiley's reaction.

"How *is* Billy?" Brooke asked. He'd been so sweet and understanding about the whole Thanksgiving visit mix-up, she almost felt bad about choosing George over him. But her heart knew what it wanted, so she had no choice but to follow it.

"He met someone on the plane on the way back to Miami," Jules said. "How funny is that? They've been dating for a month and he thinks she might be 'the one.' He said to tell you thank you."

"Are we really going to talk about Billy McCann right now?" Lexi interrupted. "I think we should talk about the millions of bucks we're on our way to pick up. Seriously, what are you guys going to buy first? I'm buying a car. A Porsche. No, wait, a vintage Mustang GT. Or maybe one of those big square Mercedes that look like toasters. Shit, how am I going to pick one?"

"You don't have to pick one," Jules reminded her. "You're about to be loaded. Splurge a little. Get two." She was snaking her way through the miserable downtown L.A. traffic, looking for a parking spot—a task not unlike finding a decent-looking pair of shoes on the clearance rack at Ross.

"Holy crap, I *don't* have to pick," Lexi shouted, amazed that it was practical, conservative Jules who'd thought of this. "You guys, I'm buying *two* cars! Maybe one of them will be a pickup truck. Or a Jeep. Or a motorcycle!"

Jules and Brooke laughed. "I guess I'll buy a house?" Brooke said with great uncertainty.

"First of all, you don't have to *buy* a house right away," Jules said. "Maybe you could rent a place and make sure you like the neighborhood and everything before making it official."

"That's a good idea," Brooke said. "That's what I'll do, then, I guess. What about you, Jules? What are you going to buy first?"

"I'm putting a pool in the backyard," Jules said.

"You're going to stay in Reseda? In that shitty little house? I mean, no offense," Lexi said. "But seriously?"

"I'm not sure where we'll move or when, and it's just something I've always wanted," Jules said, flipping on her blinker. Finally, she'd found a car about to pull out of a metered spot. "I'll make sure when we sell the house that the buyer has kids. Every kid wants a swimming pool, right?" Lexi and Brooke nodded in agreement.

They got out of the car and Jules led her sisters purposefully toward the same building they'd entered a year—or was it a lifetime?—ago. She threw open the door and motioned her sisters ahead of her.

"Let's do this," Lexi said, grabbing one of each of her sisters' hands and pulling them toward the elevator bank. They made a stunning, formidable trio.

They sat for what felt like an eternity in Mr. Wiley's waiting room. Finally, his secretary announced that he was ready to see them.

"Jules, Brooke, Alexis—" Mr. Wiley did a terrible job hiding his shock at the transformation in Brooke and Lexi. "You ladies all look wonderful, wonderful! And congratulations on all of your accomplishments. Please, have a seat."

The sisters lowered themselves expectantly into the three chairs across from him. Mr. Wiley pulled out two large envelopes, scanned some notes written on the outside of each and put one back into his drawer. He tapped the edge of the second one on his desk.

"I guess we should just get straight to it, then," he said. The girls nodded in agreement. Mr. Wiley took a slender silver letter opener from a cup on his desk and sliced the envelope open, handing copies of the letter inside to each of them to read. He cleared his throat and began:

Dear Julia, Brooke and Alexis,

If you're listening to these words, that can only mean one thing: You've met the conditions I laid out for each of you. I will admit that if I were alive, I'd be surprised. In fact, I've written another letter in the event of a failure, but this is the one I certainly hope you'll hear.

Before I go any further, let me say this: I know that all three of you blame and resent me for the way your lives turned out, but I did the best that I could, and I have only ever wanted what I thought was best for you all. Maybe now that you've enjoyed these achievements, you will finally believe that.

You've probably spent the better part of this past year imagining your affluent futures, and I'm sure those images motivated you when you were struggling to succeed— which was my intent. Because your successes are my gift to each of you. My legacy, if you will. Your inheritance. I hope that achieving these goals brings you great happiness, because the truth is, there isn't any money. There wasn't any life insurance policy. Your father and I were young and foolish and never dreamed we'd need one. Depending on the circumstances of my death, there may be a small sum of cash to be distributed—probably in the five-digit range—as well as my condo and the Caprice. Mr. Wiley can help you divide these things should there be any contention. I'm hoping there won't be.

I understand that you might be angry at me, especially when I tell you that if I did have millions of dollars, I wouldn't leave them to you, because money cannot buy happiness. I want you each to have something that you made for yourselves, something that can never be taken away. In all truth, I believe what I've given you is a far greater gift than any dollar figure could ever be.

You're welcome,
Mom

Mr. Wiley cleared his throat. The girls sat in stunned silence, each poring over her own copy of their mother's letter, looking for a loophole or a punch line or, better yet, a "Gotcha!" None could be found.

"Any questions, comments?" Mr. Wiley asked nervously.

Brooke was dumbstruck; Jules opened and closed her mouth several times but no words would come out.

"That fucking bitch," Lexi finally said. But she was smiling when she said it, and her sisters laughed.

Readers Guide for

Everything's Relative

by Jenna McCarthy

DISCUSSION QUESTIONS

1. From the opening chapter of the book, the three sisters epitomize the common traits that studies on the relationship between birth order and personality suggest: Jules is the eldest and a classic type A, responsible and a bit controlling; Brooke is the middle child, the people pleaser and peacemaker; and Lexi, the youngest, is rebellious and self-centered, with an "everything will work out" worldview. Do you see any of these common birth-order traits in your family or in families of those you know?

2. When the girls' father died, they lost their mother, too. She became overly critical and controlling while at the same time handing over many of the motherly duties to Jules, who was only twelve. Losing a spouse is one of the most traumatic events in a person's life, but it is clear that Juliana never fully recovered, nor did she help her children through the grieving process. Do you empathize with her and feel she did the best she could, or do you feel her actions are inexcusable? Did your feelings about her change from the beginning of the book to the end?

3. Jules had to write a book and try to sell it, Brooke had to dump Jake and date someone more deserving and train for a race, while Lexi had to begin using her full name—Alexis—and get a real job. These are very specific requirements that only a person who knew the sisters well could have set. What does this level of knowledge about their personal lives demonstrate about Juliana and the relationship that she had with her daughters, despite the difficulties they experienced? What sort of final conditions would your parents put on an inheritance in this same style? What changes or goals do you think they would demand of you?

4. Juliana's controlling nature seems to be born from some desire to control the uncontrollable in the wake of her husband's senseless and unexpected death. Do you think Juliana's critical and harsh words for her daughters were meant to, in some way, keep them safe? Can you think of a time when either you as a parent or your own parents reacted harshly or explosively to some mistake or event that you or they later admitted was more about fear than the actual mistake or event?

5. Jules's relationship to her sisters feels more like a parent-child relationship at the beginning of the book, and Lexi especially treats her like an overbearing mother figure. Do you feel those relationships change and become more sisterly as the novel goes on? And if so, what are some key moments when this change occurs?

6. When Jules is young, she sacrifices a lot to care for her sisters, and even as an adult, she can't seem to shake the habit of sacrificing the little comforts—for example, a fresh, warm towel—in order to achieve some tiny practical goal that may seem insignificant to those around her. Why do you think Jules continues to do this into her adult years? What little sacrifices did your parent or parents make for you, or what sacrifices have you made as a parent?

7. Brooke's relationship with her deadbeat boyfriend Jake seems, at first, to make little sense. Why would someone stay with a guy who is so obviously a leech on her life? But this type of relationship is all too common. Why do you think Brooke was settling for Jake? How do you think Brooke's childhood contributed to this habit of allowing herself to be taken advantage of?

8. Brooke has a tough start fulfilling her running goals, but as soon as she sees ways that she can help her sisters satisfy their requirements of the will, she is extremely motivated to create a portfolio for Lexi and get herself into some awkward situations trying to sell Jules's book for her. What do you think this says about Brooke as a person?

9. Meanwhile, Jules is trying to play cupid for her sister with her long-lost high school sweetheart via Facebook. What do you think of this meddling—is it the same as what Brooke is doing, or does the dating/romance aspect set it in a different category?

10. Growing up as the youngest sister, Lexi has no memory of her family as a happy, functioning unit, and it's clear from the opening scene of the book that she has always been a headstrong and rebellious person. How does that add up to the Lexi we meet around the time of her mother's death: a party girl who swaps sex for favors and can barely hold down a job at a dive bar? What do you think are the root causes behind Lexi's self-destructive behavior, and how do you think a mother's controlling nature may have led to her daughter's wild ways?

11. Why do you think Lexi never explored her talent as an artist when she was younger? Did it just not fit into the "tough chick" image she had cultivated for herself, or was it something more? Based on her behavior, how do you think Lexi estimates her self-worth?

12. Why do you think it was so natural for Lexi to jump to conclusions about Rob's Thanksgiving plans? How do you think you would have reacted in her situation—when someone says he is going to one place and then you find out he's somewhere else?

13. All of the girls idolize their father—Jules perhaps the most of all, as she yearns to follow in his footsteps and become a writer. It's impossible to know what their actual relationship would have looked like, but it's obviously important to Jules to keep his memory alive. Is there anyone like this in your life? Someone whom you barely remember or never knew but whom you think about each day and imagine *What if?* and contemplate the guidance or support he or she would give you?

14. How did you feel about the ending? Were you expecting it or surprised? How would you feel if you were one of the sisters?

15. What do you think the other letter said, the letter that the lawyer was meant to read to the sisters if they did not complete their tasks?

16. What do you see in the future for these characters? Do you think they have created solid, lasting bonds and will continue to work on their relationships and strive toward their goals, or will they go on to lead separate lives?